I0663035

The Hounds of Hell

THE BEAST WITHIN

TERRA LAURENT

THE BEAST WITHIN

Dedication

For my readers. Thank you.

Chapter One

The Transfer

"Damn." Aaron kicked the pile of discarded clothes out of the way, snapped off the light and slammed the closet door shut.

He tossed the clothes toward the bed as he headed for the shower. They landed on Carlos' side. He stared at the empty space, as if wishing for Carlos would make him appear. He hadn't expected a boyfriend of such short duration to leave his home for Maryland, not with the family still there in California, and especially not after all Aaron had put him through. He hadn't expected, but he had hoped. He shook his head at all of the unanswered questions raised by the unused pillow and smooth patch of covers, and headed for the shower.

He let the water heat while he brushed his teeth. He kept his head slanted left so he didn't have to see the scar. Even under the work-appropriate length of sandy stubble, the angry jagged line remained highly visible. Seeing it roused the dark thing inside him.

Aaron stepped out of his boxer briefs and into the steaming shower. He let the water sluice over him. He lathered his hair with shampoo as the spray battered his chest. The scars there tingled with sensitivity, but no longer hurt—not in the traditional sense, at any rate. Nerves rattled through him. What if they resented the fact a position had been created just to accommodate him? What if he couldn't fit in? What if they asked too many questions? What if they wanted to know about California? About him? He squeezed his eyes tight against the burning suds dripping down his face and rocked his forehead against the tiles. The familiar panic clawed its way up through him. His body reacted to his fear with another, stronger pull, one guaranteed to devour him if he let it.

Calm down. Calm down. He repeated it like a mantra as his forehead teetered in the wide swath of dark grout. The edges of the granite tiles bit into his skin. He wanted to press against them until he bled, anything to drown the sensation filling his chest. Showing up at the new workplace a half an hour late with twin stripes of blood stained on his face would probably not make the best first impression. And if he wanted to save his career, he needed to impress them. No. Impress wasn't the right word. *Reassure.* Yes, he had to reassure them.

Aaron reached down and took his cock in his hand. He stroked it idly, distractedly, comforting himself as he hummed a tuneless sound in his throat. His dick responded to his fingers, slowly hardening under their light touch. He ran his hand through the suds in his hair and gripped his shaft with his slicked fingers. The bubbles made a somewhat rough lubricant, but he did not mind. The mild burning distracted him, kept his focus on safe things, like erections and orgasms.

He splayed his fingers against the tiles, braced himself with his arm. He let his head droop into the hot stream of water and continued working his hand up his shaft in quick, short strokes, pausing every few times to run his cupped palm over the enlarged head. He kept the water rushing around his ears, drowning out the calls of the foreign birds roosting in his lone tree and the regional twang of the people passing on the sidewalk outside. He concentrated on the mounting sensation in his groin, the pleasurable tightness that increased in waves and attempted to buckle his knees. He played with the tip, running his fingers around the circumference.

"That cock is a beautiful thing, mi hombre guapo." Carlos' rumbling voice entered his head with such clarity that Aaron jolted and snapped back the shower curtain. Water spilt out. Aaron stared at the puddle as it spread across the deserted floor.

This wasn't a good way to start his new life as a sane person.

Was Dr Ingrahm right about rushing back into work, a new life? Were the hallucinations returning with the increased stress?

No. Aaron forced his panic back into its home at the very farthest corner of his mind. Eight months was too long for his life to hang suspended. He had to take back what they had stolen from him.

Aaron dried off, smeared some product to calm the humidity-induced frizz from his wavy hair, and dressed quickly. He gave a glance at the bag of English muffins sitting on the counter, but discarded the notion of breakfast as his stomach lurched. Eating food meant giving his body something to bring up later. He slung the bag with his pitiful number of personal desk items over his shoulder, then walked out of his condo. He returned a moment later, grabbed a tie for good measure, choked down the last of his fear and left for work.

Chapter Two

First Impressions

Aaron trailed behind the director. He concentrated on her small frame, the neat lines of her suit, the white hair tied in a no-nonsense knot at the nape of her neck, the subtle amber notes of her sparingly applied perfume, everything but the many pairs of eyes flicking up from the bustling bull pen to track his progress through its midst, and the dead silence that accompanied his passing.

"I trust your relocation went as well as possible?" Annalise Braven's English accent clipped along with her rapid, high-heeled stride.

"Yes, ma'am."

"Very good. You have taken the full month to settle in and adjust to your new surroundings?"

"Yes."

"And you passed your re-assessments with excellent marks. Well done."

"Thank you." Aaron had undergone three weeks of rigorous physical, mental and field-testing before Director Braven would even look at his file or even consider taking him on board. Up until ten minutes ago he hadn't seen the inside of Grange's Kapre branch, his new workplace. With everything that had happened, however, he found he couldn't fault her desire for utmost security. In fact, it reassured him.

"And you have found your meetings with our counselor helpful, Agent Marvell?"

"She has cleared me for the field, and I agree with her decision." He squelched his internal protest of doubt and gave the director his most reassuring smile.

"Very good. Let's get to business. You have undoubtedly noticed the Grange branch of Kapre is far different from your previous office." She waved at the clustered utilitarian desks and their inhabitants. "We do not believe in the excess or frivolity of some of our larger branches. Here, efficiency and safety are our priority, not posh offices and cushy chairs. We are vigilant, and are exceedingly intent upon security. We will not suffer an incident like the one in Salyer, California."

Aaron's face burnt. It started his scar throbbing. From the murmur rising behind him, the rest of his new colleagues were now discussing the very event he wished so desperately to avoid. Of course they knew what had happened. Even in an organization as secretive as Kapre Security the news of an entire office's annihilation could not be kept down. The dark thing lurking deep inside Aaron bristled.

"You'd think someone who looked like a hot grandma would act a little nicer," someone said close to Aaron's ear. A man had caught up with them and was now walking in lock step with Aaron. "She means well, in her horrible, crushing, troll-like way." He hopped up beside Aaron, gave a friendly smile, extended his hand and raised his voice to a normal level. "Tony Harper. Pleased to meet you."

Director Braven looked around and raked a disapproving gaze up the athletically framed, handsome man. "Congratulations on joining us before noon, agent."

"You're welcome, ma'am," Tony replied with a grin.

"One would think you would have enough respect to show up on time to greet your new partner."

Aaron swallowed hard. *Partner.* He'd known it would happen. No agent worked alone in Acquisitions and Exterminations. Still, the concreteness of Director Braven's words turned his insides to liquid. Aaron cast a glance at the man walking beside him. Who had this guy pissed off to deserve such an albatross?

"Well, I figured I'd let you have him for a while, boss. After that I'd look like the best co-worker on earth." Tony disarmed Braven's scowl with another boyish grin. He turned the smile on Aaron. An almost palpable warmth radiated from that expression. "I was right, wasn't I? I look pretty good now, don't I?"

With a strong jaw, aquiline nose and icy blue eyes framed by a short crop of chestnut hair, Tony looked more than good. Caught in his new partner's magnetic pull, Aaron struggled to make even the slightest sound. Before Aaron could force his vocal cords to obey, Tony recast his line in the direction of a cute, clearly non-field rated young female employee carrying a box of doughnuts.

"Hey, Claire. Hold up a minute." Tony trotted off after the doughnut girl. He caught her at her desk, flashed her the same disarming grin that stretched up into those same disarming eyes. If Aaron's reaction was anywhere close to that of the now flustered young woman juggling the doughnuts, he had made a complete fool of himself.

"Charismatic, that one." Director Braven's voice brought Aaron back to his orientation. "He plays up the coy angle, but he's a solid specialist, well-grounded where it matters. He is a perfect match for you."

The solid guy. A perfect match for the unstable one. The director didn't need to say it for it to be true.

"My office is this way," Braven continued. "Let's have a chat before your compatriot wrestles his focus into check and returns to finish your tour."

Aaron followed Braven to an office adjacent to the bullpen. His last glimpse of his new partner was of Tony leaning against the female specialist's desk, bitten doughnut in hand, laughing at the deep blush creeping up the pretty woman's face. Aaron felt a flash of something akin to disappointment, and shuttered it off immediately. He turned into Braven's office. She was already seated behind a plain wooden desk. Spartan bookshelves spanned the windowless wall behind her. She gestured for him to take one of the wooden chairs facing her. As he sat, Braven fiddled with the silver bracelet on her arm as a pretense at distraction. Aaron knew better.

"Tell me what happened in Salyer," she began.

"I'm sure you read the file." Aaron's stomach clenched like a fist.

"Humor me," Braven replied.

"We had picked up a case regarding unlawful supernatural activity maybe a month prior." Aaron remained stoically focused on his superior, even though his legs trembled with the urge to bolt. *Slow and steady, avoid details. Don't let the memories creep back in.* "The suspects involved were volatile to say the least." *Good. Keep going, don't think about the screams. The blood. The smell. The pain.* "They returned our interest in them with increasing enthusiasm. We reacted too late. People died."

"And yet in the ensuing chaos, you alone emerged triumphant?"

"Triumphant?" Aaron blinked as if her upbeat summation were a physical slap. "No."

"Alive, then," she corrected without apology.

"Yes. Alive."

"Well." Braven let go of her bracelet and began organizing a pile of papers already so neatly stacked they looked like an engineer had laid them out. "You may rest assured an event like that will not occur here."

As assured as I was five months ago that it would never happen in California? Aaron was certain a question like that would only result in his being sent back to the staff psychiatrist for a re-eval, so he said nothing.

From the din beyond the closed door, a familiar voice made itself known. Aaron froze in his seat.

"I'll leave you to get settled," Braven said. "Agent Harper will see you find your desk. And you will be relieved to know a friendly face among us strangers." Braven gestured to the windows separating her from the bullpen. As she did, that voice wormed its way into his ears, pitched high with excitement and full of forced earnestness.

Aaron turned and followed Braven's finger, a knot of dread in his stomach telegraphing suspicion of his worst fear. There he was, standing amongst a group of agents, animatedly gesturing with his coffee mug. From his antics and the captive expressions on the agents' faces, it was clear he was telling a story. Aaron knew from the heads swiveling toward Braven's office, which tale he told. The storyteller turned, and suddenly Aaron met the gaze of the last person on earth he'd ever wanted to see again.

Spencer Ellison.

The second, and final, survivor of Kapre Security, Salyer, California.

Chapter Three

Partners

"There he is, the man himself." Spencer Ellison swept in and latched his clammy, coffee mug warmed hand around the back of Aaron's neck as he stepped out of Braven's office. "Hey, Ar, come meet the guys."

The forced familiarity. The casual greeting. The master-hound control. It was too much. Aaron tensed. They were all watching him. He couldn't resist Ellison's pull without coming off as a self-important jerk. Ellison's hand burnt against his skin. His scent, caustic like he had scrubbed with industrial cleaners, filled Aaron's nostrils. It took all of his willpower to not shake free and let the beast inside him tear the asshole apart.

"This is Specialist Aaron Marvell, my pal from back in Cali." Ellison steered Aaron into the middle of the bullpen. "He's a good boy."

The dark thing snarled at the insinuation. Aaron clamped down on his teeth so the sound wouldn't pass his throat.

"How 'bout you give him a nice reception?" Ellison blithely continued. For a wonderful, fleeting moment there was silence, then their voices erupted like lava from a volcano.

"What was it like in there?"

"How did you get away?"

"Did they come in changed, or did they do it right there?"

"I heard it was orchestrated higher up. National level, maybe?"

Questions and comments swirled around Aaron like a tornado. The force of their words picked at his mind, prying away the protective layers, exposing raw, terrible memories. Aaron shook his head against the onslaught of images, placed first a hand, then a hip against a nearby desk to steady him. His stomach roiled. The dark thing shifted impatiently, anxious to break free and revel in their blood. Aaron felt a wild impulse to let it happen, but Carlos' previous warnings arose in his mind.

'It isn't just about you, mi hombre guapo. Not anymore.'

Carlos was right. More injuries, more bodies would only mean trouble for all of the afflicted ones, even those who had no desire to hunt humans. Especially for them. They were wholly unprepared to be thrown into the race war that would undoubtedly arise if more humans died. Aaron clamped down on his violent desire. The dark thing raged in protest. His body trembled. Sweat broke out over his forehead. No one noticed. They kept prodding and poking while Ellison exposed both the subject and his ignorance with bawdy enthusiasm, his hand on Aaron's neck, working the room on his behalf like a ventriloquist with a dummy.

"What was it like, seeing them come at you all at once?"

"I heard you have scars on your body that make that one on your face look like a scratch."

"What do you remember?"

Aaron's avoidance of breakfast no longer mattered. He was going to vomit, empty stomach or not.

"What do you all remember about doing your jobs?" The challenge drowned all out the other voices. The room fell silent. Tension filled the bullpen as twelve agents glared at Aaron's new partner. Tony strode toward them, his face a dark cloud, challenging each in turn. One by one, the other agents broke eye contact. They returned to their desks, muttering amongst themselves. Except for Ellison. He remained right where he was, a tight grin stuck to his face, his fingers still digging deep into Aaron's neck.

"You sure know how to bring down a party," Ellison said. "Is that a specialty of yours?"

"Is being a coward yours?" Tony asked. He flicked Ellison's arm away from Aaron's neck.

"You're a dick," Ellison said. "Or, is it just that you suck it?"

Aaron knew by the stillness in the room that everyone was awaiting Tony's response.

"Both," Tony agreed lightly. "And if you actually had one you might be in trouble, sailor." Tony gave an exaggerated wink, then dismissed Ellison by turning his torso, shuttering him off from Aaron's sight. He caught Aaron's eyes, reeled him in and steadied him with his gaze. "Containment has just reported a new entry incident across town. The scene is locked down, waiting for us. You want to take a minute and see your desk, or get out of here?"

"Out of here." Aaron tried to force the words into sounding normal, but the last came out with something nearing a growl.

"My sentiments, exactly."

Tony stretched out his arm. Aaron expected another hand to clamp onto his neck. Was it customary in Maryland to steer people around as if they had no means of self-propulsion? Or was it just his unique condition that made them feel as if he should be taken for a walk? Instead of touching him, though, Tony gestured toward the foyer.

"Let's get you to op-tech and then we'll take a drive."

Chapter Four

Triggered

Op-tech turned out to be a fairly large, but spartanly outfitted lab tucked behind the main offices, in the opposite direction of the elevators. In California op-tech had been an entire floor with ten scientists, three engineers, eight mages and an ever-changing parade of assistants and interns. Here, a lone, wiry redhead in a lab coat answered the door buzzer and ushered them back to the requisition desk, past rows of counters overflowing with tools and gadgets.

"Keep to this side of the line, please," the tech said as Aaron wandered too close to one of the tables. At the desk, he gave Aaron the briefest of curious glances before pushing a clipboard toward him. "Sign where indicated. I'll get your field equipment."

As Aaron scrawled his name on the sheet, Tony chatted away at the man, eventually wheedling his way past the orange stripe cordoning off the authorized-personnel-only space to better discuss the trigger mechanism on a new floor-mounted mass containment unit. Excited by his design, or lonely from life in a stainless steel isolation tank, the clerk leaped headfirst into Tony's web, and proceeded to ramble on about his newest combinations of technology and mysticism. Tony encouraged his excitement by asking perfectly timed questions, always punctuated by a winning smile or impressed nod. In less than five minutes, the op-technician was fluttering from item to item, gushing information. Aaron watched with a mixture of amusement and irritation as he loaded the magazine and slid the gun into his new shoulder holster, then hoisted the provided kit bag onto his shoulder.

"Well, that ought to do it, huh, Aaron?" Tony called out suddenly from across the room.

"I've got everything I need," he answered, confused.

"Let me know when that disruptor is ready to field test, Rob," Tony said as he returned to the front of the counter.

Aaron felt a hand slip into his pocket. Tony, back at his side and still blathering, gave no hint of awareness of what his own hand was doing as it withdrew. A small object rested against Aaron's hip. Aaron glanced at his partner, but Tony studiously avoided his observation.

"I'd love to check out another of your genius inventions," Tony finished.

"You got it, hoss," the scientist answered, a grin splitting his face from ear to ear. "Bring back something big and squishy-explody to test it on."

Aaron trailed Tony to the car pool, where the same situation played out all over again. Aaron signed the clipboard as Tony charmed his way into the best car the requisition clerk had on the lot.

"Do you do this all the time?" Aaron asked as he settled in the passenger seat.

"Do what?" Tony replied as he turned on the engine, then pulled out of the parking garage.

"Finagle your way into everyone's goodwill?"

"Finagle?" Tony laughed. "Are you a seventy-year-old Englishman?"

"You're avoiding the question."

"I'm charming. What can I say?"

"Seems borderline manipulative to me."

"Manipulative?" Tony stopped at a red light and gave Aaron an uncomfortably prolonged appraising glance. "Don't you ever use your persuasive skills in acquisitions and exterminations?"

"Always. You need every edge you can get working acqxterm cases."

"So, why is it different socially?"

"Because they're human beings you're in contact with on a daily basis, not malicious demons that require unique talents to capture and kill."

"The intent is the same."

"That's not a valid justification."

"You have a lot of opinions for someone who just started this morning."

"I *started* eight years ago." The dark thing shifted inside him.

Be careful. The warning voice inside his head was less frightening than it had been in the shower. Devoid of Carlos' actual advice, his subconscious had clearly chosen Carlos as its spokesman. While the intruding voice was jarring, it was better than the ones he had heard directly after the attack. Unlike those others, Carlos' voice offered support, rather than suggestions on how Aaron should end his miserable life.

Tony shrugged, as if Aaron's total experience, or opinion, mattered little. Aaron clamped down on the dark thing, shoved his shoulders back into the upholstery and stared out of the window. Tony fiddled with the radio. With each passing block the tension in the car mounted, growing impossibly thick until Aaron found himself fiddling with the window button with the desire to press it and let the oppressive cloud disperse.

It wasn't smart coming into a new workplace and attacking the morals of his new partner, especially when Tony had gone out of his way to protect him from Ellison. This man was his one shot to prove he was normal, that he wasn't a monster, even though he was — technically. Everyone suspected what had happened in California, each had a similar theory about how he alone had survived. If he wanted to maintain his facade of normalcy, he had to resume work like nothing had ever happened to him, like he was still the same person he'd been before the attack, no matter how ridiculous the notion. Making friends with his new partner would add an extra layer of protection he desperately needed. Besides, Tony seemed like a nice guy. Aaron glanced over at his partner.

A really nice looking, nice guy.

A few minutes later Tony pulled the car up to a curb outside a row of derelict warehouses. The street was vacant, save for a police barricade horseshoeing one entrance. Tony shut off the car without a word and climbed out. Aaron followed. He wanted to say something to erase the damage he had inflicted, but Tony had already ducked under the yellow tape. Aaron pulled the kit bag from the back of the car and followed Tony inside.

Dust motes danced in the dim light cast by frosted windows set high on the walls. The only other source of light in the room came from the golden glow of the Thurisaz cast onto the concrete floor. It was a mystic rune of protection and Kapre Security's personal sigil, a visual warning that was triggered whenever an otherworldly presence had appeared and was acting against the universally adopted behavioural guidelines set forth by the British Anglo-Demonic Pact of 1864. Cops saw the Thurisaz, hightailed it and called Kapre.

"Look at this," Tony called as he squatted over a dark area on the floor.

Aaron came closer, but he didn't need to look to know what it was Tony had found. He could smell it from where he stood. Sulfur. Trace amounts, but enough for his keen sense of smell to pick up. Fear bubbled in his gut. Images triggered by the scent swirled in his mind. A tugging sensation encircled his gut and pulled him toward the ashen pile. The floor wobbled. He disguised the buckling of his knees with kneeling next to Tony. His partner glanced at him, clearly concerned. Aaron waved it off. Tony nodded and pointed at the ashen substance smeared across the floor.

"Brimstone," Tony said. "Fresh."

Aaron pulled in his focus. *Just the details. Look at the particles, not the bigger picture.* The tug in his stomach eased a little. He pulled a flashlight from the kit bag and trained the light on the stain.

"Not all fresh." Aaron pointed at a section of the mark. "Here, and here, you can see faint brush marks etched into the surface."

"Someone tried to sweep up brimstone?" Tony leaned in closer to inspect. His hair brushed Aaron's cheek. "Is anyone that stupid?" He turned to look at Aaron as he spoke. His face was only inches away.

"Not tried. Did." Aaron pulled his gaze from Tony's with difficulty. Fortunately the lighting was dim, so Tony likely could not see the burning heat that traveled from Aaron's groin to rest in his face. "Like I said, those marks are etched into the surface, carved into an older stain. There is some residual powder here that's fresh, as you pointed out, but not nearly enough to be even the by-product of a hamster opening a portal."

"You think something large passed through?" Tony asked. He pulled the bag from Aaron's shoulder and unzipped it. As he fished around inside he said, "There are lots of nasty visitors that are rodent-sized and smaller."

"Yes, but this older residue surface area is much larger."

"And most invasions start small—preparation spells and whatnot—and end up big, with the arrival of whatever entity has been summoned."

"Exactly."

"So why is the fresher mark smaller?"

"I don't know. Strengthening the original summoning spell? Reversing it?" Aaron shrugged. "Whatever the intent, I doubt it worked. "

"Let's take a sample to the lab and see what we're looking for today."

Aaron scraped a small amount of the powder with a thick steel implement. The sulfurous odor strengthened. The rotten egg stench held softer notes of cinnamon, dragon's blood and earth. He made a note of the scent. Each mystical being's power had a distinct smell. The more palatable notes in the powder comprised the signature of the one who cast the spell. It was all but buried in the noxious powder, but his sensitive nose had little trouble filtering out the aromatic fingerprint. If, after using magic, the caster were ever to cross paths with him, he would catch the same scent. He dropped the powdery contents into a mystically charged pouch. Even though he trusted his sense of smell over the lab geeks any day, it wouldn't hurt to have forensics run a profile on the powder in case they could match the residue to an already documented entity. The end of the scraper began to glow. He sealed the pouch and dropped it into the lead lined kit bag and discarded the scraper a good distance away from the evidence. Red embers consumed the metal and turned it to ash in seconds.

"Hopefully we'll get a lead from this." Tony shifted on his heels, clearly anxious to be up and doing something.

"We already have one." Aaron pointed again at the brush marks. "Remember? Someone *swept* this residue away."

"Right..." His partner stopped, clearly at a loss how to tie the information together.

"So what does that tell you?" Aaron moved his extended finger to indicate the ashen remains of the scraper.

"Good broom?" Tony ventured.

"Very good broom. Metal bristles. Durable. Probably out-of-dimension materials, considering the depth of the etch marks."

"Few individuals in town that can produce a broom heavy duty enough to sweep up brimstone."

"Maybe we should head in, check the files," Aaron suggested. He looked at Tony. He was an all right enough guy. Smart, not as cocky on the scene as he was in the office. Braven was right. A good agent. "Look, Tony. About what I said in the car. I'm sorry. I'm on edge today, clearly. It's not an excuse, but—"

"Ellison is a jackass," Tony supplied. "And I was showing off for you. Not the best welcome." Tony smiled and extended his hand. "So, we'll start over. I'm Tony Harper, your new partner. How would you like to go shake some trees and see what falls out?"

"Aaron Marvell. Nice to meet you." Aaron met Tony's hand with his own and it was like a shock of electricity bolted through him at the touch. "Let's take a drive."

As they walked back to the car Aaron couldn't concentrate on any of the morning's details save one.

He was showing off for me.

Chapter Five

Laundry

"So, where are we going?" Aaron asked as Tony guided the car through the street.

"To the Laundromat."

"Laundromat? That's where we'll find our broom salesman?"

"No." Tony steered out of Grange's city center and took several turns down dingy one-way streets cast into twilight by the flanking buildings. "Remember, we're just shaking trees right now."

Tony stopped ahead of a street parking space in front of a ragged building called Shirley's Swish-n-Suds. Tony flung his hand in the direction of Aaron's head. It smelled of fresh soap, and an underlying hint of salt and musk. It had been hot in the warehouse. Aaron's heart tripped as he imagined that hand, glistening with sweat, cupping the base of his skull, using it to guide him closer, pull him in for a prolonged kiss. Aaron quickly shifted to conceal his hardening cock.

"I wasn't going to hit you." Tony grinned at his reaction. He locked his hand behind Aaron's headrest and looked back to guide the car into the parking space.

"I know," Aaron replied, glad to make use of the cover Tony'd provided. "Just reflex."

"I like a partner with good reflexes," Tony quipped.

Aaron watched Tony climb from the car. That was three times in one day Tony had flirted with him.

Had he?

Aaron joined Tony at the curb. He studied his partner's expression, but was met with only the same chipper demeanor.

He hadn't.

"As long as those reflexes don't include gagging." Tony winked and started toward the humidity fogged Laundromat door.

Well, fuck me. He had. Aaron shook his head as he followed his partner. He scanned the V of his torso, the perfectly rounded ass punctuating it, and shook his head against the next, very unprofessional thought that surfaced. *Seriously. Please, fuck me.*

Tony opened the door and a blast of rank air hit Aaron full in the face. The atmosphere hung thick with mildew and decay. He covered his nose with his arm, fighting back a retch. So, that's what Tony had been talking about with gagging. Not sucking cock, but disgusting demon rot.

"What are you doing in here?" a woman screeched from someplace distant and echoic. "Out. Get out."

The sound of claws against glass brought Aaron to the washing machines against the opposite wall. A woman—or a creature somewhat featured like a woman—crouched inside the machine, her knees, hands, and face pressed against the dewed window.

"There you are, Mildred," Tony said brightly. "I thought you'd be in number forty-two today."

"Occupied," the woman spat.

Aaron glanced over at the washer in question. Something lumpy and brown stared out at them with overlarge eyes. An expression akin to a scowl worked its way into the shapeless tissue folds. All through the Laundromat the other machines gently sloshed filthy water around glaring, amorphous masses of life forms.

"I'm looking for Qi. Seen him around?"

"Get out."

"He's a person of interest in a recent event and we'd like to talk to him about his broomcraft. Since you know everything about everyone that goes bump in the night—or day—I daresay you could point us in the right direction."

"I told you to leave, Kapre murderer. We don't help those who hunt us."

"You do today," Tony said with a grin. "Because it would be a shame for your clientele to get wind of Kapre employees using your facilities." Tony raised his voice so everything within earshot could clearly hear his words.

"That's why you need to leave now," the woman shrieked and banged on the glass. Up close she looked like a rank, sodden sponge, the many crannies in her flesh filled with all sorts of foul matter. "You can't search here without an order from your main office. I know my rights."

"True enough." Tony plucked a cup off a nearby bench and dumped the contents down the front of his shirt. A viscous liquid that may have once been coffee—or could have been something entirely worse—soaked into the fabric. "But I'm here as a customer. I have a really bad stain I need to get out."

Tony stripped the shirt from his torso, revealing heavy pecs, a well-defined six-pack and a pair of external obliques so precisely sculpted they might as well have been twin neon arrows pointing toward his dick. Aaron realized he was staring, and glanced away, only to find Mildred regarding him with wry amusement.

"Which washer is free?" Tony asked. He started over to a bank of dryers at his side. "This one?" He opened the lid, releasing a waft of foul warm air. Whatever was inside shrieked.

"Leave 'em alone. What do you want?"

"Just to wash my shirt. Or, if you'd rather I take my business elsewhere, tell me where to find Qi."

"He doesn't wander around town, shopping at grocery stores and getting his nails done." Mildred's face crumpled in a scowl so deep it looked like she was wringing herself out.

"No? Then, how? A word of power?"

Mildred's silence confirmed Tony's guess.

"What word summons him, Mildred?"

Mildred pressed her face against the glass and bared teeth like rotten sticks.

"Well, let's see where I can put this shirt, then." Tony moved through the aisles, popping open washer doors, lifting lids. The sounds of intense disquietude filled the Laundromat.

Mildred fixed her furious stare on Aaron as if faulting him for the entire matter. He returned her scrutiny, a memory playing at the edges of his consciousness. He had seen a similar muddy countenance before. It came to him in an instant. During his first year he had been sent on a termination assignment in the Bell Swamps. His team had tracked the offending demon for days through the forest and muck. One day he had seen them, eyes like Mildred's gazing up at him from the ooze.

'*Selart demons,*' his mentor had told him. '*Familial, self-protecting and industrious if needs be. Not worth bothering with, though. They don't mess with humans.*'

"Why are you here?" Aaron asked her.

"You're the one trespassing." Mildred huffed. A patch of condensation obscured her face, then melted away.

"You lost your habitat, didn't you? Had to improvise. Found some cozy apartments where you could individually regulate your environment to your liking?" Mildred did not deny his theory, so he continued, "You kept your family together, the way a matriarch is supposed to. What would they do without you?"

Outperformed, Tony stopped meddling with the machines and turned to watch their interaction. All eyes were on Aaron. He pulled from his pocket the object Tony had slipped in there at op-tech. It was round, the size of a Ping-Pong ball, and chalky white.

"You Selart can adapt to almost any living condition, I've heard." Aaron held up the ball.

Tony gave a sharp intake of breath, then covered it with a laugh. His initial reaction was enough for Aaron to take note of the warning it held. He shifted it so he gripped it more securely.

"Anything but salt water habitats," Aaron finished as he yanked open the door.

Mildred screeched and clawed at the opening in a vain effort to seal it against his assault. Aaron drew back his hand as if to toss in the object. Tony was at his back, gripping his shirt, ready to tear him away should he release whatever danger rested inside the innocuous-seeming object.

"Messifluotitious!" Mildred screamed. "Meditate on your intent, light seven black candles and say the word, then call on Qi. He will come if he wills it."

At her surrender the entire Laundromat came alive. A din of voices shouted the word of power. Washers rocked on their legs. Dryers rattled against the bolts holding them to the walls.

"We'd better go," Tony said, lowering Aaron's arm. He covered Aaron's hand with his own and pressed his fingers tighter around the ball. It was just the two of them in that moment, hands together, eyes locked.

The doors of a nearby washer blew off its hinges. A mass of brown ooze puddled out. It coalesced as it hit the floor, forming a taloned foot well over three feet in length. The ooze continued to pour forth, forming a dripping leg. Two arms, each easily the size of a human, slid out next. They latched onto the faces of the adjacent machines and pulled. With a grotesque pop, an elongated head appeared. The creature pulled its other leg free and stood erect, its head grazing the fluorescent lights.

"Oh, shit," Tony said. "Bigger family than you thought."

Aaron stole a glance at his partner. Tony was grinning.

The creature roared.

"We really have to go." Now Tony laughed outright, his voice as joyous as a kid's on Christmas morning.

The creature leaned in, its breath stinking of earth and decay. It swiped its long arm at them. Tony ducked under. Aaron dove back out of reach. The creature swiped again, this time sending a row of machines flying into the aisle, blocking Aaron from his partner.

"Tony, watch out," he called as the creature sent a fist squelching down into the floor just a foot from where Tony had just been. Aaron scrambled around another bank of machines, searching for his partner, just as the overlarge Selart began to do the same. It stepped over the rows, one after the other, dripping head scanning left and right. The creature's contained family hooted and howled inside their refuges, concealing the sound of Tony's retreat, which was useful in keeping him safe from his pursuer, but made it difficult for Aaron to spot him.

"Aaron." Tony popped up from behind a long bench near the front. "Use the ball."

The creature whipped around at the sound of Tony's voice and barreled toward him.

"How?" Aaron shouted. He turned the object over in his hand, but it gave no hints as to its detonation.

The creature continued on its path toward Tony.

"How do I use this thing?" Aaron repeated. It didn't matter. The creature was too close. He pulled out his sidearm. Regular bullets. Generally useless. He didn't have much of a choice. He discharged the entire clip into the Selart's back. It barely grunted from the impact. He re-holstered and ran toward Tony.

The creature scooped up the bench and raised it over its head. The sight of Tony crouched at the creature's mercy sent a reverberation through Aaron.

"No," he called out. His voice was already lowered, guttural. He raced ahead, his joints cracking and shifting painfully.

"Control, mi hombre guapo. Control."

Tony scurried out of the way as the makeshift weapon came crashing down. The tiles where he had been crouching splintered. Frustrated, the Selart struck again and again, pounding down the heavy seat as Tony scuttled out of the way, each time coming closer to being crushed.

Aaron's fingers popped and cracked. Their shifting makeup made it nearly impossible to hold the sphere, let alone examine it.

"Come on, Tony. Answer me. How do I use this thing?"

"Throw," Tony sputtered as an edge of the wood grazed his ribs. Crimson blossomed across his side.

"You're in the way," Aaron countered. His voice was a true growl, now. "Get out of the way."

"I'm trying." The amusement had gone from Tony's voice. He ducked a blow, then another, moving back each time, cornering himself against the front window.

"No! Get out of there," Aaron yelled.

The Selart swung again. Tony jumped out of the way. The bench crashed through the window, and Tony followed it outside to safety.

"Now," Tony shouted.

Aaron threw the ball. The creature stabbed its hand through the glass shards in an effort to seize Tony. It didn't see the spreading, mutating net of light emanating from the sphere. The mystical webbing slammed into the Selart, then sliced through him. Cubes of substance fell to the floor and splashed as mud. The outcry from the machines rose to a murderous combined scream. Death filled Aaron's nostrils. Overcome with the scent of the kill and his morphing body, he threw back his head and howled. He clamped his hands over his mouth, praying the interior din absorbed the sound as one of its own.

"Aaron," Tony shouted from outside.

"Don't' let him see, mi hombre guapo."

"I'm fine. The creature's down. I'm coming out," Aaron shouted.

The beasts in the machines banged and wailed, but no others emerged to confront him as he backed toward the door. Why would they? He was of their world, and they knew what his kind was capable of. Mildred — his thoughts led him to seek her out — was a sodden lump in the bottom of the washer, regarding him with something akin to pity. More likely she was simply despondent over her fallen family member and the damage done to their refuge. Either way, he was not welcome, monster or no.

With the immediacy of the kill over, Aaron pulled in his focus. One by one his joints slid back into place. The coarse black hairs that had begun to protrude from his flesh receded. He cleared his throat, relieved when a normal sound emerged. He hit the door and backpedalled out.

"Sticky Fingers one, Mud Butt zero," Tony said from the curb, his joviality already on the rebound.

Aaron double-checked the interior to be sure they weren't being pursued, then turned to his partner. Tony had pulled himself over to a defunct parking meter and leaned against the pole, examining his side by poking at it with a filthy finger.

"Stop touching it," Adam said.

"Bug you, the squishy stuff?" Tony grinned. He looked up at Aaron. His merriment briefly faltered, but returned in a flash.

"Systemic infections bug you?" Aaron retorted. "God knows what we touched in there." He kept his voice light, but worry gnawed at his gut. Somehow, Tony had seen. But he wasn't mentioning it, yet. Why?

"Good point." Tony dropped his hand. "Well, that went well."

Aaron couldn't fathom the depth of the remark, so he did not answer.

"Come on. No long faces. We scored one for us," Tony said. He pushed off the concrete and stood, wobbly legged.

Aaron reached out and secured his partner's arm. Tony gave him a brief glance, his expression inscrutable, then let Aaron help him into the passenger seat, and turned over the keys without comment.

"What now?" Aaron asked. "You need a hospital?"

"Nah, this is an easy one. I have medicine at home I lifted from op-tech that'll seal this right up."

"You steal a lot from op-tech?"

"Only what I need. Or want. Didn't see you complaining a minute ago."

"Why don't you just requisition it?" Aaron pulled the car away from the curb as quickly as possible. He checked the rear-view, but the street was clear, as he had expected.

"Braven has become a little stingy with what weapons we can and can't take out of the office. Doesn't want our stores too stripped in the case of emergency."

"Like what happened in California?"

"Yep."

"She said she was vigilant."

"That's an understatement if I ever heard one. Turn right, there." Tony pointed to a street. As Aaron followed his directions, he continued, "She's become obsessed with doomsday protocols."

"Where are we going, exactly?" Aaron asked. Avoiding discussing California had become an art form for him.

"To summon Qi."

"Where do we go for that?"

"Anywhere. That's the beauty of the power word Mildred just gave us, it opens a portal for Qi anywhere the summoner wants. There's a bit of a lag time, though, between the summoning and the arriving, so I thought we could get comfortable and have some food."

"Okay," Aaron agreed. "Where to?"

"Like I said, I have some stuff at home to patch up my side. Thanks to my brilliant navigation skills we are already on the way there, so turning around would be a waste of company gas. You don't want that do you?" He flashed a smile that struck Aaron in the chest and warmed him all the way to his groin. "Plus, I'm injured and shirtless. I'm going to need you to help me fix that."

Cleaning up Tony he would happily do. Putting a shirt back on him, though, well that was a damn shame.

"We can order in. There are some really good restaurants that deliver nearby. We can fill up and wait."

"Sounds like a plan." Aaron followed Tony's next gesture and pulled up in front of a three-story brick building. A deserted shoe store occupied the ground level.

"Entrance is around back," Tony said as he hefted himself from the car with a groan of pain.

Aaron shut off the car and came around to the other side to help Tony. His partner draped an arm around his neck with a grateful nod.

"Lost more blood than I thought. No worries, though, we'll fix that soon." Tony settled into Adam's shoulder and let him take some of his weight. "It's a steep staircase."

"It's okay." *More than okay. Heaven.* "I'm stronger than I look."

"I'll bet."

Aaron again had to wonder what his partner had seen, how much he suspected. Since he was a special agent who put the mystical two and two together every day, Aaron was certain he had come up with the correct answer. Hell, most people at Kapre probably suspected the answer already. The question was, what would his new partner do with the information? Aaron couldn't expect him to sit on it out of loyalty. They had only been working together half a day, and half of that half Aaron had dedicated to being obnoxious and judgmental. He shook off the gloom. There was nothing he could do except prepare to bolt if the worst happened and an acqxterm team was sent to retrieve him. Until then, he had a beautiful man leaning on him and a promise of sponge baths and dinner. Not too bad for a last night before criminal exile.

Even with sweat and blood and tiny stabbing flecks of glass rasping across his skin from Tony's battered body, it was the best few minutes Aaron had spent since Carlos had practically packed his bags and pushed him onto a plane to Maryland. He helped Tony around to the back. Tony opened a narrow door with a key he pulled out from behind the light fixture.

"Very secure," Aaron commented as Tony worked the lock.

"I figure I can handle any human that enters, and anything else that is going to come in won't be deterred by a deadbolt."

Aaron couldn't argue the logic, so he shut the door behind them and helped his partner up the metal stairs. The door at the top was unlocked and Tony waved him inside.

"Do you snore?" Tony asked as he disengaged himself from Aaron and turned to face him.

"Why?"

"We might be waiting a long time for Qi." He gave Aaron a wink. "I'm going to call in to Braven, let her know we won't be in the rest of the day."

Oh good God. Aaron marveled at the sculpted bare back of his partner as Tony turned and pulled out his cell phone. Heat and foolish excitement raced through his veins at the thought of a private night spent in the company of Tony Harper.

Chapter Six

Summoning Desire

An open steel staircase bisected the downstairs living area, leaving the kitchen with its elongated island counter on one side, the couch and television on the other. A makeshift gym stood behind the stairs. Acrobatics mats covered the floor in the area. A boxing dummy stood sentry outside the glass door of the bathroom, his menacing countenance daring Aaron to pass. Jump ropes, weights and medicine balls all hung from an organized hook and shelf system on the far wall. Tony was a man who liked to keep in shape. But, then again, that was obvious to anyone with functioning eyeballs. Aaron glanced back at his partner. Blood still trickled down his side unchecked. If he lost much more he would likely pass out. Aaron gave the dummy a half-hearted swipe to the nose as he entered the bathroom in search of wound care supplies. The medicine cabinet held a ridiculous number of cologne bottles, the vanity drawers and cabinets only grooming supplies.

"Yes ma'am. We will have a full report to you in the morning." Tony's voice became clearer as he approached the bathroom. He appeared in the doorway, cradling an impressive number of black candles in one arm. He clicked off his cell phone and jammed it into his pants. He grinned like a kid who had just convinced his mother he needed a sick day.

"Now let's make a call to Qi."

"What about your wound?"

"It can wait a minute." Tony stood the black vigil candles on the vanity. He pulled a lighter from his pocket and began setting the wicks aflame. Aaron watched the light dance across Tony's features, softening the angled cheeks and jaw with its glow. "I want to get Qi here tonight. We need to figure out who came through that portal, and what amateur mystical jackass was trying to clean it up."

"Or was rushed into cleaning it up. Maybe they got interrupted."

"That, too. Only one way to know for sure. Close your eyes and concentrate on Qi."

Aaron obeyed. Tony lit the last candle and let his own lids fall shut.

"Messifluotitious," he chanted softly. "I use the word of power to summon Qi. Qi, come forth. It is my will and command."

"That's it? Qi's not one for pomp ceremony, huh?" Aaron remarked after it became clear the ritual had ended.

"Apparently not, which is good because I really don't want to have to get chicken blood out of the grout again."

Aaron made a face.

"And chickens smell disgusting even before they're disemboweled. Speaking of, this thing on my side doesn't smell too pretty, either."

"No wonder. You were digging at it with your cesspool fingers. Who knows what came off of those washing machine lids you touched. Let's get you cleaned up. Where do you keep your medical supplies?"

"Over there, by the tub." Tony said as he sat down on the closed toilet seat.

"You mean the indoor pool?" Aaron remarked. The bathtub was the jetted kind, large enough to comfortably accommodate two large men and whatever activity they could together imagine. Aaron's groin tightened. He fought not to look back at his partner lest his own imaginings — or worse, desperation for them to come true — conveyed on his face. Instead, he opened the door of an antique dentist cabinet. The shelves held boxes of bandages and tape, bottles of antiseptic and an array of brown jars each marked with odd symbols.

"That one," Tony said as Aaron touched a larger jar. "The one with the flattened smiley face looking symbol on it."

Aaron took the container and a roll of bandages.

"Won't need those."

Aaron glanced back at his partner. He was poking the bloody gash in his side once again. Fresh blood trickled out.

"What about the peroxide?" He wrinkled his nose in distaste at Tony's dirty fingers probing the open wound.

"Nah. This stuff'll do the trick. Takes care of most everything."

Despite Tony's confidence, Aaron brought a packet of gauze pads and the peroxide along just the same. He washed his hands at the sink, singing his arm hair on a candle in the process, then knelt by Tony's side.

"Arm up," he commanded.

"You always this bossy around half naked men?" Tony teased.

"You should see me when they're fully naked." The words were out of his mouth before he could stop them. He bit his tongue and went to work cleaning the wound. To his credit, Tony did not wince or groan when he poured the peroxide across the tender flesh.

"Now the ointment." Tony's voice was low, intimate in proximity.

Aaron couldn't force his gaze upward to meet Tony's. He concentrated on the gash, using the corner of a clean piece of gauze to spread it across Tony's side. The medicine slid easily across the flesh, warming as it touched the damaged areas. The heat below his fingers became searing. Tony stiffened, grabbed the edges of the toilet seat with both hands. A sound of pure agony built in his throat, tearing from his mouth in a ragged scream. His feet lashed out, missing Aaron by a scant inch.

"What's wrong? What's it doing? Should I wash it off?" Aaron shouted over Tony's misery.

"Leave. It," Tony managed to say past gritted teeth. "Melts."

Aaron nodded and moved to Tony's front, placing himself between his knees as a brace so he didn't slide off onto the floor. The flesh on Tony's side became molten. Tony howled as his skin sizzled. Sweat covered his pale face. He leaned forward, buried his head in Aaron's shoulder. Aaron cupped his neck and held him as he screamed. The steaming, liquid flesh flowed together across his ribcage, sealing closed as if by an invisible zipper. The last of the wound disappeared, leaving a red-hot patch of unmarred skin. Tony's shoulders relaxed and he slumped into

Aaron's arms, panting. The angry inflammation quickly faded. A moment later, Tony sighed in relief and pulled back enough to look Aaron in the eyes. Without the cocky radiance, they were soft, vulnerable. Aaron became aware of his hand's lingering presence on the back of Tony's head, and even more so of the desire to keep it there.

"Thanks for that," Tony said. His voice was worn, raspy from the screams.

"You could have warned me," Aaron whispered back. Something fragile seemed to hover in the air around them, something that even one harshly voiced syllable could shatter into irretrievable pieces.

"And miss this?" Tony reached out and stroked Aaron's face. He slid his thumb along the hollow of Aaron's cheek, once, then again.

Aaron closed the distance between them in a swift, sure motion. He covered Tony's mouth with his own. Tony responded, pushing his tongue past Aaron's lips, gliding it along his tongue with deep intensity while he spread his legs farther apart to accommodate Aaron's body against his own. Even as Aaron slid his hands to either side of Tony's face to control the pressure of his lips, he could not wrap his mind around what he was doing. Tony was his partner. His *new* partner. In a new town. This was more than breaking the rules, it was snapping them into tiny pieces and tap dancing on them. Aaron pulled back.

"Tony," he said, his tone hardly a firm one. "Tony?"

"Yes?" Tony stroked Aaron's arms, ran light fingers down to his clenched fists, which rested between his legs. Tony played with the balled digits. "You were going to say this is wrong and we shouldn't."

"Yes." Aaron watched the hands playing with his own, then looked beyond to the unmistakable bulge resting against Tony's thigh. "The rules —"

"The rules are stupid," Tony interrupted. "They tell us we can't be involved as it presents a safety hazard. But, let me ask you this, would you protect me less if we were fucking?"

A blush rose to Aaron's face. He couldn't hide it. Decided he didn't need to.

"Would you be so busy looking at my ass that you wouldn't see a ghoul coming at us?"

"I might." Aaron gave a wicked smile.

"Fair enough." Tony grinned back. "How fast would you move to rectify that situation, were you distracted as described?"

"Fast."

"Well, then. If you are as bound by desire as you are the rules to protect me, as you attest" — Tony bent and kissed his eyelid — "I don't see a problem." He planted a kiss on Aaron's other lid. "Do you?"

Aaron looked up into Tony's face. His smile grew so large he thought his face might split.

Tony nodded, satisfied, then lunged forward. He caught Aaron's head in his hand as he drove him backwards, his mouth crushing his lips, legs straddling his body. The force slammed them against the tub. Aaron took little notice. All that mattered was Tony pressed against him, his warm, sweat-dampened chest sliding against his shirt.

Tony's kiss was deep and skilled. With each caress of his tongue, a jolt of electric pleasure shot down Aaron's abdomen to his groin. His dick stiffened. Tony moved to his neck and he licked and kissed along his jugular, lapping slow and cat-like. Aaron clenched Tony's arms. The muscles rippled beneath his hand. Tony arched in, and pressed his cock against Aaron's. Aaron's dick jumped at the proximity. He reached for Tony's pants, but he was slapped gently away. Tony grazed Aaron's neck with his teeth as he smiled against it, letting out a little laugh.

"How do you like it?" he whispered in Aaron's ear. Dizzying blood pounded there at the question.

"I just want you," was all Aaron could answer. His body trembled with anticipation.

Tony trailed along Aaron's jaw, up to his mouth. He kissed him lightly, still smiling. His teeth snapped over Aaron's lip, biting hard. Aaron cried out in surprise. A moment later, Tony's hand cupped his balls and rubbed gently. Pleasure coursed through his cock.

"Do you want me like this?"

Aaron didn't trust himself to speak. He had never been with someone so confident, so sure of what would bring his own body pleasure. The dark thing roiled against Tony's alpha play. Anything the nastiness inside him disliked, Aaron found appealing. Besides, the look in Tony's eyes and the delicious tingle in his lip and crotch were too much to resist.

"How about this?" Tony grinned and pulled the Class-A restraints out of his belt.

Enthralled by Tony's charm, and aroused beyond reason, Aaron held out his hands. The creature inside him growled, but desire drowned the protest.

Tony closed the distance between them with a kiss. As he explored Aaron's mouth with his tongue, he worked his hands down Aaron's arms. The cold metal shackles clamped around one of his wrists. The magic within them hummed pleasantly against his flesh. Tony kissed his neck, brought his hands to the side to a loop of pipe protruding from the floor. He threaded the restraints through the pipe and clamped the restraint over Aaron's other hand. A moment later, the pleasure turned to stabbing pain. The dark thing howled in fury. Aaron had been tricked.

"What are you?" Tony pulled back, all trace of warmth gone from his face.

"What do you mean?"

"When you came out of the Laundromat your eyes were yellow. Why?"

Aaron shook his head.

"I could have called Acquisitions to come get you right then. But I didn't. I wanted to give you a chance to explain. So don't throw my generosity back in my face with stupid blank stares and lame shrugs. What are you?"

"You know." Aaron sagged into his restraints. The humiliation of being lured into confinement in an obvious holding device in his partner's bathroom was nothing compared to the fact he was to face this reality with a still raging hard on. His sins of omission had come home to roost far sooner than he'd expected. "Everyone suspects it. How else could I survive an attack of the Six Rivers clan? You know as well as anyone in our line of work that a werewolf bite is lethal unless you are that one person in twenty-five thousand who has the gateway gene. Everyone in my office had werewolf bites."

"And you're not dead."

"No, I'm not." Aaron gave a small smile. "Although there were times in the beginning I wished I were."

"Why didn't you tell me?"

"And say what? Hi, I'm Aaron Marvell, werewolf, and your new partner? Or should I have turned right there in the bullpen? That's what Ellison was angling for, you know. He was trying to humiliate me into turning. A couple of months ago it would have worked."

"You have better control that that, though?"

"Now, yes. Thanks to Carlos, my ex. He reached out to me after the attack. His clan had heard about what happened, that there was a survivor. He found me and counseled me about the change. Fortunately the full moon had just gone, so I had a few weeks to wrap my head around it before the first shift took me. Carlos and the others made sure I was secluded and safe for that first transformation. They guided me through the process. Carlos then mentored me, taught me what it was like to live as a werewolf in modern society, to avoid doing the things that make people like you and me head out on a termination hunt."

"But he didn't come with you to Maryland?"

"No." Aaron sensed a shift in Tony's line of questioning. It was a sign of hope. "We ended up together too soon after the attack. Some days I was fine, almost normal. Other days I had horrific nightmares, panic attacks where I screamed my head off for hours on end, general freak-outs where I forgot where I was, who my friends were." Aaron shifted in an unsuccessful attempt to ease the cramp growing in his side. "I often shifted during those times. I couldn't control it. After the initial transformation my shifts became violent, unpredictable. The full moon guaranteed a shift for me, but the rest of the month was not a change-free period for me the way it is for other weres."

"Why not?" Tony asked.

"I don't know. Nobody does. But, that's how it was—is—for me." His answering shrug sent a wave of pain down his wrists from the restraints. He stopped moving. "They locked me up in Carlos' house and kept a guard on me twenty-four hours a day. I would change unprovoked, and attack whichever pack member was assigned to babysit me. Carlos had to shoot me with tranqs to keep me down. And then I would shift back, wake up with blood staining my mouth and cry for hours, begging Carlos to kill me."

Begging was the mildest term for it. Naked, snot running from his nose and drool dribbling down his chin, screaming unintelligible words as he slammed his head into the wall in the hopes of dashing his brains out of his skull... Aaron fought off a chill at the memory.

"We did have a few good days out of the five months we were together. I clung to the memories of them while Carlos grew brooding and unreachable, haunted by the countless days that were nowhere near happy. Even though I eventually gained control of myself, it was too late for us. Carlos had given me everything he had, and in return I emptied him like a soda can and crushed him for good measure. When the transfer order came, he encouraged me to head out and give my life another shot. He was relieved."

"Did you ask him to come with you?"

"Of course. And of course he said no."

Tony watched him for a few moments, his expression softening. Finally, he said, "What's Ellison's beef with you?"

"Who knows?" Aaron laughed. "He's been a jackass since day one. I lost track of him after the attack. Thought shaking loose of his endlessly running mouth was the one small blessing I'd earned in this mess. But no, here he is. Maybe he resents me for what happened to our co-workers. More likely he resents I was the one lauded as a hero when he was off taking a sick day and missing the slaughter. He definitely suspects I've become a were. Maybe he's waiting for his golden opportunity to shift the paradigm, turn himself into the hero that saves the Grange branch from the nasty werewolf."

The floor trembled, cutting off Tony's reply.

"Qi?" Aaron asked, although he was certain he knew the answer. His stomach knotted once more, urged him to escape his bonds and make for the sulfurous gateway that had just opened. The awareness of that odd sensation faded as the shaking increased. The lights in the main room flickered. The furniture jounced.

"I'd say so," Tony replied.

"Let me out, then." Aaron jangled his restraints. "You need me for backup."

Tony cast a critical glance at him, then at the restraints. He opened his mouth again to speak, then shut it and shook his head.

"You don't trust me. I get it." Aaron pressed. "But, I had your back today in the Laundromat. And what I agreed to, about always having it, I meant. Whatever bullshit game you were playing with me through the past twenty minutes, I don't care. I meant what I said. If nothing else that happened between us matters, fine. But, I am your partner. Sworn and bound to protect you from harm." His voice rose as doubt flashed across Tony's expression. "Sworn and bound. And I can't do a thing about it with my damn hands cuffed to a pipe."

"Sorry," Tony said. "I have to concentrate on one potential threat at a time." With that, he rose and left the room, pulling the door closed behind him.

Aaron didn't bother to struggle against the restraints. They were magically sealed and intuitive to the size and potential lethality of their captives. The more flexing and prying he did, the tighter the bond, the more severe the electrical shocks would become. He scooted to a full sitting position and sat cross-legged and sullen, listening to the commotion outside.

The shaking escalated until the light bulbs rattled in their sockets, then died off, replaced by voices. Although Aaron couldn't make out the words, he could hear the charming, enticing lilt in Tony's voice, and the contrasting sandpaper-across-concrete rasp of Qi's. After a few moments of back and forth, the grating voice began to rise in agitation. Aaron leaned forward to try to hear what was being said. The restraints tightened with his movement.

"...not your problem..." A few of Tony's words made their way to Aaron's ears. "...broom...who bought...?"

Qi's rumbling grew louder, more menacing. Aaron scooted forward, his arms now uncomfortably strained to one side, his wrists pulled tight against the cuffs. His joints screamed against the strain, his hands burnt with electrical fire.

"Who hired—?" Tony was suddenly cut off. A fraction of a second later, something crashed into a piece of furniture, splintering it. "Hang on a second, Qi. Hang on." Tony's weakened voice came from another area of the room. The sour note of panic drifted under the door to his nose.

Aaron struggled against his bonds. The restraints tightened until his fingers grew purple. From outside came another crash, followed by a human yell. The grating rumble became a torrent, sounding like a garbage disposal gnawing away at a ceaseless supply of waste. Tony's placations turned to shouted threats, useless ones, apparently, as the sounds of destruction grew more violent. Tony's voice faded away as he either fought or fled his attacker. Wood splintered. Glass shattered. Tony's pained shout cut through the building like a knife.

Aaron's composure fell away at the sound. His bones shifted, popped and slid into their new positions. Hair sprouted along his body. He knelt against the floor, bowing his head and keeping his back straight, aiding the shift as Carlos had taught. Even with his mind eager for the change, his muscles primed to accept the transition, it was agony. Aaron's face elongated. Tissue crackled under his thickening skin. His sinuses stretched. His clothes tore from his body as his muscles changed and bulged. Sulfur and the scent of Tony's fear filled his nose. His thumbs faded under the shaggy black fur of his foot.

Fully shifted, he pulled against the restraint, but it had already adapted to his changed physiology. On his first clan-approved outing he had accidentally peed on an electric fence. The agony of that was nothing compared to the frantic bolts of power shooting into his forelegs. The struggle outside was growing sporadic. He could hear Tony's heart racing, could feel the fatigue in his limbs. The wolf in him knew when a kill was certain, and it recognized it now. Tony was prey.

Aaron pulled against the restraints. The cuffs cut into his thick fur, then into his skin, all the while shooting volts into his body. He snarled and bore down, pulling with all of his enhanced strength as his muscles twitched involuntarily with the ceaseless shocks. The tiles around the pipe cracked. A chunk of porcelain flew into the air. Aaron pulled harder. The pipe inched upwards, buckling the floor, splintering grout. Tony had grown quiet. His heart was slowing. His breathing rasped and sputtered, then halted.

Aaron gave one last massive heave and the pipe clattered free. He crashed into the floor.

Tony's breathing resumed in a coughing fit that echoed like a windstorm in Aaron's perked ears.

A shadow darkened the glass door.

Aaron had earned Qi's attention.

With front paws still bound together, Aaron sat back onto his powerful haunches, propelled out of the shoes still clinging to his back paws and leaped through the glass.

Chapter Seven

Dogs Like You

Glass clung to his fur and stabbed at his muzzle as Aaron sailed through the opening he had made. Qi, flat-faced, nearly as black as Aaron's pitch fur and as big as a pair of NFL linebackers, was not prepared to meet a werewolf. The demon shouted in utter astonishment and backpedalled. Teeth bared, Aaron flung his monstrous lupine bulk into Qi. He drove the demon to the ground. His bound front paws slipped on the wood floor, but he caught himself by burying his teeth in Qi's neck. The whites of Qi's eyes shined wide with panic, but the demon made no sound. Aaron kept the pressure tight on Qi's neck, agonizing, terrifying, but not deadly. Not yet. Foul blood trickled onto his tongue. Aaron searched the room for Tony. His partner was sitting on the floor like a rag doll that had been dumped by a fickle child. A deep purple bruise ringed his neck where Qi had choked him. His breath wheezed past the injured windpipe. Aaron whined for him. Tony shook his head as if to clear it, then looked dazedly at Aaron. His jaw dropped as Aaron regarded him with yellow wolf eyes.

"Oh, shit."

If Aaron could have smiled, he would have. Instead he looked down at the demon, then back at Tony. He whined and perked his ears questioningly.

"Let him up," Tony said.

Aaron snarled a warning at the dangerous hulk sprawled under him.

"It's okay," Tony replied. "We've got this. Let him up."

Aaron quickly released Qi. He leaped back from the rising demon. His bound paws caused him to land awkwardly at Tony's feet. He curled around in front of his partner, shoulders brushing Tony's hips, and faced the demon, snarling loudly.

"Looks like you tell me who ordered that broom from you, or you become puppy chow," Tony said. He placed his hand on Aaron's head, ran his fingers through the coarse fur until they contacted skin.

Aaron thrilled at the touch. To Qi, he offered a growl that rumbled deep in his throat and nearly vibrated the floor.

Qi glanced from Tony to Aaron, clearly assessing the threat.

Aaron raised his hackles. The demon in front of him was not a true predator. He could sense it. For all of his brawn, Qi didn't have much in the way of real power. He was a metal smith with a single specific magical ability, nothing more. When faced with equal strength, werewolf strength, he would back down. Aaron put on his best menacing predator expression.

"Private transaction," the demon relented.

"I'd guess all of your transactions are under the table," Tony replied. "Try giving us something a little more specific."

"Dumbass humans, always getting in where you don't belong," Qi muttered. When Aaron growled again, he changed his tone. "All I know is someone came to me wearing a glamour. It was a male, I'm pretty sure. Human, from the smell of him." The nostril slits on his face flared. "Pushy. Wanted a rushed job. I gave him one. Double price. He paid half up front, welched on the second." Qi smiled around a mouthful of rotten teeth. "Bet those bristles cut real deep in the floor, didn't they? Left all sorts of telltale marks."

"They did, at that," Tony agreed. "You made him a shoddy broom on purpose?"

"I get insulted, I get distracted." Qi gave a shrug. "My work suffers."

"You made sure those bristles dug into the concrete. You wanted us to find you?"

"Me? No. Not particularly." Qi gave another shrug. "Just the one who hired me. I figured he deserved a run in with you assholes after walking off without paying me in full. But, instead of finding him, you geniuses found me... How did you find me, by the way? I'm hard to track, you know. Only former clients can call my 'number'." He jabbed a meaty fist at the splintered bathroom door and the candles flickering beyond.

"We received a tip."

"An informant? Demon, no doubt." Qi's featureless face crumpled in disgust. A moment later, he shook off his irritation. "Oh, well. I'll just change my word of power, *again*."

"How would you like it if we did what you wanted and caught this guy? Maybe insulted him the way he insulted you?"

"Go on."

"We catch this guy, make him confess. Hold him in a cell for who knows how long. Could even become a termination job. You'd like that, big guy?"

Qi grinned.

"We get this human, we get our rocks off, you get your rocks off. Everyone is happy. And we don't come looking for you ever again. You can keep making your hellfire brooms with no interference from Kapre Security, Maryland. You have free rein to conduct your business as you please while we turn a blind eye. C'mon, Qi, it's the cherry on the proverbial shake."

"Cake," Qi corrected.

"Demons now know clichés?"

"I make it my business to sound hospitable to my potential clients. Being familiar with human lingo helps me fit in."

"You must do a lot of your work over the phone," Tony remarked as he surveyed the massive, midnight-hued demon. "Anyway, I don't like cake. I like shakes. Now, how about your buyer? Any specifics you can remember?"

"I give you information, then it gets out that my reputation for being closed-mouth goes down the drain. That's not good for business. Killing you here and now, well, that might be a better way of putting a stopper in this leaking jar."

Aaron stepped forward, snarling. His mouth watered for the taste of blood.

"Easy, now," Tony said, keeping his hand entwined in Aaron's scruff. "My friend is getting anxious for answers. Look, we only need a hint, a push in the right direction. That's all."

"Like I said, he had on a glamour. Couldn't see past it. But, he was talking a lot about dogs."

"Dogs?" Tony tightened his fist in Aaron's fur.

"Not just any dogs." Qi fixed Aaron with a grin. "Dogs like you."

Aaron perked his ears.

"You don't know?" Qi let out a booming laugh. "You don't know!"

"Cut the shit, Qi," Tony said. His fingers were so tightly laced in Aaron's hair it hurt.

"I'll give you the one bit of information that'll get you going, plus ease the curiosity of your pointy-eared friend, here. And then I'll be on my way, undisturbed. Is that a deal?"

"Deal."

"You're not just any oversized wolf, my panting friend." Qi leaned in close. "Oh, no. There are lots of different doggies out there, and your bite came from pretty high on the supernatural food chain."

A whine escaped Aaron's throat before he could squelch it. The sound brought the smile back to Qi's face.

"You're welcome." Qi gave a small, mocking bow, then disappeared.

Chapter Eight

Mixed Messages

Qi's departure left behind a stench of burning sulfur. Tony immediately removed his hand from Aaron's scruff. Aaron looked up at him, but Tony avoided his gaze. A moment later the Thurisaz sigil appeared, glowing softly in the exact spot the demon had been standing. Qi's appearance at—and assumed intended compliance to—human command was listed on the exhaustingly long list of official bad ideas noted in the British Anglo-Demonic Pact.

"I should call that in before Braven sends a team out here," Tony said. He bent down and unfastened the restraints, then stood and moved away. "Why don't you change? There are clothes in the bedroom closet. Take whatever you want." He gestured up the stairs, fished his phone out of his pocket and gave Aaron his back.

Aaron watched him dial the switchboard number and give his access code. Would Tony include him in his call-in? Would he report that he had a werewolf for a partner? Aaron decided he didn't want to hear. He trudged up the steps, Tony's voice fading only slightly due to his excellent hearing. Once he'd changed, however, his human ears wouldn't be able to pick up the sounds of his partner turning him over to Braven.

Aaron wasn't looking forward to shifting back into human form. As a wolf he was still dimly aware of his alter ego's concerns, but the wolf mind had little time for trivialities like feelings of disappointment, betrayal, humiliation. The man part of Aaron, though, would keenly know each of those feelings, and would undoubtedly wish to wallow in one or more of them. The dark thing, spurred by the terror of Qi's insinuation that he was no ordinary werewolf, urged him not to bother with any of it a moment longer. It told him to run off into the night, find the deepest, most secluded patch of woods and happily hunt rabbits until he died. Aaron had to admit it sounded nice, except the shift couldn't last forever. He was human first, wolf second. So to human he would always revert, no matter how much he fought, how much control he exerted. At some point his body would force itself back into its natural state, then he would be a naked man squatting in the woods with a dead rabbit hanging from his mouth.

As if this last thought flipped a switch in his head, his bones began to grind. A whine escaped from his tightly clamped muzzle. His chest heaved with repressed panting. The thick hair covering his body retracted. His skin stretched with the extension of his skeleton. Tendons groaned under the pressure of his shifting structure. His face raged with agony as his muzzle pulled back into his sinuses. His eye sockets shifted, the pressure stuffing up his diminishing nose. He kept his focus away from the standing mirror in the corner of the open loft bedroom. He had once made the mistake of catching a reflected glimpse of this current stage of his transformation. Patchy, with clumps of fur hanging from his body, bent at the waist with half human, half canine appendages, face a wreck of a hodgepodge, fangs overlying human lips. It was a sight he never wished to see again.

The final sinews popped into place. Aaron collapsed onto his side. The return shift always took more out of him. He laid there for a few minutes, marveling at his fingers and the precise control they had—so different from the ungainly paws—and ignored the warning sirens wailing in his mind. If Tony had called Kapre, if an acqxterm team was on their way, there was little he could do about it. The bulk of his supernatural power lasted only as long as the shift, and burned up much of his regular human energy to boot. It was one of those secrets Carlos had warned him the general public could never hear of. They had to think werewolves' strength persisted at all times. If word got out that werewolves suffered a weak period after shifting, then the humans hunting them would alter their attack strategies, much to the detriment of the weres.

And so the nagging human thoughts resume. Aaron pried himself off the floor.

"Normalcy wins every time, mi hombre guapo." Carlos' voice joined his own thoughts.

Giving in, he staggered over to the European closets lining half of the far wall. He pulled open the doors of the first cabinets and grabbed a T-shirt and a pair of track pants, both of which hung neatly on hangars. Despite his gloomy mood, he chuckled. He had never seen anyone hang sweats before. It was downright strange. He glanced down at the long single row of drawers at the base of the cabinets. Could a man have so many pairs of underwear and socks that he needed every drawer? It was too tempting a question not to look.

With a quick glance at the open railing and stairs, Aaron squatted and pulled open the first drawer. Socks. He moved to the next. Instead of the expectant underwear, he discovered a pile of porn DVDs, each of them showing beautiful men being pleasured by heavily muscled gods. Cocks in asses. Cocks in mouths. Cum on lips and tongues. Ropes and handcuffs dominated the covers. It turned his thoughts to earlier, and despite the negative situation, the memory of the restraints buzzing against his wrists sent a thrill through him. Before Carlos, he had been content to simply find a nice guy who had his own job and apartment, could tolerate his frequent sudden and mysterious career-related travel and was content to throw a weekly quick fuck and maybe a blow job into the equation. After his transformation, life had been exciting enough. Restraints were for keeping mad weres like him from killing people. Using them for anything else had never entered his mind. Even now he found it difficult separating the notion of sexual bondage from hostile prisoner status. But looking down at the images on the movie covers he felt a stirring of curiosity, the same excitement he had felt earlier with Tony, titillation at the confident certainty of purpose and pleasure the covers conveyed. While he wasn't keen on being hogtied anytime soon, he wondered what it would be like to tie up Tony and do to him some of the things the photos suggested. The notion made him hard.

"I see you found my...clothes."

Aaron turned his head to find Tony standing at the top of the stairs. He hastily bunched the pants and shirt in front of him to hide his erection.

"Do they fit?" Once again Tony was wearing that confident, charming smile, the one that sought to assure him they were friends.

This time, however, Aaron wasn't sure he could buy it.

"I think you and my things are a perfect fit."

"Again with the double talk," Aaron snapped. "Here you are hitting on me, or pretending to hit on me, and you just called me in to Kapre. Is this another trick? See if I'm dumb enough to let you tie me up and wait for the cavalry again?"

"I didn't report you." Tony moved closer. He tossed Aaron's phone on the bed so he could reach it. "Didn't turn on your red alert tracker, either."

"Why not?" Aaron tried to hide the relief from his voice as he turned his back and pulled on the clothes. He faced Tony as he secured his phone in his waistband, thankful the pants were baggy enough to conceal his fading erection.

"Why should I? You were the victim of an attack. And I've seen you shifted. You were no threat to me just now. Just the opposite. You saved my life. Qi was going to choke me to death."

"I know."

"So, I'm sorry."

"You're sorry you seduced me and made me look like a fool? Or, you're sorry because you were nearly killed and I had the decency to stop it, despite your asinine behavior?"

"Both."

"Well, then." Aaron turned away and began closing the drawers. "I'll have your clothes clean and waiting for you on your desk tomorrow. Braven will have my resignation on hers."

"No, she won't."

Tony's hand dropped down onto his shoulder. He shook it off.

"I'm sorry I did those things as part of my stupid trick, but I'm not sorry I did them," Tony said. "And I'm not sorry we're partners. And I'm not sorry for this." Tony dropped to his knees. Before Aaron could react, his face was cupped in Tony's hands. Tony covered his mouth, kissing him deeply. His scent, his taste, the nearness of his heartbeat, they all overwhelmed Aaron's thoughts, stirred inside him the dark thing who had so recently been put to bed. Carried on a wave of animalistic desire, Aaron opened his mouth to Tony. A moment later the wave crashed, and human logic hit. Aaron pulled away.

"I've gotta go," he said. "I can't do this. Not with you. Not after all of this."

"Don't go," Tony said.

"What right do you have to ask that of me?"

"None." Tony spread his hands in a pleading gesture. "But I didn't mean..."

"Your intent doesn't matter." Aaron stood to loom over Tony, who cleverly remained kneeling, penitent and subservient, at his feet. It pleased the wolf. The human, however, was far less easily swayed. "You hurt me, whether you wanted to or not. You made me feel good about my job and myself for the first time in a long while. Maybe that's my fault for letting someone I met six hours ago have that kind of influence over my happiness... Of course it is. But, I'm not going to let that happen again. I understand you're sorry, and I accept it. And I'm going home."

"You don't have your car." Tony tried one last angle. "Let me drive you, at least."

"I'll catch a cab."

Tony made a helpless sound and shrugged, clearly out of tactics. The gesture lifted his pecs, heightened the definition of his shoulders and tightened his sculptural abs. The patch of skin Aaron had doctored earlier shined pink and new — a swipe of imperfection that merely accentuated the divinity of form around it. A ragged breath escaped Aaron's throat. His gut twisted like an invisible fishing line had secured around it. It tugged with an almost violent desire. With a force of will that depleted his remaining strength, Aaron turned to the stairs. He clattered down the treads two at a time, lest his weakness land him in trouble yet again.

Chapter Nine

Dredging up the Past

Even through the cloying 'Sunshine Rain' scent of his detergent, Tony's aroma screamed at Aaron. The richness of musk and man swirled through his head like an exotic dancer, teasing, promising, inviting. A deep chill pervaded the air, and Aaron set off for home, determined to let the cold and exhaustion work out his frustrations. He made it just three blocks without his shoes before he pulled his cell out of his waistband and resignedly called a cab.

The driver's mass spilled over the front seat across the armrest. His eyes, constantly flicking up to the rear-view to observe Aaron, were vacant and unsettling. The monster inside him labeled the man a predator, but not the sort he was used to dealing with. Aaron made a mental note of the driver's posted information and jammed himself as far into the corner of the back seat and door as possible and let the scenery tick by.

"Belle Woods, that's the new apartments out there on Backfin Road?" the driver asked.

Aaron nodded.

The dark thing snarled.

A few minutes later the cab pulled up into the apartment complex. Aaron motioned for him to stop in front of the clubhouse. He did not want this man knowing where he lived. He passed a twenty up to the driver and climbed out. He hesitated a moment, then swung back to the car. The driver rolled the window down, his expression as blank as before. Aaron relaxed just enough for his alter ego to scrabble for control. He directed its power, felt the shift in his vision. The driver's sudden slacked jaw and smell of terror confirmed they had turned wolfish, deadly.

"Whatever it is you're doing, or planning on doing, you should stop." Aaron leaned closer, sucking air into his nose with a loud sniff. "I can smell the evil on you. It's a distinct odor, one I won't have any trouble at all tracking should the need arise." He channeled Tony's easy grin as he pulled away from the window and gave the vinyl a slap. "You have a good night, now."

The driver, pale and sweaty, peeled out of the parking lot and sped away.

The encounter left the dark thing unsettled. As he made his way along the labyrinth of sidewalks, Aaron's senses slammed into overdrive. Each scent that drifted to him was that of another predator, each rustle of shrubbery and elongated shadow an ambush. His childhood dog used to snap at leaves borne on the wind, whipping this way and that to snatch the threatening objects out of the air, never gaining hold of one because another fluttering object caught his attention mid-attack. This was how the monster in him now reacted, racing in metaphorical circles, gnashing teeth at every imagined aggressor. By the time Aaron reached his door, his heart was racing.

Overcome by the multitude of alarms wailing in his brain he pushed into the bathroom and slammed the door behind him. His hands were shaking. Letting the dark thing rise so soon after a full shift had been a bad idea. It knew he was tired and his focus shattered. And it was wide awake.

Right after he was bitten the creature would fight him for control, try to gain dominance in their relationship. Unlike Carlos and his weres, Aaron was not the wolf. It wasn't simply a facet of him, nor he a facet of it. The thing living inside him was entirely independent and viewed him and his body as nothing more than a defiant member of its pack who did not know its hierarchical place. All of these attempts at subjugation made Aaron frantic and added to his erratic behavior, which was already in overdrive from the PTSD. Carlos had helped, taught him ways to turn back the rising tide of panic and prevent it from gaining control.

Aaron snapped open the shower curtain and turned the cold water on full blast. The spray splattered against the fiberglass in a familiar rhythmic tattoo. He sat down, side pressed against the tub. A fine, cool mist tickled his face. He leaned his head against the side and let the noise drown out all external sounds. It soothed him, denied the hungry beast the adrenaline it thrived on. Deprived of mental and physical stimulation, the dark thing soon subsided. Overwhelmed with exhaustion, Aaron leaned back against the tub and closed his eyes.

* * * *

Aaron awakened to the sound of soft laughter.

"Left you tied up there too long?" Tony *stood over him, his shirtless torso gleaming with sweat.*

Confused, Aaron blinked away the sleepiness. His hands tingled from the restraints and his arms ached from their awkward slant. The massive tub chilled his back. He rattled the restraints against the pipe. They held fast. His mind churned with the slowness of first awakening. He was home, wasn't he? Hadn't he already been chained up? Hadn't he already escaped and saved Tony from Qi?

"That demon put up a helluva fight," Tony said, as if reading his thoughts. "I got him subdued, though. Got the information we needed." He knelt beside Aaron, his crystalline eyes sparkling. He held out a bloody knife. Its handle declared 'www.KapreSecureNation.com' in tacky trade show font. "Then I put this in his brain."

Aaron stared. This wasn't right. It didn't happen this way.

"Come on, don't be mad," Tony said, sidling up against him. He pressed his lips to Aaron's neck. "I only restrained you to keep you out of the way. You know Qi couldn't see you like this. It was his birthday, after all."

Aaron looked down. His entire body was covered in wolfish fur. Through the riot of horrified confusion in his head he managed, "No, I guess I'm not dressed right."

"That's more like it." Tony smiled and cupped his face in his hands. "Let's get you taken care of, hoss."

Hoss?

Tony's mouth came down on his with brutal force, his teeth crushing Aaron's lips. Blood trickled into Aaron's mouth. The wolf howled for more, and he shuddered.

"Are you cold?" Tony pulled away. "Let's get you into the tub. It'll be full in just a sec."

Tony reached over and unclasped the restraints. Aaron's arms fell dead in his lap. Tony ran his hands down Aaron's furred extremities, stroking circulation back into them. His fingers screamed with tingling pain, but he didn't mind as long as Tony continued running his hands along them. His cock jumped to life at the thought of those caressing hands wandering elsewhere. Panic filled him. What if he was still a wolf...down there? Aaron squirmed, wanted to run and hide, but there was nowhere to retreat. Tony had him pinned against the side of the massive tub.

"Let's get this off of you." Tony kissed him again, then began snatching away chunks of his fur.

Aaron cried out in anticipatory agony, but his wolfish coat fell away in painless tufts, leaving behind bare, undamaged skin. Tony grinned with delight. He leaned in and ran his tongue along Aaron's chest. He teased his nipples with his teeth, then dropped his head and kissed a trail from his sternum to belly button. Tony dipped lower and Aaron thrust his hips to meet Tony's open mouth. He groaned as Tony covered the head of his engorged cock and suckled gently. Tony pulled away and licked the base a few teasing times, then ran his tongue up the shaft in long, slow strokes. Aaron threw back his head. His hair trailed in the metallic smelling water sloshing against the edge. Tony pulled at the tip with firm, sure pressure as his tongue teased the ridge. Aaron let his head fall to the side as he gave in to the pleasure. His unfocused vision caught a burst of color in the otherwise stark white room, but then Tony was running his mouth along the entirety of his shaft and he drifted away on a new wave of ecstasy.

Tony found his sac and cradled it gently, squeezing lightly as Tony took all of his cock into his throat. Tony pulled back, suctioning with his full lips closed tightly around his shaft, then plunged down again, taking him deep into his throat. Aaron moaned. Tony moved faster, pulling and sucking.

An intense pressure built just beneath his head. Aaron's shaft spasmed. He flung back his grasping hands, seeking support as his cum shot into Tony's waiting mouth and the orgasm shuddered through his body with driving pleasure.

His flailing hands hit the water. It splashed across the floor. A few drops spattered along Tony's back. They were red.

"Tony?"

Tony continued working at his still shuddering organ. The sensation was quickly fading to something bordering on pain.

He grabbed Tony's shoulder. His hand was covered in viscous red. With a startled shout, he looked back. The tub brimmed with blood. The heads of his former colleagues bobbed on its surface. They bumped around, knocked loudly against the sides. He screamed. Tony consolingly lapped his dick.

"Tony!"

He looked down to see the black wolf sitting between his knees, licking red from its muzzle.

Aaron awakened, screaming and clawing at the air. His feet, acting on his brain's instinctive commands, scrabbled against the damp tiles in an effort to flee, but his trembling legs would not let him stand. The screams came from his throat in short, desperate bursts. The scent of the wolf lingered in his nose. The knocking of the heads in the tub continued, grew in volume until they crashed like splintering wood.

"Aaron!" a voice that was not Tony's cried out.

The floor shook with advancing footsteps. Aaron tried to muffle his screams with his fist. A man burst through the door, slid on the film of overspray from the shower, and fell, sprawling on the tiles next to Aaron.

"Mi hombre, it's me. It's me," the man said as he wrangled his long limbs under him.

The words scratched the surface of his hysteria enough for Aaron to realize he was curled on the bathroom floor in the middle of a hysterical fit. Carlos was now on his knees, leaning protectively over him, his dark curls sticking to his forehead and stubbly cheeks, performing his practiced search of Aaron's face for signs of lucidity. For a moment Aaron thought he was still asleep, that this was some new and torturous aspect of the dream, but then came the other voice.

"Is he okay?" Matthew, the Trinity Clan's second-in-command asked from the doorway.

Tall and fit, with slicked blond hair and pale blue eyes, he was the negative mirror to Carlos in every physical way, the white chess king to the black. As Matthew watched Carlos cradle Aaron, Aaron's tormented mind wrenched into overdrive. He smelled the truth of the matter on the man even before he saw Carlos' expression soften slightly when he returned the glance. He knew it before the words came out of Carlos' mouth.

"Give us some time, *Cielito*."

"All right." Matthew's gaze flicked between the pair of them and finally settled, confidant and trusting, on Carlos. "I'll go get you a replacement front door. This one is beyond repair."

Carlos gestured to his back pocket where his wallet rested. Matthew waved it away with a smile. It was all too comfortable. Too familiar. Aaron looked at the tiles.

"I'll be back in twenty." Matthew pulled the bathroom door shut behind him.

Chapter Ten

Trinity

"'Sweetheart'?" It was the first coherent word that crawled out of his terror-paralyzed mouth, and Aaron wanted to shove it back in there with the screams that still bubbled at the edge of his throat.

"Aaron..." Carlos began.

"No." Aaron waved a hand. *You cared for me, but didn't love me. I made it too hard to be loved. I was a freak having regular freak-outs. I attacked members of your clan, your family. You fought for me, risked your position, your authority, your respect. You protected me from everyone, including myself. If I ever loved you, and I know I did, I can't deny you happiness now. Even though it pisses me off to no extent, go ahead and be happy.* All of these things were what he was supposed to say. They rushed through his mind in a split-second, but never made it to his lips. "No. It's okay."

Aaron stood and turned off the shower. The overspray had soaked the floor at the tub's edge. He dropped a towel onto the puddle and mopped it up with his foot, grateful for a reason not to look at Carlos.

"Are you all right?" Carlos asked.

"Better now," he said. "Why are you here?"

"I came because we have wolf business to discuss. I didn't bring Matthew to rub anything in. I would have left him home if I could. But, he is Beta, and is the second strongest in the pack. I needed that."

"I don't understand." Aaron picked up the sodden towel and slung it over the curtain rod. He wanted to ask about the threat Carlos spoke of, but his mind couldn't leave Matthew. "You two were alpha and beta for how many years?"

"Forty."

"And you never got together until just a month after I left town? That's odd, to say the least." He had a hard time hiding the hurt in his voice. It didn't matter. Carlos was well aware of how he expressed pain. Aaron was certain it was written all over his body, redolent in his scent.

"We had been together well before that."

"Are you saying you cheated on him with me?" Now Aaron was looking at Carlos, and the expression on his former lover's face did nothing to ease his internal torment. "Right in front of him?"

"*Mi hombre*, sixty years is a long time for a couple to be together without growing bored. Matthew and I have drifted apart and back together several times."

Aaron studied his former lover's slender face. Carlos was nearly a hundred years old. The wolf was deeply ingrained within him. Matthew was not much younger, and also a very lupine man. It made sense they would be together, for no one could understand the mind of an alpha like another male of near age and status, not even an alpha female — which was a historically scarce thing in Carlos' clan. Pack business forced the leaders to be close, to develop a tight bond of mutual trust which undoubtedly fostered other feelings of closeness. As much as he hated it, Aaron understood that part. What he was having trouble with was how they could forsake each other over and over, yet still come back together like nothing was wrong. That, and how his entire relationship with Carlos now seemed contrived, scheduled to fail.

His mind inadvertently turned to Tony, and the hurt he would feel if Tony were to spurn him out of boredom. Although it was an unpleasant sensation, it somehow made facing Carlos a little easier.

"So then why are you and Matthew here?"

"Can we go somewhere else?" Carlos gestured to their surroundings with a wry grin.

Aaron took in the dripping showerhead, the limp towel, his borrowed and now thoroughly dampened track pants. He couldn't resist a small smile in return. "So, my standards aren't high enough for the alpha of the Trinity Clan?"

"Your standards are perfect," Carlos said. His face sobered. "I'm sorry it turned out like this."

Aaron nodded. "Go on into the living room. There are sodas and stuff in the fridge, harder stuff in the far left upper cabinet if you want. I'm going to change my clothes and then I'll be out."

Once safe behind the closed bedroom door, Aaron exhaled a shaky breath.

"Shit." He borrowed Tony's interjection, breathed it softly so Carlos' wolf ears didn't pick it up. He leaned against the jamb for a moment until the shakiness subsided. He hadn't had a panic attack since he'd left California. It was strange he would relapse on the night Carlos came to town. Maybe some connection inside him noted the pack leader's presence, stirred up the old ghost.

He pulled a pair of clean jeans from his dresser and a loose button-up from his closet. He left his feet bare, as the dark thing had taught him distaste for suffocating shoes. He looked in the mirror and gave a quick swipe to his hair. The banal sandy locks fell right back into chaos, and he let them be. He wasn't trying to impress anyone. Not anymore.

He opened the door to find Carlos on the couch, a mixed drink in hand. He watched Aaron approach, swirling the glass so the ice clinked rhythmically against the glass.

"You look good, *mi hombre*," he said as Aaron sat in the armchair opposite him.

No more 'guapo' for you. Out loud, Aaron replied, "I feel good. Aside from tonight's little freak fest, I've been in control."

"You shifted today." It wasn't a question.

"Earlier. To save my partner."

"You let a Kapre agent see you shift?" Carlos' voice lost the friendly edge and took on the authoritative growl of the alpha.

"It was necessary. He won't say anything."

"How do you know that?"

Because he already had me handcuffed to a pipe and didn't bother to call it in. "We're friends."

"Fast friends, eh?" Carlos agitated the ice cubes until they rattled like teeth in the cold. "People who are quick to help oftentimes want something from you."

"Kind of like how you were quick to take me in?"

"Ah, you get sharper every day." Carlos smiled. "Do you remember how I found you?"

"How can I forget?"

"You were in the hospital, under observation. They had you listed as a bear-mauling survivor. But I had heard of the real attack and was looking out for survivors…"

"You mean new pack members."

"Yes," Carlos agreed. "When I got word of you, I came to see you."

"You looked like an English teacher with those little round vanity glasses and that stupid brown sweater."

"You asked me if I was the chaplain, if I remember correctly. Said you wanted nothing to do with God."

"No, I said God wanted nothing to do with me."

"That's right." Carlos nodded. "That's right. But, even in your despondency you talked with me for a bit, about how you felt inside. I told you I could smell the wolf in you, mixing in with your human blood. I've never smelled it stronger within a person. It was fighting with you, devouring you. You wanted it to."

"Death would have been preferable in those first days." Aaron leaned forward. "You talked me out of killing myself what? Four? Five times? And then once you got me released from the hospital I tried death by werewolf with pretty much everyone in the pack."

"They all knew your pain and were sorry for it. They never would have killed you." Carlos chuckled. "Kicked your ass, yes. But never murdered you."

"You treated me well. When we ended, I knew it was for the best, for you especially. We both needed new starts. I came here a month ago and earned clearance, one grueling test at a time. I started my new job and have had a supremely interesting first day. The thing is, I trust my new partner instinctually, the way I trusted you. You're going to have to accept that. I left California and the Trinity Clan. You're not my alpha, anymore, and there are no clans around here. That means this town is my territory. My decisions hold sway in Grange, not yours. I'll listen to your advice, but you're not in charge. If I say I trust Tony, then that's the end of it."

"Very well." Carlos' expression was difficult to read, but he remained seated. Aaron took it as a good sign.

"I like it here. I have a home, and a job I enjoy. All of the wounds of the past eight months were finally healing, but then you showed up and in twenty minutes have managed to rip most of them open again." Carlos moved to speak, but he cut him off. "It's okay, if what you're here for is important." He took a deep breath and fixed Carlos with a glare he hoped was more intimidating than it felt. "It had better be important, Carlos."

They stared at each other, tension building between them. Carlos was sizing him up, wondering if he was challenging his position in the Trinity Clan, posturing for a fight. Aaron did not look away, but also did not make any move that could be construed as aggression. He didn't want a fight. He didn't want to make up. He just wanted Carlos gone as soon as possible.

Something banged at the bottom of the entrance stairwell. They both froze, nostrils flaring, ears tuned to the sound. A few clangs later, Matthew appeared, a white exterior door in his hands.

"I found a match pretty easily at the home improvement store around the corner. Apparently all of these new apartments use one standard door ty…" Matthew trailed off. "I'll, uh, just install this later, then?" He stood awkwardly holding the door as if he hoped to disappear behind it.

Like all werewolves, Matthew appeared to be much younger than his actual nonagenarian status. His sun-bleached wavy hair and bronze tan made it seem as if the fine lines etched above his high cheekbones were from two decades spent squinting against the sun from a surfboard, rather than from an old werewolf finally showing the first signs of age. He had a good-natured, honest personality that had endeared itself to Aaron, made him one of his preferred babysitters when he was going off the deep end.

"Aaron," Matthew said, putting aside the door and coming to stand beside his chair. "I'm sorry for any pain my presence is causing you. Carlos wanted me here, so I'm here. But, I can be outside the door—once I fix it—and still be here. I won't blame you for not welcoming me into your home."

"Would you two stop being so nice?" Aaron blurted. His burst of irritation faded as he looked from one surprised face to the other. "I'm sorry. Sit down, Matthew. Just, can we please get to why you're here?"

Carlos nodded at his second, and Matthew took his place beside the alpha, sitting close enough to convey the sense of a unified front, but nothing more.

"When Kapre California was attacked, we knew that it was the doing of the Six Rivers clan," Carlos began. "Six Rivers and Trinity have always had an uneasy co-existence. When their Alpha died a year ago, we knew there would be eventual problems."

"You said their new alpha was the best turd in a pool of assholes," Aaron said.

Carlos laughed. "Did I phrase it so gracefully?"

Matthew nodded in confirmation.

"Well, it is the truth," Carlos said. "They have more wolves than we. More money. More power. The leaders have chosen to raise their pups as privileged little brats who think nothing of kin and clan, but only of themselves. Their greed and aversion to hard work is outmatched only by their ignorance. Once Steven Wilkes died, apparently the Six Rivers clan went through a period of extreme upheaval, where fast succession of leaders took place. In the end, two older wolves died, most of us believe suspiciously. When Wilkes' pups had finished duking it out, two of them were dead as well, and one was severely disfigured. Brandon—Steven's most spoiled, irresponsible, inexperienced middle pup—somehow emerged as alpha. Then he got straight to fucking things up.

"When Kapre fell, we assumed it was a strike coordinated by Brandon. However, some of the nuances of the attack didn't fit Brandon's M O."

"Like how it is an almost Herculean task for Brandon to multiply seven times nine," Matthew offered. "And then there's the fact he got past Kapre's extensive security system, something only a cleared Kapre agent or a powerful mage could accomplish. We've talked about this before, Carlos. Brandon is not competent enough to haven taken down Kapre on his own."

"And I still agree with you," Carlos answered. He turned to Aaron. "The rest of the clan is beginning to see our point of view, as well. Six Rivers is on the move."

"What do you mean?" Aaron asked.

"They've struck camp, bailed out of California," Matthew replied.

"Where are they heading?"

"Where they have gone is the better question," Carlos said. He swirled his drink. His lupine-warm hand had all but melted the ice and it clinked weakly against the sides. "They are here, *mi hombre*. They have come to the home of Kapre's Maryland branch."

"Why?" Aaron looked from one were to the other. Anxiety built in his chest as his thoughts secured around the most likely scenario.

"We think they're looking to take out Kapre once again."

The room dimmed. Aaron's vision pulled in until Carlos' face was a blur at the end of a long, black tunnel.

It couldn't be. Not again. He couldn't...

Aaron jumped up and ran to the bathroom. He flipped the toilet lid and retched all his empty stomach had to offer—a thin stream of bile—into the bowl. He flushed the toilet with a shaking hand, then turned on the tap.

Carlos and Matthew murmured together on the couch. Aaron couldn't make out most of the words, but what did convey was doubt regarding his mental strength.

He rinsed his mouth and looked up to meet the wide, brown eyes staring back at him.

Like a deer caught in headlights. Rather, like a deer before the wolf's mouth closes around its jugular.

Except this time you're not a deer.

The latter thought, surfacing from nowhere, caused Aaron to straighten and look harder at his reflection. He could almost see the shadow of the beast shifting behind his gaze. He relaxed his mind, then let surface the anxiety and anger that had been building in him since Carlos broke down his door. His vision momentarily blurred, then keenly sharpened. He stared at the transformation staring back at him— yellow orbs bisected with a pitch ellipse.

He had endured torture under the fangs and claws of the Six Rivers Clan. He had watched his friends and colleagues die as he gasped and writhed beneath a jostling pile of fur and muscles, sloshing like a landed fish in a pool of his own blood. So many of them had sunk their teeth into his flesh that he had blacked out from the agony. His last conscious thought before coming to in the hospital had been, *I'm dying.*

He had awakened to a new nightmare reality, one where everything he had, everything he had been, was lost forever. The wolf was an unbearable presence inside him, something to be squelched if not put down entirely. He had been cared for and pitied, called a victim for so long he accepted the label as truth. But the dark thing now arose to reject that notion. It growled as he studied the reflection of his lupine eyes, a reminder he had power few others could claim.

Aaron took a deep breath and pushed back his feral companion, gently this time. *Soon*, he promised.

Whatever was going on with the Six Rivers Clan and the Trinity Clan, Aaron wasn't going to let it affect Kapre. Whoever was orchestrating this extermination was not going to succeed, not again. Despite the power coursing through his veins, he knew he couldn't handle a full invasion on his own. He thought of the weres sitting on the other side of his closed door. He needed someone he could trust — someone who would have his back. That was a tall order for a werewolf in strange city, surrounded by strangers. Everyone he knew had given him reason to not trust them in the past twenty-four hours alone. But if he couldn't go with his head, he would go with his instinct.

Aaron opened the bathroom door. He avoided the curious glances shot his way and retreated once again into the master bedroom. He grabbed his phone from the dresser. An apologetic text glowed on the screen. It cemented his decision. He nodded to himself and hit the 'call' button.

Chapter Eleven

An Uneasy Alliance

Aaron watched as Tony scanned the splintered wood hanging from the hinges, the broken door lying across the threshold and the two men sitting on the couch, with a grin. His gaze skimmed past them and met Aaron's. Despite the jolt that brief intimacy shot through his heart, Aaron returned the look with equanimity.

"Should've invited me to the party sooner," Tony said, throwing him a wink.

"Tony, this is Carlos Mendes and Matthew Shipley," Aaron supplied. "They are here about a growing werewolf problem here."

"Nice to meet you." Tony swooped into the room, stepping across the shattered door like it was a red carpet. "Aaron mentioned you," he said to Carlos. He tossed a Matthew a cheeky wink. "Not you, though. Are you unimportant to this tale, or a recent development?"

Matthew's expression darkened.

"Ease up, Tony," Aaron said with false reproach.

"Sorry. I had a crazy day," Tony picked up this new conversation thread as if he had done nothing untoward. "Got pummeled by two demons in less than two hours. Who would have thought that could happen over one routine sweep? Terrible odds." He shrugged and moved to the bottle of Jack that Carlos had left out on the kitchen counter. He poured himself a generous glass then plopped onto the far end of the couch beside Matthew. "Have you ever seen a pissed off Gerodon demon? I had one in my living room. Not the best place for them, believe me. They reek. And they break *everything*." He flung his arm over the couch behind Matthew's head. He turned, leaned around Matthew to put his face within inches of Carlos'. "So, what kind of shit are you trying to drag my partner into?"

Carlos raised an eyebrow, but did not move away from Tony. The two simply stared at one another for a very long, uncomfortable minute. Matthew feigned adjusting his shoelace to break the standoff. Tony leaned back, flashed them both a disarming grin and began the second great inquisition.

Twenty minutes passed as Tony grilled the weres about their presence in Grange. Carlos and Matthew haplessly tumbled into Tony's usual trap, nipping and biting at the agent's goading bait, then bristling to the point of rage as Tony reeled them in with his wit and finally let them go with a carefully placed chipper remark. By the time the weres' story was re-told everyone in the room but Tony—who was beaming like a kid coming off a rollercoaster—was exhausted.

"Let's let all this sink in and regroup tomorrow night," Aaron said, rising from his seat.

"We can meet at my house," Tony offered. He explained to the weres, "It's more secure. Sometimes

Kapre sends wellness agents out to check on officers who are post-traumatic-incident. We don't need you two hanging around here if or when one shows up."

"I'll text you the address and his phone number, Carlos." Aaron nodded his appreciation at Tony.

"Will you bring us to meet with your superiors?" Carlos asked, standing to face him.

"Not yet. We have no proof, other than you, and what you have is only hearsay and heavy speculation. Besides there is my own personal condition that would come to light. I'd rather we find the Six Rivers weres before we do anything. Considering the full moon is the night after tomorrow, they'll be forced to shift. We can track them better then, if all else fails."

"You know I'd rather clan business stay in the clan, but we need to move fast," Carlos said. "Waiting may not be the best option for your people."

"If it becomes clear Kapre is under direct threat, then we will all go to Kapre's director," Aaron answered. "I have to warn you, though, at that point Kapre's Acqxterm agents will wage a full-out war."

"Which doesn't bode well for any of you," Tony added. "Acqxterm will see a wolf as a wolf. You and Matthew here will most likely get caught up in the extermination campaign."

"We expect no less," Matthew said. "We understand your people have to protect their own. The only reason we have involved ourselves at all is because we feel there is a growing threat to all weres. Finding out what their endgame is and stopping it is our only priority, even if it costs Trinity its leaders."

"Then we'll get in touch with you tomorrow after work and we can go from there," Aaron said. He nodded to Carlos and shook Matthew's hand. The dark thing approved of the beta's willingness to protect his clan. Aaron grudgingly agreed.

"I hope our working together…" Matthew trailed off. "I don't know what I was going to say. Nothing that could make this any better, for sure. Thank you for your hospitality." To Aaron's shock the beta gave a small bow of his head, a lower-ranked wolf's acknowledgment of Aaron's alpha status.

"Good night, *mi hombre*," Carlos said as he followed Matthew out into the hall.

Their footsteps dwindled down the stairs. The scent of wolf drifted behind them out of the open door, leaving only the crisp, intoxicating scent of Tony.

"Do you believe them?" Tony asked.

"They have no reason to lie," he replied as he turned. Tony was right there, his ice blue eyes burning into Aaron's own. His momentary hesitation, or maybe his expression of poorly controlled lust, caused Tony to quirk his lips. Aaron shook his head and stepped away. "Look, I called you because for some stupid reason I trust you in this wolf business. However"—he gave Tony a glare—"I am not an amnesiac. I don't know what's between us, if there can ever be anything other than professional reliability, and you grinning at me and giving me the once-over is not going to change that."

"I'm here because I want to prove to you I can be a good partner. That I am reliable. I know what Braven calls me. She thinks I'm a clown, wandering around the office spraying everyone with my loose cannon of bullshit."

"She said you were a solid agent. Coy, but reliable."

Tony's mouth curled in amused disbelief.

"She said we were a good match as partners." *The perfect match, actually.* "I'm inclined to go with her experience and trust you to do this with me."

"I won't let you down again." Tony paused as if wanting to say something more, but then turned toward the exit. "We haven't eaten today."

Aaron froze, dreading the push that was coming.

Tony watched him, his expression almost forlorn. "You should get some food before you go to bed," was all he said. "Do you need help with this?" He gestured to the splintered wood on the floor.

"No. I've got it."

"Tomorrow, then." Devoid of an audience for his showmanship, Tony picked his way across the shattered remains and disappeared into the hall.

Aaron set to cleaning up and hanging his new front door. Despite Aaron's initial dread at the idea of dinner with Tony, the fact his partner had not offered up the invitation gnawed at Aaron. But, he told himself, there were weres out there who wanted to destroy them all. He didn't have time for dating, anyway.

Chapter Twelve

Back to Nature

"Hey, Ar."

The last chunk of pumpernickel bagel stuck in Aaron's throat at the sound of Ellison's voice. He choked down the bread as Ellison barged into the break room and made a beeline for the coffee maker. Aaron had smelled the man's acidic chemical solvent scent moments earlier, but had attributed it to residue from some detonated op-tech device. He would have to remember the man's odd stench and use it as an early warning device from now on.

"I heard you had a run-in with the demons at Shirley's." Ellison scooted the nearly empty coffee pot out of the way to divert the fresh stream of percolating java into his mug. "Not the best idea to get into it with those mudfuckers."

"Language, Ellison," Director Braven said as she clipped by the door. Her voice rang out as her diminutive body disappeared from sight. "Agent Marvell, when your partner arrives please direct him and yourself to my office."

"Yes, ma'am." Aaron's chest pounded. Had Tony, embarrassed by his rebuff, told their supervisor he was a werewolf? Was this early morning meeting to be his trial and conviction? The thought made the cream cheese spread curdle in his stomach.

"What a dragon lady." Ellison rolled his eyes at Aaron in an attempt at commiseration. "At least out in good ol' Cali we had bosses who were laid back."

"You mean our dead bosses?" Aaron snapped. "Yeah, they were pretty relaxed until they were eaten alive." He didn't know why he said it. It was wrong on many levels. And he was already treading dangerous ground without shooting off at the mouth.

"Not cool, man. Not cool." Ellison dumped creamer into his coffee and huffed toward the door, his expression one of deep dudgeon. A moment later a pretty, buxom, tracking tech swished into his path, and the two-cent grin returned to Ellison's face. He swung around, coffee cup curled in front of him like a trophy, pinning the blonde into the corner by the door. He said something low, his voice and scent vibrating with pent-up sexual frustration. The young woman laughed uncomfortably and extracted herself. Once she was clear of Ellison's trap and safe with a pot of lava-hot coffee in her hand, Aaron retreated to the hallway. Behind him, Ellison rattled on, oblivious to the young lady's repulsion, already recovered from his fit of offended mourning. Aaron snarled. If ever a genuine feeling ever passed through Ellison's heart the underused organ would most likely stop beating on the spot from shock.

"Admiring the dulcet sounds of your best friend?" Tony's voice was at his ear. "Or plotting a quiet murder?"

"Which do you think?" Aaron turned. "That man grates my nerves."

Although only Tony occupied the hallway with him, it seemed too full, too close. The walls had somehow pushed in, leaving only enough room for them to stand with a foot of space between them. Tony's voice had been light, casual, but in his eyes' clear depths a silent plea rested. Aaron sighed. Earlier that morning he had promised himself two things—first, to put aside the previous day's confusing events and focus on the agreed-upon plan of discovering what Six Rivers was planning, and second, not to fall for Tony's charm. He found simply occupying the same space in the very public hallway swayed—if not bent to the snapping point—the latter vow.

Despite his feelings, his desires mattered little. He needed Tony to help him keep Maryland's Kapre branch alive. And even though just looking at his partner made Aaron want to tear off that crisp white shirt, throw him to the ground and work his cock until he begged for release, need currently overrode want.

Aaron checked his longing and continued down the hallway. Tony followed, his delirium-inducing scent filling the corridor like a cloud. For the second time in sixty seconds Aaron sighed. To get through this he would have to execute iron control and above all else feign normalcy. Fortunately, he had become accustomed to doing both over the past several months.

"Our desks are over there," Tony remarked as Aaron overshot the bullpen.

"Braven wants us in her office." He tried to keep the sound of accusation from his voice.

"I didn't say anything, I swear." Tony's hand was on his arm in a flash. "This isn't about you. At least not about *that*."

"Okay." Aaron didn't trust himself to say more.

Braven waved them inside her office and gestured for them to sit. With her wraithlike hands folded over an open binder, she fixed them with a glare as steely and severe as her hair.

"At three a.m. I was awakened by a phone request for a containment unit to respond to the scene of a grisly attack in the conservation forest just west of town."

Aaron's heart seized in panic.

"We don't have grizzlies here, Director." Tony winked at Aaron, his impish grin concealing an urgent message. *Be cool.* "We *bear*-ly have any predators at all."

Braven shot Tony a withering glare. "Do you mean aside from demons, ghouls, poltergeists and weres?" There was no lack of stress on the last word. "Now, if you are quite done being simpleminded, I would like to know why a pair of seasoned agents with — I would hope — a pair of brains between the two of them would think it acceptable to ignore protocol and not report an influx of werewolves in our territory?"

Aaron glanced at Tony, who was gazing levelly at Braven. He took his partner's cue and concentrated on the Director.

"Because we were afraid there might be an information leak," Tony replied.

Aaron whiplashed his head to stare at his partner, mouth agape.

"And by we, I mean *I*, ma'am," Tony continued. "Providing that information to this office could have contributed to the finalization of certain plans I believe are in the works."

"Are you saying that you think we have a double agent in this office?"

"In one of our offices, yes. But I have nothing more than a hunch to go on. I'm sure you agree you wouldn't want me to start crying, uh, wolf, without solid evidence."

"And you are aware of your partner's hunch, Agent Marvell?"

Aaron glanced from one to the other. "I…"

"Of course not. He just got here yesterday." Tony drummed the desk's edge with his fingertips. "He's still figuring out which side of his computer monitor he wants his pen holder to sit on."

"Well, you are quite the secretive man as of late, Agent Harper. Perhaps you will find the consideration to enlighten me of your agency-impacting notions now and again. Now, in fact, would be nice." Braven leaned back in her chair, her stern rigidity eased.

Aaron nearly slumped with relief. The dark thing found it amusing that he was so unnerved by a diminutive older woman in high heels, but Aaron found nothing funny about her at all. Everyone credited Red Riding Hood as the victor, but it was the granny who had survived the interior of the Big Bad for an entire day and emerged unscathed. Aaron was fairly certain if his wolf was ever forced into a showdown with Braven, she wouldn't stay down very easily, either.

"From reviewing the files on the California incident prior to being partnered with Agent Marvell, and from information I acquired during our investigation of the inter-dimensional doorway we were assigned yesterday, I am nearly certain there has been a breach somewhere within Kapre, and one of our agents is working against us."

"Why were you reading files on California?" Braven asked.

Aaron tensed.

"Morbid curiosity, ma'am, as always," Tony replied.

"Indeed." Braven nodded. The corner of her mouth twitched slightly. Apparently, there was a running joke—or at least anecdote—in regard to Tony's interest in the particularly grim.

Aaron let out the breath he had been holding. His partner knew Braven. It was a slow, cautious twist, but Tony was wrapping her around his finger just the same as he did everyone else.

"And you feel this leak is related to the doorway?" Braven continued.

"It takes a good deal of magical skill and energy to open a door like that," Tony replied.

"Magic some demons possess."

"It was cleaned up after," Aaron interjected. Both the director and his partner looked at him. "Yesterday in the warehouse I noted brush marks in the brimstone. We followed the lead to a disgruntled mystical broom manufacturer. The crafter didn't give us specifics, but whoever hired him wanted a fast, clean job. The client got only one of his wishes. There might as well been a sign hanging that said, 'Otherworldly entry, here'."

"So we have a portal opened and a shoddy attempt to conceal the fact?" Braven asked.

"Most demons don't bother with hiding their doors," Tony said.

"There are still a hundred reasons that something would want evidence of their entry into our world expunged."

"Which is why I said I had a hunch, and nothing else."

For whatever reason, Tony was not bringing up the fact that Qi had all but confirmed a human had opened the portal. It didn't make sense to admit all of these other theories and leave out the one bit of evidence they had actually gleaned, but Aaron was not about to argue when Tony had steered the conversation from disastrous to nearly congenial in less than five minutes.

"What does this portal have to do with the weres coming into our territory? What do you know about their activity?"

Aaron caught Tony's furtive glance. He couldn't shake his head, or give any sign without tipping off Braven, so he simply sat still and hoped Tony knew that to give up information on the invading weres would risk giving him up, as well.

"Nothing substantial." Tony answered. "But after a quiet few months to have this happen in such close order it seems likely to be related."

"True enough." Braven pushed away from her desk and stood. She came around the desk and loomed over Tony and him. "I am going to make myself very clear. Your first priority is finding out why these weres are here and what they are doing. A pack of wild dogs have been slaughtered in the conservation forest. The weres are staking out territory. I need not remind you there are park rangers in there, as well. It is only a matter of time before one of them is attacked." Braven waited for his reaction. Her point hit home, and he made sure it reflected on his face. Satisfied, she continued, "Once your bums are out of my seats they will be in a car headed for the conservation forest. The Thurisaz has been removed by our technicians so as not to attract any more attention to you than necessary. You will enter quietly and scour the area for any and all intelligence you can obtain regarding our new alien residents. You will remain unobtrusive. Do not engage, but rather bring your findings back to me alone. Everyone else will believe you are still following up on the warehouse summoning. Once you have done that, then, and only if you tread very, very carefully, will you pursue your little 'hunch'. Do I make myself clear, gentlemen?"

"Yes, ma'am," they answered in unison as they stood.

"Oh, and Agent Marvell?"

"Ma'am?" Aaron turned back from the door as Tony passed through ahead of him.

"Since you are right-handed, logic and convenience mandate you store your pen holder on the right side of your screen. Now that that's settled, you can get to work with an eased mind."

"Yes, ma'am," Aaron said. Despite his attempts at control, his mouth twitched upwards. Maybe he would yet breach that private buddy club Tony and she shared. "I will move it immediately."

Chapter Thirteen

Six Rivers

Dappled with light and riddled with potholes, the road snaked beneath the trees into the heart of the conservation area. Tony watched the mystically enhanced GPS while Aaron drove, head tilted toward the open window, ready to catch a scent of the interlopers.

"Turn here," Tony pointed. "The Thurisaz went up just beyond this access road's end. Kapre's taken it down, like Braven said, but the GPS has its residual signature pinpointed. We can walk into the woods from there, see if we can track the wolves back to their den."

Aaron steered the car onto the dirt lane. Clouds of dust plumed around the tires, funneling into the windows. With nostrils full of chalky dirt, he abandoned the sensory search and rolled up the windows.

"The tranqs are loaded," Tony said.

Aaron turned the car around at the end of the lane. Ease of escape was always crucial in case advantage was lost. He put the car in park and shut off the engine. He checked his sidearm and accepted the tranquilizer gun Tony passed him from the back seat.

"Remember, the tranqs will work if they're in human form, but as wolves only a permanent disruption of their nervous system will kill them definitely. Heart and other organ wounds might heal. Depending on the age of the wolf, they might heal fast enough to remain a threat." Aaron felt a pang of guilt in discussing the slaughter of his own kind, but it wasn't like he was sharing anything new. The methodology of werewolf slaying was well established. Not even rookies fell for the silver bullet routine anymore. "Since it's the week of the full moon, the strongest one or two might be able to shift already, so be careful."

"Do you think they're just hiding out in the woods, plotting evil deeds?" Tony asked as he climbed from the car. "Living under the trees like Robin Hood's band of merry puppies?"

"The Six Rivers clan has historically been different than most modern werewolves. They're clan purists. They put their faith only in their own pack. They may interact with the rest of the world to make money and buy items they can't make for themselves, but for the most part they feel they are wolves first, humans second," Aaron answered. He shouldered the tranq gun and checked his sidearm. "From what Carlos has told me, though, they—especially the younger ones—aren't against having big houses, nice cars and good clothes. They're a wealthy clan, one that could have bought half a dozen vacant buildings in town to hide out in. But, they're here instead, which means they either they have a very specific need to be in this forest, or they are hoping if their plan falls apart, the woods will provide them a quicker, quieter getaway in wolf form."

"Well, let's find out which."

"I'll take point," Aaron said, tapping his nose.

"What other heightened senses does being a were give you?" Tony asked. He fell in beside Aaron.

"Vision and hearing. Taste is slightly more intense, though not as much as I'd thought. But I once drank poisoned beer, so..."

Tony raised an eyebrow.

"When I was fresh out of boot camp and before all of this happened to me, I held the same opinion of myself that all recent grads have of themselves— I thought I was hot shit. And thinking this, I made a bet against a demon in a bar. If I win, he comes quietly with me. I lose, he can try to beat the holy crap out of me before I acquisition him."

"And you lost?"

"He stuck his poison tongue in my drink when I wasn't looking."

Tony let out a full-throated laugh. Unlike that of his glib, chipper persona, this expression of mirth was joyful, honest. It was the first true glimpse of Tony Aaron felt he had witnessed. He liked it.

"I spent a week in the infirmary, drinking counter-cures that stripped the taste buds right off of my tongue. So now, despite my newly acquired senses, my taste is a little questionable sometimes."

"Not your taste in clothes," Tony said. "I noticed that outfit you had on yesterday morning. Sharp."

"I guess the werewolf heightened my sense of style, too," Aaron deflected the compliment.

"Really? I thought all weres dressed like lumberjacks."

Aaron grinned. "Hardly. Although, there are a good number of…outdoorsy types. Goes with the territory, I guess."

"Speaking of territory, does killing wild dogs fall in line with how weres usually act?"

"Not especially." Aaron pointed to a slightly beaten patch of brush. They paused. He took a few deep inhales. The musk of wolf hung faintly in the air in that direction. "This way."

They ducked the overgrowth and emerged onto a freshly made path of trampled vegetation. "Like I said, Six Rivers is more of a back-to-basics group. And they're more than a little crazy I'm beginning to think. Rousting the local competition for game doesn't really fall into most weres' interests. We're more of a sharing-the-resources type."

"Rousting?" Tony grinned. "There's that old Englishman in you again."

"I've had one of those," Aaron quipped. "Well, not so much old, as older." He tried to explain away the joke when Tony looked at him askance.

"Relax. You can joke around me. I'm on your side, promise. I screwed up before, but I want to be your friend." The look on Tony's face, a mixture of desperation and desire, said he wanted even more than he was admitting.

"All we've done is piss each other off since I got here." Aaron turned to face him, his frustration mounting. "And I don't want to do that anymore. I want to be friends. Maybe we can try sometime, start again, but not now. I just can't…"

Tony cut him off by shoving him against a tree. He started to protest the untimely advance, but Tony clamped a hand over his mouth. Tony pressed his face closer. He used the forefinger laying across Aaron's mouth to press his own lips in a silencing gesture. Tony unsnapped Aaron's holster with his free hand then reached for his own weapon. His eyes slid to the right, indicating Aaron should do the same. Aaron obeyed. A trio of figures walked through the woods, headed away from them. Two appeared male, one female.

Dammit. He should have heard them coming. Too busy playing round three of High School Angst with his partner of two whole days.

Aaron nodded his understanding of their situation and peeled Tony's hand away. The wind was blowing in their direction. Aaron lifted his face into it. Sure enough, the scent of the trio drifted into his nostrils. Weres, all of them. The Six Rivers camp had to be close.

"Quietly, slowly." His hushed voice at Tony's ear was the lightest tickle of wind. "We're going to back out of their sight and scent lines."

Aaron guided Tony backwards, stepping over twigs, carefully placing his feet in soft mounds of pine needles. He pulled Tony into the spots his feet had occupied. He tried not to think of the prominent hipbones beneath his palms, the firm oblique muscles that refused to yield to his fingers' pressure. Even as he kept wary note of the weres disappearing into the trees, his mind threw out wild images of him toppling back, pulling Tony on top of him, landing in a pile of leaves, suddenly, gloriously naked, their bodies pressed together, rigid dicks hot against their bellies...

A twig snapped under his foot. He pulled Tony down, twisting his body to control their descent. Instead of his mind's dreamy, slow motion fall, it was a sudden collapse of intertwined limbs as he twisted them around into an advantageous position. He punched Tony's shoulder as he reached out to halt their fall, while Tony's head whiplashed up to hit his upper lip. He pressed over Tony to view the slight ridge they had fortunately landed behind, his belt buckle surely digging into one of his partner's ribs. He moved carefully. If his excellent vision could pick out the weres, they certainly could see him in return. They had paused, possibly at the sound of their descent, but were now moving on. He turned his head, listening. Their muted voices carried through the quiet.

"...more rabbits..." One of the males gestured to where he and Tony hid.

"...others will be back...dinner..." the female said.

"...will be a good hunt..." the third agreed.

Their conversation lulled. The weres disappeared from view. It was odd for them to hunt when not shifted. Six Rivers, with their purist ideals, most assuredly wouldn't be hunting with bows, guns or snares. So, what, then, did they use? A muffled groan reminded him he was still sprawled across his partner's body.

"You okay?" Aaron pulled back enough to look at his partner. He knew he should climb off, but his limbs refused to obey his commands. Instead, he remained where he was and stared like a fool at his partner.

"Yeah. Just got a root or something in the back. Hurts."

"Let me see." He grabbed Tony's shoulder and pulled.

"I'm fine," Tony protested, but raised his torso for Aaron to see. His abdomen rippled under the thin white T-shirt he wore.

Aaron clamped down on the wave of lust the sight aroused and instead focused on peering over Tony's shoulder. "No blood." He ran a hand down Tony's back. "Yeah, you've got a lump here. Probably going to be a big bruise."

"It's all right." Tony's voice sounded odd.

"What's wrong?" He moved back to get a better view of his partner.

"I've ruined it." Tony gestured helplessly at how Aaron's legs spread across his lap, groin pressed against his lower stomach, one hand braced against the ground, the other still cradling his back. "It's what I do. I act stupidly and ruin my chances. And then I make a joke about it."

"Tony..."

"Nothing to joke about now." Tony gently extracted himself and stood. He attempted a smile. It cracked against the wretched backdrop of his face. "It's okay. I'm good."

Aaron couldn't think of anything to say, so he turned and started toward the spot the three weres had come from. Their scents were stronger in that direction, which meant they were walking away from their camp, not toward it. Or, at least he hoped.

The brush grew thicker. Thorny vines riddled the narrow gaps between the trees. They picked their way carefully, silently, through the foliage. After another ten minutes' walking, the moss-covered roof of a building came into view. Buried within a mass of kudzu vine and brambles sat a battered, wooden single story structure. A ground level porch spanned the front of the building. A pair of grimy windows and a metal door punctuated the facade. It seemed a building more suitable as a hideout for drug runners—or renegade werewolves—than even the most rugged outdoorsman's woodland retreat. A myriad of scents lingered in the air, but none of them as fresh as those belonging to the three recently departed weres. Aaron placed a hand in front of Tony, signaling him to stop.

"I think it's empty right now, but I should shift and get a closer view," he said.

"What if it's not? Won't they smell you?"

"It's easier for me to run in wolf form if I need to, and they'll smell me just as much shifted as not. Even if I come across a were or two, it'll unlikely be the alpha, which means no one will be able to challenge me in wolf form."

"And what if they just pull out a bunch of guns?"

"Well, then they shoot at me."

"I don't like it," Tony groused.

"I'm not a big fan of it, either, but I don't know what else to do. You move quiet enough for a human, but to a werewolf's ears you might as well be open-mouthed crunching potato chips in an art museum."

"What if I take off my shoes?"

"Slightly stale potato chips."

"Oh." Tony frowned. "I always thought I was good at the covert stuff."

"Like I said, you are—for a human. Werewolf hearing is at a completely different level." Aaron took off his weapons, then bent down and pulled his shoes and socks from his feet. "And if any of them are in the cabin, then I need to be the one approaching it. They might mistake my scent for another of their own."

Tony's expression said he didn't buy his bluff.

"Just keep your weapons ready in case."

Tony unslung his tranq rifle, slid the bolt into place then put it back over his shoulder. Aaron continued stripping. He warmed under Tony's surveillance, suddenly, terribly uncomfortable. He looked up, sensing the sorrowful expression before he saw it.

"They don't even ache anymore." He gestured to the mass of puckered scars lining his torso and legs. "If I had been a were when I got these they would have healed into perfect skin. But, since these were my transforming bites, they didn't... But they don't hurt, just tingle sometimes. They're mostly just ugly now."

Tony studied them for a long moment before replying, "I don't mind them."

Aaron would have usually flinched at another's direct mention of his scars, but the way Tony said it, so simply and honestly, took away the usual sting. He swallowed against the knot in his throat and pulled off his underwear. As if his scars weren't enough cause for feeling more naked than naked, casually standing in front of the man he desperately desired with his cock hanging out sent a flood of heat into his cheeks. Tony appraised his body, slowly, sensually. Aaron thanked the heavens he was a shower and not a grower — or worse, a shrinker.

"When I give the all clear, you can come on up," he said, bundling his clothes into Tony's arms. "And bring these with you, or it'll be a naked house search."

"And if I should drop a key article or two?" Tony asked lightly.

"Just look away, please." Aaron gave a low growl and let the dark thing inside him rise with the sound.

As Tony made a pretense of studying the cabin, Aaron let the transformation pull him to his knees. His body re-shaped itself as if it were made of clay. The agonizing tearing and popping of his joints and bones made him wish it were. Within a few moments, however, the pain eased and he sniffed the ground in front of him simply for the joy of taking in the hundreds of subtle layers of scent the forest floor provided.

"Hi, again," Tony said above him. "Your fur is prettier in the sunlight than it was in my place. Lots of variations in that black coat I didn't see before."

Aaron looked up at his partner. Tony held his revolver lightly in his right hand, clutched Aaron's discarded clothes and handgun in the other arm.

Aaron gestured to the pile, where his boxer briefs sat in a crumpled heap on top.

"Yeah, I'll try to bring these, too, but they're kinda small." Tony grinned. "I might lose them in the fray."

Aaron growled and nipped at Tony's leg, coming close enough to brush his trouser leg, nothing more. Even so, he gave a wag of his tail to show he meant no real aggression. Sometimes it was hard for humans to get past the whole wolf thing. Little Red didn't do much to help that particular cause. He turned and ducked into the undergrowth.

"Be careful," Tony softly called out behind him, all traces of levity gone from his voice.

The clumps of vine and brush gave excellent cover all the way to the side of the porch. He stopped, tested the air with his nose. Satisfied no one was around, he placed his front paws on the rotted decking boards and slid under the rails. He glanced back at the forest. He could smell Tony, but no one else. His heart pounded, but it was the wolf's excitement at the potential hunt, and not his human fear, that spurred the sensation. The dark thing hoped other wolves prowled the unlit interior of the building. It wanted a fight. Wanted blood in its mouth. The problem was, it was Aaron's mouth, too, and he had no interest in tasting human flesh. And that was what it was, regardless of what Six Rivers believed. Beneath the curse, disease, whatever the fad was to call it, weres were still humans.

He crossed toward the first window. Dirt caked it in such thick layers it was opaque. He moved to the next, careful to give a wide birth to the closed door. This window was as filthy as the previous, but a small corner of glass had broken out of the lower pane. Aaron stood on his hind legs and peered through the opening. No bodies moved inside. A small closet had lost its door at some point. Junk tumbled unchecked out of the recess and spilt across the floor. The only other visible room was an unoccupied small bathroom in the far corner.

He dropped to all fours then turned to face the location of Tony's cover. He lifted up onto his haunches once again, and pawed at the air like a dog trying to 'shake'. It was the closest thing to a wave he could muster. The intended message conveyed, because a moment later Tony began working through the brambles. To his ears the sound was like a bear pirouetting across matchsticks.

"All clear?" Tony asked as he appeared from the shrubs, looking like some sort of mythic adventurer on a laundry errand. The tranqs dangled from each side of him like a pair of gigantic earrings. Aaron's clothes and weapon were bundled under his arm. His service weapon hung freely in his grip. He swung up onto the porch and made his way to the door. It was locked.

"People don't lock things they don't care about. They're staying in this dump," Tony said. He placed Aaron's clothes on the porch floor, holstered his weapon and began to dig in his pocket. "I can pick it, if you want to go ahead and shift. I'll need thirty seconds."

Aaron relaxed his mind and let the transformation take him. As the usual pain took over, he began to panic. He had forgotten to tell... No, he hadn't. He had *omitted* his temporary weakness after shifting back into human form. Part of him still didn't trust Tony, and revealing to an Acqxterm agent a crucial werewolf weakness was something he couldn't muster. Once again, he would have to pretend everything was fine. His shift finalised and the usual barrage of unsettling thoughts raged into his skull.

"And what if the wolves return before you can leave, mi hombre?" Considering Aaron had been talking about slaughtering weres, Carlos' voice was a startling appearance as devil's advocate. *"You will be weak. You and your partner could be killed."*

"It's a risk I had to take. For us."

"There is no 'us' anymore, mi hombre."

"There is a werewolf 'us'."

"No, beautiful man, there isn't."

He was lying face down on the floor, arms splayed out at his side. His mind spun as if he had been drinking for the past several hours. He wasn't sure if it was the shift, or his imagined conversation with Carlos. The change from wolf mind to human mind oftentimes brought out suppressed thoughts and emotions. While the imaginary Carlos' implication that he was not part of the werewolf clan was unsettling, his subconscious insecurity would have to wait. He pushed onto his knees. His arms trembled with the effort. In front of him, Tony cursed mildly and worked the lock with a tension wrench and pick. Aaron grabbed his clothes and staggered to his feet. By the time he had one leg in his underwear, the lock gave way with a click.

Tony turned, a triumphant smile on his face. It faded when he saw Aaron. "You look like shit."

"Rough change," he answered as he struggled to control his shaking foot enough to land it in the other leg opening.

"No, you looked this bad last night, too. After you were done."

"It's because I'm new. The shift is hard on me. And it's not a full moon." It was a half-truth, an admission that protected his clan, yet allowed him to conceal the worst of his guilt behind a guileless expression.

"Should've told me that before we started. Could be real trouble if we get in a pinch." Tony grabbed his arm and helped him inside. He seated him in a chair and began to slide his legs into his pants.

"Sorry," Aaron replied. He allowed himself to lean on Tony's shoulder as his partner slid socks and shoes onto his feet. "It was my mistake."

"I can't blame you. You're a seal swimming in a shark tank. The fact you get a paycheck for it still doesn't negate the—"

"Stupidity?"

"I was going to say, 'Need for caution'." Tony handed him his shirt and let him finish dressing as he checked the windows for signs of outside movement. "We look clear, but who knows when they're coming back. You up to doing some searching?"

Aaron nodded and stood. He buttoned his jeans and fixed his holster in place. Tony pulled one of the tranqs off his shoulder and passed it to him.

"I'll take right, you take left. Keep checking the windows."

While Tony rifled through the kitchenette, Aaron shifted his focus to the burgeoning closet. Clothes of many different types and sizes lay piled in forgotten heaps. A layer of dust had settled across the topmost layer. He searched the most apparent pockets then abandoned the task. Whatever the Six Rivers clan was doing was recent, and this pile had been untouched long enough that most of the owners' scents had gone from the fibers. Another jumble of fabric lay in the corner beyond. He moved over to inspect it. Here was the scent he had expected from the closet. The stench of were filled the jumble of shredded blankets, worn sheets and old coats. This was where the Six Rivers spent their nights, in a dog pile at the back of their lair.

"They're sleeping here," he said over his shoulder. "This isn't the comfort-loving clan Carlos was talking about."

"Probably has something to do with this." Tony held up a battered piece of parchment he had pulled from a lidded tin. "What's that say up at the top there?"

"It's demonic." Aaron came closer and scowled at the lettering.

His crash courses in demonic languages took place mainly in the field, as there were too many tongues with too many dialects for an agent in a twelve-month training course to even begin studying. Those who wished to be translators skipped early field internships for the opportunity to learn a chosen language set, but even they never really mastered more than one language out of a hundred thousand. A number of signatures, looking as if they were penned in blood, filled the bottom third of the page. A symbol he didn't recognize sat beneath the scrawled names. He flipped the document over.

"Here, on the back. It's a sticky note. Looks like someone jotted down the key points to remember."

"Seriously? Wow, these guys are really not bright," Tony said. He began reading over Aaron's shoulder. "Bill of Renunciation. Dated a month before the Kapre California attack, calling all true weres to rid themselves of humanity's shackles and live like the wolves nature intended them to be, and to convert or exterminate any recalcitrant shifters."

"Look here. Goes well with this, I'd think." Tony held up a small bound book, opened to a page. He held up it up for Aaron to see.

"Pocket grimoire," Aaron replied.

"Not just for any old wart-removing spells, though. This one is a summoning spell. A big one."

"So, the wolves have decided become nature-lovers and slaughter any weres that disagree."

"Seems like." Tony plucked the parchment from his hand and slid it into his back pocket.

"What are you doing? Braven said observe only."

"They've already killed off one of our branches. Now they're here to do in another. *My* branch. We have very few leads, aside from the paper and this book. We need them." He paused to pocket the little tome. "And you're telling me they're not going to smell we've been here?"

Aaron couldn't argue his last point.

"At least now they'll know we're onto them. Maybe they'll change course."

"Or accelerate their plans."

"Tomorrow's the full moon. I'd say their plans are as accelerated as they can get."

"Well then, let's get out of here," Aaron replied. "We'll keep the papers until Carlos and Matthew have seen them tonight. Maybe they can tell us more about what's written in here.

"Wait." Aaron held up a hand. "You hear that?"

Tony shook his head.

"They're coming." He sniffed the air leaking through the many gaps in the worn construction. "Fast. They smell us. Just two of them, for now."

"Any windows aside from out front?" Tony asked, even as he bolted to the bathroom to check for himself. "No. Nothing."

"I can't shift," Aaron said. "Damn. I'm so stupid."

"We're not dead in the water," Tony replied. He pulled the tranq from his shoulder. "We've been doing this longer than you've had the ability to get furry. We can make it, maybe even get one for questioning in the bargain."

"We're about to find out," Aaron said.

He had enough time to pull his weapon before the door exploded from its rotten frame.

Chapter Fourteen

An Unexpected Turn

They raised their guns as the female and one male barreled through the doorway, propelled by the force they'd used to break down the door. They dropped to the floor hips low, knees bent. Their hands splayed across the floorboards, the blades they had crudely affixed to them as makeshift talons dug into the wood. Naked and slavering, they lifted their spines like hackles, growling low in their throats. Their eyes were the yellow of lupine, but the rest of their bodies remained unshifted, human.

"They're not alphas," Aaron said to Tony. "They can't shift."

"They're not *un-shifted*, either," Tony protested in disbelief.

"We are above human, above common werewolf," the female spit. "We are gifted."

The stench of musk and rank body odor filled the cabin when she spoke. Decay teased Aaron's nostrils. The female pulled back her lips in a snarl and he learnt from where the rot originated. Her teeth had been filed into dagger points. Chunks of uncooked meat jammed the interstices. She dropped her weight back onto her heels. As if in silent communication, the pair launched at the same time, the male for Tony, the female for Aaron.

Tony fired first. The tranq lodged in the male's neck. He yelped and toppled to the floor. Aaron shot a moment later. The dart flew from the gun. The female twisted. The dart sailed past her and lodged in the wall. She was on him before he had time to reload. The blades at her fingertips dug into his shoulders as she rode him to the floor. His sidearm was out of reach. She lunged for his jugular, mouth open. The dark thing raged inside him. His vision shifted, and he knew his eyes now matched hers—wild and furious. But his body was helpless to accommodate the wolf, too drained from the earlier shift to aid in another transformation.

Before he could fully curse his stupidity, a gunshot rang out. The female gave a bloodcurdling scream. She toppled off Aaron and fell to her side, clutching her bleeding lower leg. Aaron scrambled to his feet. The female snapped at his ankle, reached out to pull his legs from under him. Aaron sidestepped her grip and landed a kick to her temple. She collapsed, unconscious.

"We have to get this guy and out of here," Tony said, propping his tranq gun against the wall so he could holster his weapon. "You all right?"

Aaron nodded, distracted. His ears rang from the gunshot, but from what he could tell the woods had gone silent. A moment later, the sound of galloping footfalls carried through the cotton muffling in his ears.

"You grab one arm, I'll get—"

"We can't take him," Aaron interrupted Tony. "Run."

Tony didn't argue, but made a beeline for the door. Aaron followed. He ditched his own tranq and pulled out his sidearm. He followed Tony down the porch steps. From the direction the two unconscious weres had arrived was a group of fifteen or so people, all naked and running with their bodies low to the ground, blades glistening dangerously from the fingertips they used to push off the forest floor. They were moving fast—wolf fast. A prod into Tony's back was all that was necessary to spur his partner into a run.

Back the way they had come, they crashed through the woods, each now making the same amount of unholy racket as the other. The shift had taken a toll on Aaron, and made him clumsy, but the adrenaline flowing through his blood pushed his exhausted body forward so he remained only a few steps behind Tony's long-legged athlete's stride.

Despite their steady sprint, the weres were quickly gaining. Was it possible this back-to-nature lifestyle put them in greater touch with their lupine side and tapped into latent powers Aaron had not yet discovered? Their pursuers' footfalls were dangerously close. Aaron could smell the sweat on their bodies, the stench of raw meat on their collective breath. They couldn't be more than fifty feet behind. He didn't dare to look. As if reading his mind, Tony turned his head to check their progress. In that fraction of a second that his concentration strayed from the treacherous beaten path, Tony's foot caught on a distended root. He lurched, touched his fingers to the ground like a football player, and pushed himself upright.

"Watch—" was all Aaron could get out.

Tony ran into the low hanging branch full force, the center of his forehead taking the brunt of the impact.

"Don't fall, don't fall," Aaron chanted as he sprinted. He caught Tony as he dipped back and righted him. "Keep moving."

Tony, dazed but conditioned by training, continued, but his stride was now as wobbly and indistinct as the path they followed.

The car was only a few hundred yards away. Aaron could see the dusty access drive and the black paint shimmering in the afternoon heat.

"Come on," he urged Tony. "You didn't hoist anything from op-tech today, did you?"

"Braven locked it down," Tony panted. His words were slurred.

"Don't pass out on me."

"'Kay," Tony replied as he stumbled on.

A lone, human-voiced howl arose behind them. It was answered in unison, the call morphing into something dark and canine as it grew. Aaron feared to look behind him lest they all had somehow shifted and now fifteen werewolves hunted them, but his head turned of its own accord. They were still too far out of range for him to see clearly, but they had not changed from human form. He snarled an answer to their cries. They returned the sound. It set the dark thing howling inside him. That strange, luring sensation filled his stomach—the same he'd felt twice the day before when around portals. A moment later his vision intensified and became the truer, clearer sight of the wolf. Something was nearby, a presence strong enough to override his own body's fatigue. In response, his jaw popped and cracked.

"No, no." He couldn't shift now. By the time he was halfway through the transformation they would be on him, and he would stand helpless witness as they used their filthy blades to disembowel Tony. "Keep it together."

Despite his reluctance, his teeth extruded, sharp canines shot from his jaws like daggers. His fingernails elongated and tapered to razor points.

While terrified at what his body was doing, he welcomed any extra edge he might gain. He could worry about the repercussions of this strange half shift after he and his partner were out of mortal danger. The weres would spread out soon, encircle them and cut off Tony from him. Tony was hurt, weak. He would be the one to fall first.

Aaron let loose a deep snarl. He grabbed Tony's arm and began propelling him forward. The muscular exhaustion from the shift had faded in this mysterious partial transformation. If it was some sort of physical response to Six Rivers' own odd display of lupine abilities, he wasn't going to condemn it. Anything to get Tony safely inside the car.

They reached the access road with only twenty feet between them and the still human weres, who had dropped to an anticipatory lope.

"Get in the car," he snapped.

Whether it was the feral tone in his voice or simply a by-product of the head injury, Tony obeyed, popping open the unlocked door and climbing inside.

Aaron whipped around to face the weres. Their predatory eyes shined with the certainty of the kill, their false fangs glinted with anticipatory froth. When they caught full sight of him, they ground to a halt. The male in front stared, uncertain. He wasn't Brandon, the alpha. He wasn't even the beta. Still, without the pack leaders present he was the highest-ranking wolf. He transferred his weight from bare, filthy foot to foot, and back again. Aaron's semi-shifted appearance made him confused, nervous. Aaron took the opportunity and snarled again, this time opening his mouth wide as he would have done with his muzzle, showing his teeth, his power.

The lead wolf looked from his blade-enhanced fingers to Aaron's own elongated claws, touched his filed teeth with his tongue.

"What do you want?" Aaron snarled.

His vocalization seemed to rouse the were from his indecision. He gave Aaron a look of utter disgust, then launched at him. Aaron caught the man mid-flight, and spun, letting the force carry them both to the side of the car. The were's knife claws raked across his arm as he rode him into the rear section. The glass shattered beneath the man's spine and part of his torso disappeared inside. He let loose a keening whine and went limp. Aaron pulled him from the jagged opening. A knife protruded from between his shoulder blades. Tony, bloody handed, twisted back around in the driver's seat and grabbed the wheel.

"Let's go, Aaron," he shouted as he started the engine.

Still howling like wolves, the pack abandoned their pseudo-quadrupedal gait and broke into a full humanoid assault. Aaron pulled out his revolver. Still with the aim of the young man who had earned top marks in his range assessments, he emptied his clip. Seven shifters dropped to the ground in rapid order. A mournful howl bellowed from the lungs of an unscathed wolf as she watched a bullet explode in the spinal column of a nearby pack mate. She sprinted toward Aaron, murderous rage etched across her face.

Tony accelerated. The front end of the car caught her at the knees with a meaty thud and sent her flying onto the hood. She rolled off and landed in an awkward heap.

The uninjured pack members kept their distance, eying Aaron with hatred, but none daring to advance. With his weapon still raised he hurried to the passenger side and slid in.

"Watch the road," he warned Tony. "There could be more coming."

They sped down the lane, tossing dusty clouds into the air behind them. Aaron surveyed the treeline on either side, waiting for the ambush. It never came. Only a few of the pack must have been left to guard their new territory. Where the rest had gotten off to was a concern, no doubt, but for now Aaron was happy for their absence.

Once Tony steered the car onto the highway, Aaron relaxed his guard. He pulled the emergency kit from the glove box and opened a packet of gauze with his teeth. He pushed back his sleeve and covered the deepest gashes with the dressing. The knife wounds on his biceps trickled blood, but were not immediately concerning.

"How's your head?" he asked.

"Which one of you two asked me that?" Tony replied, shooting him a quick grin before returning his eyes to the road. "I've had worse."

Aaron nodded, his thoughts already drifting to the werewolves. Their behavior was unlike any were he had ever known. He had to talk to Carlos. The Trinity alpha would know what in the hell was going on.

"Aaron?" His partner gave him a nervous glance. "Was that the Six Rivers Clan?"

"I'm pretty sure."

"What's happened to them?"

"I haven't the slightest idea, but it scares the shit out of me."

Chapter Fifteen

The Hound of Hell

"Let me get that arm fixed up for you right." Tony tossed the car keys on the kitchen counter as he passed, and headed off to the bathroom.

"I don't want that skin melting stuff," he called after Tony. "It's not bad enough to warrant that kind of pain."

None of the cuts were deep enough to need stitches, and because the shifter's talons had been blades instead of wide claws, they were much cleaner. In fact, his skin had pressed the gashes closed already. Usually he would have to shift to see such remarkable healing. It was another oddity to add to the day's pile.

He walked over to Tony's gym setup and leaned against the scowling dummy. What had happened to the Six Rivers clan to make them act like wolves all the time? Was it voluntary, or some sort of magical interference? Either way, this wasn't the work of Brandon, their entitled, self-serving new alpha. There was definitely another factor in this equation, the same factor, he would bet, that had helped Six Rivers get into Kapre California. A connection began to form in his mind, but it fizzled into nothingness before he could grasp it. With all of the chasing and fighting over with, he realized he was tired to the bone. He pressed his forehead against that of the dummy.

"You okay?" Tony emerged from the bathroom with a packet of gauze and a self-adhesive bandage roll in his hands.

"Yeah. Tired, that's all." He unbuttoned his shirt and slid his arms out of it.

Tony took the shirt and draped it over the dummy while Aaron pulled the piece of gauze away from the wound.

"That looks pretty good," Tony remarked. "Really good, in fact."

"Unsettlingly good?"

Tony avoided looking at him.

"It's okay. I was thinking the same thing." Aaron watched Tony change the gauze pad and begin rolling the puckered bandage around his tricep. "Those weres ran like wolves. I don't mean just in the way they used their arms as forelegs, but how fast they went. It was like they were shifted when they weren't. Even the night before a full moon, Carlos doesn't get any wolfier in terms of skill and speed. And he's old."

"And there's how your face changed." Tony caught his surprise. "Yeah, I saw. Your face didn't shift, just your eyes and teeth. And you had claws, but no fur. That's not normal for you, is it?"

"No." The unsettled feeling that had been growing in his stomach since they had found the cabin in the woods turned to twisting fear. "I'm changing. Something's changing me. And I think it's the same thing that's changing Six Rivers. In fact, I think it changed me right when we were being chased. Something was nearby. I could feel it."

"Do you think it could have affected Carlos, or any of your clan?"

"We'll ask tonight." Aaron put a hand on his forehead. His thoughts turned to dull slush in his head. "Is it okay if I—?"

"Go get some rest in my bed," Tony offered. He didn't follow up with any wisecracks. "I'll wake you if anything exciting happens. Or if I order pizza, which is pretty much the same thing."

Aaron smiled. Without thinking he reached out and brushed Tony's face with his fingers. Embarrassed, he let his hand drop away.

"Let me know if you need me," Aaron said. Realizing the second inferable meaning to this, he quickly turned and headed for the staircase.

Aaron kicked off his shoes and climbed onto the steel gray comforter. The pillow smelled of Tony, warm and manly, with a slight hint of crisp aftershave. He pressed his cheek against the cool cotton. Egyptian. Tony liked his luxuries. His mind drifted to the drawer of DVDs he had found the day before, and again a deep curiosity stirred inside him. The dark thing once again suggested maybe Tony should be the one pinned down, mastered, fucked. His dick rose to half-mast before sleep began pulling at him.

Why didn't he give Tony another chance? After today it was clear he was an ally. And the thought of driving himself into that perfect ass was enough to make him half-crazy with lust. He ran his hand over his sensitive, but still frustratingly softening cock. Why didn't he...?

He drifted away, lulled by the metallic snap of Tony loading clips in the room below.

* * * *

Children in wolf skins ran around a campfire, howling and snarling at the shadow lurking deep inside the flames. The beast rose up with the conflagration, spreading its arms to the sky, blocking out the stars. The only brightness came from the fire at its feet, yet even that no longer shed light on the children. The shadow being plucked them up, one at a time, and tossed them down its pitch throat. It rumbled in pleasure, the sound at first like that of an approaching train, but as it built turned into a howl so piercing it shattered the black sky, raining down chunks of midnight glass, exposing the gaping abyss above.

Aaron thrashed awake, unable to stop the strangled cry before it escaped his mouth.

"It's okay," Tony's voice came from the far side of the darkened loft.

"What…? What time is it?" he croaked, sitting up.

"Late." Tony came closer, his body a shadow over the bed. "You were dreaming."

"The light, please." After his nightmares the darkness was always too dark. A lamp clicked on to show Tony standing bare-chested above him. "Thank you."

"Better?" Tony sat down on the edge of the bed. His hip rested against Aaron's leg.

"Yes."

"Better than this?" Tony leaned in and touched Aaron's mouth with his own. It was a light, tentative touch. He pulled back just enough for Aaron to focus on his face.

Aaron shook his head, too afraid to speak.

"Even better, this way?" Tony leaned in again and ran his tongue slowly across the line of Aaron's closed lips.

He gave in to the pressure of the caress and let Tony press his mouth against his and kiss him deeply. Aaron's cock jolted. His entire lower body seemed comprised of one screaming nerve that ran directly into his dick. With each *stroke of Tony's tongue against his own, the nerves shot a wave of cramping pleasure into his groin.*

He broke contact, moved to the hot skin beneath Tony's ear and moaned his partner's name.

"Tony."

* * * *

"I like it when you say my name that way."

Aaron awoke to Tony's gentle shake. Tony was sitting on the edge of the bed, his hip pressed against Aaron's thigh. Aaron looked at Tony, unsure of what to say. He could deny the dream, or at least the meaning behind his moaning Tony's name like a cat in heat, but the obvious proof to the contrary rested a few inches west of Tony's hip, where a monstrous bulge strained against the confines of his pants. He was so hard he could see the contours of his cock head.

So that was it. Keep denying his wishes, denying himself, or… He lurched to a sitting position and put his hand on Tony's neck.

"I want you," was all he said.

"Carlos is here."

Tony's words sliced through the fog of desire. Aaron took a steadying breath and nodded.

"I told them about the forest today. But you should get yourself together and come down." Tony's expression mirrored Aaron's frustration, disappointment and hesitancy. After a moment Tony moved to stand, but Aaron tightened his grip and pulled him in closer so his ear brushed his mouth.

"I want to trust you." His voice was a growl in Tony's ear. His teeth elongated and he let them graze Tony's neck.

"I'll earn it. I will." Tony stood and gestured toward the door, indicating that he would handle things downstairs while Aaron put himself to rights.

"Remember when you said you always screwed things up?" Aaron asked softly. "Why is that?"

"I don't know. Abandonment, mommy and daddy issues." Tony gave him a shaky grin. "The usual, boring story."

"I'd like to hear it sometime."

Tony winced as if in pain. After a prolonged moment of silence he acquiesced. "Yeah, okay."

"You know this, right here and now?" Aaron added. "This isn't screwed up."

"Says the Acqxterm agent slash shapeshifter hanging out in my bed." Even though Tony replied with his usual deflective grin, his eyes were sober. He patted Aaron's hand. "Let's go talk about our wolf problem."

* * * *

"May I see it?" Carlos avoided looking at Aaron as he came down the stairs and instead held out his hand to Tony.

From his place on the couch next to Carlos, Matthew looked from his lover to Aaron and back, lips pursed. Whether it was in amusement or irritation, Aaron couldn't tell. He didn't know Matthew well enough to recognize his subtleties. Tony passed Carlos the parchment they had retrieved from the Trinity clan's cabin and sat down in one of the opposite chairs. Aaron took the other.

"Hello, Carlos, Matthew," he said.

"Hello, Aaron," Carlos said, glancing up only momentarily.

Carlos never called him by his given name, had always used some endearment or another. The fact he used Aaron's name now meant he had heard the exchange between Tony and him. Aaron didn't care about being vindictive, nor was his interest in Tony a device for getting Carlos' attention, but still he couldn't deny he was a little pleased the alpha, too, felt the sting of an ex-lover rebounding with whiplash speed.

"Good evening," Matthew said as he leaned over Carlos' shoulder to study the parchment. His expression immediately clouded. "Oh."

"What is it?" Carlos asked.

"The symbol," Matthew said. He traced the form with his finger. "It's a mark of Hell."

"Hell?" Tony repeated.

"That would explain the brimstone at Kapre California, and here," Aaron said. "But, what do denizens of Hell want with werewolves? Aren't they lower beings to them?"

"I should have clarified," Matthew said. "It is a mark of a high ranking demon. The legendary father of the wolves."

"Cerberus?" Carlos asked. "Are you sure?"

Matthew nodded as he frowned at the mark.

"Cerberus, the three-headed dog that guards the gates of the Underworld?" Tony asked.

"Cerberus, or Kerberos, was the multi-headed hound of the underworld of the Greek and Roman mythology, yes," Carlos answered. "But that is just a legend, a facet of his true identity worked into their personal religion. There are numerous accounts of hellhounds across all cultures, most of them due in some part to Cerberus' actual influence over past events."

"But," Matthew picked up the thread, "he is a very real demon of the highest order. He has access to all of the links between dimensions, and is thusly the guardian of the gates, which is where his Greek title comes into play."

"He's in many stories, including werewolf legend," Carlos said. He placed the parchment on the coffee table. "Did I ever tell you the legend of the first wolf, Aaron?"

"I don't think so. I remember you telling me lots of stories when I was having my panic attacks, but I don't remember anything about a wolf."

"I guess it wouldn't have been a soothing topic," Carlos agreed. "Well, there is a tale that has been handed down through the werewolf lines. It was, like the tale of Cerberus, once taken as gospel but slowly became myth among shifters and nothing more. The old ones told it like this—

"The first were was a demon, a massive doglike creature that skulked through the blackness that lies between dimensions"—Carlos relaxed back into his chair, his voice taking on the melodic rhythm that had many nights eased into Aaron's world of unspeakable terror and lulled him for a short while—"always cold, always yearning to fill the vortex in his chest caused by the isolation of his depthless home, the creature prowled the dimensions, wishing for warmth, searching for companionship. When it reached our world it saw the sun and rushed out to greet it. But, the light caused it great pain and burned its fur black. The creature retreated to the gateway and hid in the shadows until nightfall. Darkness came, and yet another bright orb lit the sky. Except this one did not burn. The creature ran under its glow, happy to feel the leaves under its paws, the trees rustling overhead, the illumination caressing its back. When daylight came, the creature retreated to its gateway to await the moon's rise. After a few nights however, the moon began to shrink, its light lessened. Soon, it became a sliver, and the next night was gone. The creature's world was again dark.

"Bereft that it was once more plunged into cold darkness, the creature began walking aimlessly. After a time it saw a warm, non-threatening glow in the distance. The creature had found humans, and fire. While it was ecstatic, the humans were terrified to see a large, black, wolflike creature stalking toward them. They grabbed branches of fire and waved them while they fled, screaming. A young woman, however, saw the grief in its eyes and took pity on the beast. She invited it to share the light of her fire. In exchange, the creature offered her his own warmth. She consented and the creature swallowed her whole. So happy was the creature to have such close company that it curled up to sleep and did not awaken even with the sunrise, and soon burned to a char. When nightfall came the unharmed young woman climbed out of the creature's ashen form. For keeping company with a devil, her people forsook her. They forced her back into the winter woodland where she lived off tree bark and pine needle tea. She suffered greatly. Twenty-eight days later, she was nearly dead of starvation. The sun set and the full moon rose overhead. The starving young woman, blessed by the creature, shifted into a wolf. She hunted that night and ate her fill of the forest's creatures. No longer trusting humans she remained in the woods, living like a wolf even in human form. She attacked any human that crossed her path while shifted. Those who survived her bites were worthy of the creature's gift, and they too, shifted at the full moon and ran through the leaves under the stars. And the creature's soul, carried in the hearts and blood of its children, was never alone again."

"Which is all utter bull, of course," Matthew said. "We have what most would call a disease, a contagious genetic mutation."

"But, where did it come from, *cielito*?" Carlos asked. "Is it simply a virus, this mystical power we have? We have seen magic. Aaron and Tony here work with it each day. Demons and other inexplicable creatures fall at their hands. We were just speaking casually of Hell. Yet you think we are just diseased?"

Carlos' indulgent smile seemed to irritate Matthew. "I'm not saying there isn't a mystical element, but when something is transmitted from person to person it's generally thought of as a virus."

"That may be so," Carlos conceded, but it was clear he did so only to placate his boyfriend rather than out of being convinced otherwise. "However we wish to view our condition, we are talking about the legend itself, and it gives us some real information about Cerberus, such as his ability to move between worlds, and the brimstone that marks his arrival. Those who have seen him appear say a shadow rises from a spontaneous deflagration that extinguishes soon after the shadowy feet leave the embers."

"Leaving behind a circle of brimstone," Tony said.

Aaron tuned them out. His mind replayed the dream of the shadow emerging from the fire and consuming the little wolf children. His thoughts turned back to the sigil on the parchment and the signatures above it, and the grimoire with the summoning spell.

"He is helping them to be better wolves. Stronger." He wasn't aware he had spoken out loud until the room quieted. "That's how the shifters in the forest could run faster. With Cerberus' help, they're making a move to unite all of the weres under Six Rivers control, and they're destroying Kapre agencies because we're the only force with enough power to stop them. Cerberus is giving them magic, or sharing his own in Matthew's germ warfare theory..." Aaron sat back, stunned.

"And this back-to-basics nonsense with Six Rivers, whose idea was that? Theirs or Cerberus'?" Tony asked.

"Does it matter?" Matthew sighed.

"It does if it means their endgames are different," Carlos answered. "We know what Six Rivers wants, control. But what about Cerberus?"

"If he isn't happy playing servant to a bunch of weres, and I don't know why he would be, then he has his own agenda. And I doubt it'll be a friendlier plan than what Six Rivers has been hatching," Tony said.

"But if a mage is controlling him?" Matthew offered. "Binding him by ritual and forcing him...?"

The words of the three men buzzed around Aaron's ears but made little sense. He had pushed to the back of his mind Qi's declaration that he was not like the other 'dogs'. It had not seemed relevant at the time. He was a werewolf. It didn't matter who had bitten him, or what their rank was. He was a werewolf, regardless. But now... Aaron stared into the polished surface of the coffee table. Behind his human facade he imagined he saw the dark thing, how it lived inside him instead of becoming part of him. His uncharacteristic black pelt. The ability to shift at any time, not just on a full moon. The rapid changes he was undergoing that coincided with the appearance of the brimstone in town—the mark of an otherworldly being entering this world.

"It's not possible." A tremor ran the length of his body.

"What?" Tony clearly noticed the distress in his voice. He turned toward Aaron, forehead drawn in concern.

"The bites were so painful I blacked out," Aaron continued, uncaring that the others were staring at him outright. "But the one, it was like fire. Like hot pokers from a blast furnace being jammed into my abdomen. It was so dark I couldn't see. I thought I was dying it was so dark. But then the hair—wiry and sparse—I saw it sticking out of the black hide."

"No, *mi hombre*." Carlos switched back to the endearment, which meant he already believed what Aaron was saying. "It can't be."

"It all makes sense, doesn't it? When you think about it?"

"There has never been a case like this before," Carlos protested.

"Well, then, meet Mr Precedent." Aaron looked across at Tony, who stared at him with concern and confusion. "I was turned by Cerberus. I'm the son of the Hound of Hell."

Chapter Sixteen

Brimstone's Child

"It's okay," Aaron said for the fifth time. And for the fifth time he remained unheard.

His revelation had brought down a chorus of inflamed protest. Matthew and Carlos exchanged a barrage of speculation while Tony interjected to argue this or that point. Their voices, meant to reassure, to share with him his pain and fear, grated against his sensitive ears like a wire brush against porcelain. Aaron listened to the weres discussing the implications of his existence, watched Tony steal surreptitious glances his way, and merely nodded, a puppet on a string, as his mouth again formed the same words.

"It's okay."

It wasn't. Not by far. But that was what people said to reassure others and themselves when life started to fall apart. It was the mystical incantation to fix everything, to convince those in horrifying situations that they would soon move through, that sunny days rested just beyond the dark tornado swirling around them. But magical thinking would not stop real magic or the demons from which it sprang. And there was his own personal demon who seemed overjoyed to find him wholly submerged in its darkness at long last.

As Aaron crashed into his emotional low, the dark thing resumed its struggle for control. It scrabbled against his insides in an effort to take over, howled and barked into the cavernous pit that had once housed his undoubtedly shredded soul. Aaron braced his back against the cushions as if physical reinforcements would help contain the unsettled monster. His impulses screamed for him to shift. Changing would satisfy the beast and squelch his riotous thoughts. But changing, he suspected, would also hand over the keys to the empire. One shift and that would be it for him. Even though he wanted rest and peace, he didn't want to earn it through being eaten alive from the inside out by a demonic dog.

"Regardless, tomorrow night is our deadline." Tony's voice cut in above the others. "If we accept our current theory that they are going after Kapre, we can also assume their attack will come when they're strongest, with the full moon at its zenith. It will also be when Kapre is at its weakest. The most qualified acqxterm agents will either be home, sleeping, or out in the field on nocturnal hunts. Braven will be gone and the night manager is mostly incompetent. The only people in the office will be rookies and non-field rated support staff. They will follow protocol and try to evacuate. By the time the alarms summon our active agents from their houses, everyone inside will be dead. Our teams will storm in with only their take home weapons. It will be a bloodbath. I'm sorry, Aaron, we can't keep Braven in the dark any longer."

"I agree." Aaron's voice sounded small against the enormity of the expectant silence pressing against him. "I'll tell Braven myself tomorrow morning."

"I'm sure she already suspects you're a werewolf, at least," Tony said.

"Probably. She didn't get to the top of the command chain by not knowing the ins and outs of supernatural beings."

"Matthew and I will be able to shift by the morning." Carlos glanced at Matthew, took a deep breath and continued, "By then the rest of the clan will be here."

"The rest...?" Aaron sputtered. "What do you mean? What did you do, Carlos?"

"What I had to do, *mi hombre*. This is a war against weres just as much as it is against Kapre. We have right to fight for ourselves."

"Bringing in the entire Trinity clan on the same day as the invasion only implicates you—us!" Aaron said.

"There is no way around it, I'm afraid," Matthew replied.

"You should have told me," he said, directing his ire at Carlos.

"You said yourself Trinity is no longer your concern."

"I also claimed this area as my territory. I have every right to view your actions as hostile."

"If that is what you wish, *mi hombre*. Your agency will be fighting Cerberus and Six Rivers, leaving you and"—he waved a hand at Tony—"possibly your partner to call Trinity out on breeching protocol. It is your right as alpha, of course, but not only will you distract my forces and let Six Rivers win, you will be severely outnumbered and your fight, however justified by clan law, will quickly become futile."

Aaron felt Tony's guard rising, sensed Matthew's desperate desire to steer the conversation back into neutrality, but neither of them mattered. There was only Carlos and him in the room. Two beasts — one an old leader, powerful in his own right — the other younger, rogue, but by his genetic makeup likely much stronger. They could shift and fight and Aaron would stand a good chance against his former lover.

A very good chance.

This revelation knocked the air from his lungs. He was Carlos' equal, if not superior. He could, if he chose, be headstrong and stupid, take his former mentor in a fight and secure control of Trinity entirely. No one could stop him. Yet, instead of heightening his aggression, this knowledge drained the tension from his body. He no longer needed to prove himself to Carlos or anyone, at least not on the physical front. How he appeared as a leader, however, was still up in the air. Acting on childish impulses would have him labeled as Six River's new alpha had already been, a useless whelp, unworthy of respect. As he was for now only a pack of one, he needed to be judicious.

As Aaron sorted this out, Carlos watched him with a shrewd expression, as if all of his thoughts were being broadcast directly into his mind. Aaron returned the scrutiny and leaned back into the cushions, relaxing into his new power and position. Carlos gave him an almost imperceptible approving nod. Even though it was clear Carlos had been steering his outlook toward this particular maturation, Aaron couldn't find the will to be aggravated by it. Regardless of how he had gotten there, he was finally free of the pack's hierarchical control.

That, however, didn't mean he didn't require assistance.

"Next time I would appreciate a heads-up on any pack movement within my territory," was all Aaron said.

"Of course," Carlos agreed, a small smile playing at his lips.

"We'll leave you, now." Matthew stood and gestured to Carlos to stand.

An alpha would usually bristle at an underling taking the lead in that manner, but Carlos merely dipped his head in acknowledgment and stood. Matthew was special, of that there was no doubt.

Tony led them to the front door. Aaron trailed the group.

"Call us after your meeting with your boss tomorrow," Carlos said. He amended with, "When it is convenient, of course."

"I will." Their new roles were going to take some getting used to on both sides, but Aaron was already pleased with the progress. No longer the pitiful head case charity, he was alpha. Alpha of what, he didn't quite know, but alpha just the same. "I'll walk you to the parking lot."

"I'll say my goodbyes here." Tony opened the door for them. He nodded at the weres, then brushed Aaron's sleeve as the three of them passed. "Will I see you tomorrow, then?"

Aaron sensed rather than saw the hesitancy in Carlos' step, the quirk of Matthew's lips as the pair continued their descent, leaving him some privacy to give Tony his answer.

"I'll be back in a minute." He returned Tony's suddenly shy smile, and followed the weres to the ground level.

As Matthew opened the ground floor door, Carlos turned to speak. A rush of wind buffeted them. They all froze. The scent of hellfire stained the back courtyard, turned the weed-choked lawn ochre in his mind.

"He's here."

The words were scarcely out of Matthew's mouth before Carlos and Aaron tore outside, nearly colliding in their rush. Carlos streaked off into the shadows, following the heaviest scent. Matthew stuck to his heels. They vaulted a privacy fence, one after the next. Aaron ignored them, ignored the smell. He could see tracks in his mind, lava orange, leading in the opposite direction, toward an adjacent parking lot. He started to call for the weres, but the words stuck in his throat. It was stupid, almost certainly mortally so, but he had to see his creator for the first time alone. He ran through the maze of cars, following the footprints burning in his skull. So intent was he on following the images in his mind he didn't see the form step out from the shadows until almost too late. He skidded to a halt a mere five feet from the hulking creature.

Black and bubbly like the exterior of a burnt marshmallow, with sparse hair dotting its scarified hide, Cerberus was a terrifying sight. Yet, even with its foul gray fangs and coral eyes, the demon dog was nothing compared to the image his inner eye showed. In his mind, the creature's blackened skin was just a thin, cracked surface overlaying a sea of shifting, burbling magma. Three heads sprouted from a charred tree trunk neck, each snapping and slavering, the viscous froth that dropped from its jowls singeing the earth beneath.

Aaron recoiled in horror. This thing couldn't be what had turned him. This foul creature could not have forged the shadow that lurked in his chest. As if to dispute this very point the dark thing inside him stretched out, sniffing and questing. It invited Cerberus closer.

The massive demon raised its snouts, nostrils flaring like furnace vents. Aaron stood frozen. An odor of deeply charred flesh and sulfur burned his throat as Cerberus moved closer. A rush of power surged through Aaron, sent electric shocks coursing through his nervous system. His muscles trembled under the dark thing's desire to greet its maker on equal footing. His vision slid, blurring a moment before sharpening keenly. Aaron steeled himself against his inner demon's onslaught. His jaw popped. His teeth stretched and elongated. His knuckles sprouted tufts of black hair.

Hair that matched the demon standing before him.

Cerberus was inches away.

Aaron trembled with the effort of restraining the dark thing.

Cerberus trailed his nose slowly up Aaron's legs, beginning at his feet, snuffling loudly, taking in the scent at his toes, shins, knees, crotch. When the demon's nose touched Aaron's stomach it gave a growl. Not menacing, but almost playful. Friendly.

The dark thing gave a violent lurch. Aaron pitched forward onto his knees, his nose almost in contact with that of Cerberus. Pain radiated through his body. Tendons stretched to near snapping. Aaron threw all his resistance into fighting the transformation. Agony shook his limbs as he and the creature inside waged war over the form his body should take. His organs shuddered beneath a contorting, rioting frame. The bones in his ribs twisted against his spine. His legs and arms shook with mounting unspent energy.

Cerberus leaned in and nuzzled deeper, like a free man speaking through the wall to a prisoner. The demonic soul howled for liberation, for its creator.

"No," Aaron yelled.

He flung himself away from Cerberus. His contorted skeleton screamed in pained protest as he landed on his back, sprawled on the pavement. The moon shined above, a luminous disc marred only by a slightly flattened left edge. He felt its strength running through his body, the undeniable power it fed the raging beast inside its humanoid cage, and knew he was indeed looking at the progenitor of all weres, the alpha of all alphas. The moon's light disappeared as a cloud swept over its face. Few lights lit the parking lot, leaving most of the illumination provided by a malign glow oozing from between the cracked patches of Cerberus' skin.

"No." This time softer, more in answer to his terror than in defiance of the hellhound.

A grating, guttural sound came from Cerberus' throat. It was laughing.

"Have it your way." The voice churned through Aaron's mind. *"See me."*

The air seemed to solidify like layer of ice over a river. The moon appeared watery, the stars mere pinpoints of light in the blurred darkness. Magma spilled from Cerberus' wolflike form, devoured the outer shell in a fiery flood. The demon's head tore into three. The mounds of fiery torn flesh transformed into three necks, three skulls. The body flowed up, the rear legs lengthened and became human, the torso and forelegs straightened and elongated. Each face smiled down at Aaron, a horrifying mix of man and wolf. The muzzle-like mouths opened wide and more abrasive laughter rolled out.

"Why did you change me?" Once the first question had passed Aaron's trembling lips the rest followed in a torrent. "Why not let the weres have me? Why did you kill the others and not me? Why did *you* change me into *this*?"

"Gifts are never appreciated." Cerberus' voice was as coarse as the flesh on his body.

"But why me?"

"Why not?" All six eyes scanned Aaron's body. The mouths snorted as if they found nothing of worth. "Tomorrow, then. Maybe you can die with the other pieces of meat."

The crystalline air shattered. The illusion of the humanoid figure vanished. Cerberus was once again a canine monstrosity. He gave Aaron one last disparaging look and turned. The demon loped several feet. A burst of flame erupted from the ground to engulf him. A wave of oddly familiar spiciness hit Aaron's nose. A moment later the stench of rotten eggs overlaid it. The fire exploded toward the sky and burnt out, fading first to the ground, then into nothingness.

Aaron got to his feet and moved to examine the asphalt. A pitch mound of brimstone rested where the demon had made his exit.

Shoes gritted against gravel at his back. Aaron turned to find Matthew.

"So, that was Cerberus?"

Aaron wanted to explain why he hadn't called for reinforcements, or why he hadn't fought the demon, but he honestly didn't know why, other than he had wanted to see Cerberus for himself, maybe just to see if the creature that had made him into a monster felt anything, anything at all for him. That sort of rationale was not one easily explained if he wanted to reassure the weres of his improved sanity. He remained silent.

Why not? The words echoed in his mind, a torment in two syllables. A verbal shrug. An acceptance of coffee with a co-worker. The declaration of a bored, apathetic monster. *Why not.*

"That was him, yeah," he said.

A large wolf, hair the gentle red and golden hues of the desert at sunset, came speeding across the parking lot.

"It's okay, Carlos. That light was Cerberus departing." Matthew looked at Aaron, then back at his lupine partner. "For now, at least."

Aaron watched the brimstone as if Cerberus would pop back out and give him a better explanation. From Matthew's expression the beta had seen most of the interaction. Aaron lifted a questioning eyebrow. Matthew shook his head almost imperceptibly. He would let Aaron have his secret. Matthew flashed him a small smile, then looked down at the alpha.

"Your shift came sooner than you thought."

"Possibly something more to do with Cerberus' presence?" Matthew posed.

The wolf gave a shake of his head, indicating his ignorance of the situation.

"Well, one thing came out of this exercise," Aaron said. "We have confirmation of tomorrow's attack."

Chapter Seventeen

Solace

Aaron walked back to the apartment complex. The dark thing howled inside him, furious at being denied emergence in the face of its creator. His legs trembled with post-adrenaline decline, or possibly terror and rage. He didn't know. For he was howling too, raging inside himself along with the demon he housed. His mind tossed out an angry imagined conversation with the hellhound.

Why not?

Seemed like a good thing to do at the time.

Why not?

You had no other plans for your life than to house a piece of my demonic soul.

Why the fuck not.

He kept his gait steady, knowing Matthew and the re-humanized Carlos watched him from the street. They smelled his emotions, no doubt, but their toll on him was what they assessed. True enough he was no longer under Trinity control and could not be barred from the following night's war, but he couldn't afford their confidence in him to slip even a little. Doubtful soldiers made dead soldiers. And it was very likely there would be deaths enough without him adding to the tally. He raised his hand without looking back and moved around the corner. A few moments later two car doors slammed and the master and second of Trinity clan drove off into the night, ready to get back to their hotel where their pack undoubtedly waited for them.

The pack. Somehow Aaron hadn't thought about them when considering the consequences of this war. Some of the shifters who had cared for him when he was at his weakest would die tomorrow. The ones who had held his hand, pinned him down or downright kicked the shit out of him during his flashbacks, they would be there fighting with him. And he would watch them die. He pulled open the door and leaned into the jamb. A fine tremble shook his body.

Orchestrate a bunch of shifters to kill each other in the name of lupine rusticism?

Why not?

His feet felt leaden as he trudged up the staircase. A scent caught his nose at the landing. A wave of emotions swept over him. Too basic and intermingled to label, they flowed through Aaron, shook him to his core. The wall supported him as the sensations crashed through his body. The door opened. Tony stood there, his elegant face a mix of concern and relief. They locked gazes and the feelings roiling inside Aaron cemented into one solid, driving force.

"I thought you had gone—"

Aaron lunged forward, grabbed Tony's neck and pulled him close, cutting off his words. Aaron pulled him in, crushed his mouth with his lips. Tony's eyes went wide with surprise, then drifted closed as he fell deeper into the kiss. Tony opened his mouth to him, and Aaron kissed him deeper. The dark thing raged and Aaron didn't try to push it away, but funneled its energy into Tony. He pushed Tony through the door, using his hips to guide Tony to the wall. They slammed into it together, bumping chins and crushing lips. Tony smiled and kissed him harder, delved his tongue deep inside his mouth. Aaron pulled at Tony's T-shirt. Tony lifted his arms, breaking the kiss only enough for his head to pass through the hole, then returned his mouth to Aaron's. Tony worked the buttons on his shirt while Aaron unzipped Tony's fly.

Aaron moved his mouth to Tony's neck. He trailed his tongue along the steady pulse, worked his lips across to the hollow in Tony's throat. Tony swallowed hard, head thrown back, hands bunched in the shirt he had shoved down around Aaron's shoulders. Aaron ran his mouth along Tony's chest, the soft down tickling his lips and nose. He flicked his tongue out to lap at first one nipple, then the other. He took one in his mouth and suckled it gently. Tony gripped his shoulders. He moved his hands, urging. Aaron followed their hint. He traced a wet line down Tony's taut abs and around his belly button, and kissed a trail toward the waist of Tony's pants.

Aaron dropped to his knees, his face even with the enticing bulge straining out from the undone zipper. He sloughed his shirt off his shoulders, then pulled Tony's pants to his ankles, freeing a generously-sized erect cock. His own dick gave a violent spasm. Aaron turned his head, kissed along the length from the base and slowly worked his way to the burgeoning tip. When he reached the extra sensitive area at the base of the engorged head, Aaron teased it with his mouth. Tony dug hard fingers into his shoulders, into the network of scars. For once, Aaron didn't care about them.

With one fist around the base, Aaron plunged down onto Tony's cock with his mouth. He sucked at it hard, letting his teeth graze against it. Tony tightened his grip and groaned. Aaron pulled harder, savoring the sensation of Tony's shaft sliding through his mouth. Tony gave a cry of pleasure. The dark thing lurched, a predator wanting prey. He released Tony's dick suddenly, and surged up, catching Tony off guard. He turned Tony, slamming him face-first against the wall. He covered Tony's back with his mouth, laying hot, desperate kisses against his skin. Aaron ached for his most sensitive places to be touched, but the dark thing wanted more. It wanted Tony begging for it.

He planted a foot against Tony's bunched pants and underwear. His voice was a harsh growl when he said, "Step out of them."

Tony did as commanded, freed his legs from the fabric at his ankles, then kicked off his shoes for good measure.

Aaron continued to devour Tony's back. He ran his hand along the defined lines, feeling the dips and swells of each muscle under his palm. He reached Tony's ass and cupped it violently. As he squeezed he worked his other hand to the front. He found the softly haired mound and stroked it. Tony's hips spasmed. He took his hand off Tony's ass and delved into the crack, forcing Tony to spread his legs. He ran his fingers along the hot opening and stroked farther to rub the tender perineum, then farther still to cup Tony's balls. He gave them a gentle squeeze then backtracked. He rubbed the warm cleft a few more times, then put his fingers to his mouth. He licked the first three, savoring the musky scent and returned them to Tony's ass. He pressed his index finger against the tight opening. It yielded easily. Tony thrust his hips back, pushing into his hand. Aaron shifted his hand from Tony's pubis to his cock. He worked it gently, moving with featherlight motions up and down, concentrating on teasing the head when Tony took his finger in the deepest. He unfolded another finger and let Tony back into it. The opening strained a little wider as he inserted the third finger. He braced his thumb against the soft skin at the base of Tony's spine and plunged deeply into his ass. Tony moaned as he worked the head into a hot, tight knob. A drop of viscous liquid seeped out onto his fingers. Aaron pressed his aching cock against Tony's hip. It seemed the heat of it would burn through the fabric of his pants.

He pressed his fingers deep inside Tony's ass, searching for the small knot of his prostate. A moment later he found it. Tony's erection jerked in his hand and Tony cried out.

"Oh god!" Tony leaned back into Aaron, arching into his shoulder and laying his head on it. "I need you to fuck me."

The dark thing howled its triumph. Aaron took his hand off Tony's member and slid his fingers out of his ass. He kissed Tony's neck, ran his face through the sweet, silky chestnut hair. With one brutal pop his teeth elongated, his eyes shifted. He growled deep in his throat.

Tony looked back at him, an expression of desire and awe suffusing his face. Aaron fed on the first, the dark thing rejoiced in the second.

"Bedroom," was all he could manage.

Tony made for the stairs, his gorgeous ass working as he took the steps. Aaron watched him ascend, watched the flex and release of his muscles, the perfect motion that highlighted the perfect body. Another growl escaped him as he stripped off his own trousers, shoes and socks. Tony looked down at him from the landing. He skimmed past the myriad of scars disfiguring his body, and came to rest on Aaron's erection. A wave of lust poured out of him. The scent filled Aaron's nose and the dark thing surged into control. Tony tore his eyes away and disappeared behind the wall.

Shifter speed got Aaron to the top of the steps before Tony could shut the nightstand drawer. Aaron was on him in a flash, eliciting a small surprised gasp from Tony. The beast inside him swelled. It had its prey. Aaron allowed it to join him. Their needs and desires finally unified, they came together in an outpouring of carnal lust. He yanked the lube and condom from Tony's hand. They didn't really need the condom, but discussing the ins and outs of werewolf immune systems was not a feral creature's priority. He unscrewed the cap. Tony half turned, but he pushed him around. On its way to brace against the wall Tony's splayed hand hit a lamp. It clattered from the table to the floor. Aaron nudged it out of the way and advanced. He tore open the package, rolled the condom onto his dick, then spread onto it a generous amount of the silky gel. Tony turned his head, concentrating on Aaron's hand and dick as he worked the lube up and down the thinly veiled shaft. Pleasure coursed through him, but his demonic passenger was growing impatient. He squeezed more onto his fingers.

He kicked Tony's ankles like he was searching a perp. The lamp sent a wash of brilliant light into his face. Aaron grabbed his chin, pulled his face around for a deep kiss. Tony opened his mouth to his and he thrust his fingers into Tony's anus. Tony moaned as Aaron worked his fingers along the warm insides. Tony's knees buckled with pleasure and Aaron withdrew his hand, catching him by the hips. He held Tony in place with one hand, his demonic muscles easily supporting his partner in case his legs failed. Aaron traced his cock down between Tony's cheeks, slid it between his thighs, caressed the underside of his sack a few times before he pulled back and plunged into Tony's warmth.

Tony cried out. His fingers whitened against the bricks. Aaron and the dark thing growled. He knew his face was half lupine. Half demon. He didn't care. For once he and the beast agreed on something — dominating this moaning, impassioned male, and pleasuring both of their bodies.

He pounded into Tony. His partner arched his back and pressed into each thrust, taking it all inside him. He reached around and grabbed Tony's dick. It was hot and hard with need. With fingers still slick from the lubricant he stroked the shaft in rhythm, tightening his fist when he pushed, forcing Tony's cock to squeeze through the narrow opening his fingers provided, then loosening as he pulled back. Tony's arms splayed rigidly across the bricks as he absorbed the impact of Aaron's wild pumping.

Aaron's loins screamed with pleasure as he worked against Tony's. With each thrust he brought the tip it to the edge of the alluringly stretched hole and thrust in again. He battered the beautiful cheeks with his hips, his balls slapped wildly against Tony's. The repressed demon in him had awoken with full force and he wouldn't be able to stop, even if Tony began voicing discomfort. He didn't.

Tony returned his thrusts with equal enthusiasm, pressing his hips back into Aaron's dick to intensify the impact. His shaft jumped under Aaron's fingers. Aaron worked it harder, sliding his hand faster and faster along the spasming erection.

"Oh god I'm coming," Tony cried in one breathless heave.

"Not yet." Aaron stopped his fingers, but still held on. Tony writhed beneath his grip and pressed his forehead into the brick.

Aaron's hips had a mind of their own. His insides screamed with feral glee. He resumed working Tony's dick, urgently stroking with his fingers. Tony pressed back into him, open, ready, cock jolting with need.

"Now," Aaron breathed against his back as his head filled with pressure.

A few more firm strokes and Tony's rod convulsed in his hand. Tony cried out. A stream of cum spattered against the bricks. Tony shuddered with his orgasm. Aaron watched his body tremble, saw the thin line of jizz trickle down the wall. His own dick exploded. He pumped manically against Tony, who cried out with him. He rode the pleasure, his groin tight, overwhelmed with sensation. He pounded out the last few waves of ecstasy, then collapsed forward. He rested his cheek against Tony's heaving, sweaty back and pulled out. Tony reached for him, grazed his fingers along his hip, and turned to face him.

Aaron leaned in and kissed Tony.

"Not that I'm complaining," Tony said with a grin, "but what about us being partners? What about you not needing this right now?"

Aaron touched his face, ran a hand through the carelessly perfect mop of hair. Something in his expression sobered Tony.

"I figure right now is all we have."

Chapter Eighteen

Tony

Aaron stood naked and awkward in the bedroom. The upstairs shower was tiny, and after his nightmare about the dismembered Kapre agents Aaron had no desire to bathe in the downstairs tub, so he resigned himself to a sweaty, sticky ten minute wait. He was afraid to touch anything so he paced a careful path in the floor, looking at the sparse collection of personal items in Tony's room. A glint of gold drew him to the bureau. A small frame, no more than two by two, sat behind a pile of supernatural books. He nudged the books away with his elbow. Inside the frame, a woman with heavily feathered brown hair, and cheeks delineated by sharp swaths of coral blush smiled down at a grinning, dark-haired toddler. It was the grin that struck a chord of recognition. The grin Aaron couldn't help but return, even to a photograph.

"She was young," Tony said. He was hovering outside the bathroom door, a towel wrapped around his waist. "Too young. Too drunk. Too addicted."

Aaron turned to face Tony. The pain in his voice was nothing compared to that in his eyes.

"She didn't love my father. At least, she didn't love him enough at eighteen to marry him. But, she did." Tony edged around him and picked up the frame, holding it so they both could look. "She was beautiful, wasn't she?"

"Very," Aaron replied.

"My father had a hair metal band, or so I'm told. Average talent, but a nice handful of groupies. He went out on gigs that lasted longer and longer. Finally, he didn't come back."

"I'm sorry."

"I wasn't old enough to remember him going. Just a little older than I was here." He tapped the photo glass. "Before he left, though, he made sure my mother had her priorities straight. Got her hooked on heroin early in their relationship. When he left and took away what little cash flow she had, she eventually went to crack. She said the booze kept her 'even' on the days she couldn't score.

"I grew up thinking that the families on TV were fantasies, as real as unicorns or anthropomorphic teddy bears. I thought all dads left and all moms were so rocked they forgot to make lunch. By the time I was nine she might as well have been dead. She occasionally did things—unladylike things—to scrape together enough change to keep us in our shitty apartment, but that's about all. Most of the time she sat in a daze while I did all of the chores I thought needed doing. I made my food, washed my clothes in the sink when I couldn't find enough quarters for the Laundromat, tried to clean the filth off the floor without waking her. I went to school and usually came home to an even bigger mess. Sometimes on her lucky days I would come home to find a strange man lying in her bed, zoned out along with her."

"How long did that go on for?" Aaron felt strange standing naked and dirty while talking about such familial intimacies, but maybe his bareness, the vulnerability suggested by his exposed network of scars, made Tony feel like he was on level ground.

"Another six months after that. Then, one day I came home and the house was clean. A chicken — I remember it, I'd never seen a whole chicken before — was roasting in the oven. She was happy and free of that glazed expression I had come to associate with her. She didn't want the 'bad stuff' anymore, she said. She was in NA, finally, but didn't really need to be. She was off everything and didn't want any of it anymore. She only wanted to make Him happy."

"I thought by *him* she meant my father. I was elated, in only the way a stupid, naïve kid can be. I took our laundry to the Laundromat and did the wash properly. I hung all of our clothes in the closet and put the fresh linens on the beds. Then I went into my room, and after I cleaned every square inch I put out my collection of his old guitar picks. Daddy was coming home.

"But what walked into the door wasn't my dad." Tony put the photo back on the dresser and slid the books back in front of them. "It was a demon named Ray." He gave a bitter smirk. "Scary name, huh?"

"Scary's not in a name," Aaron said.

"No, it's not. Scary, in this instance, was in Ray. He was an incubus vampire, an old one. He had ensnared my mother. He got off on controlling her, forcing her to purify her blood while making her crawl after him like a lust-filled teenager. He got off on me seeing it all and being able to do nothing about it. He fucked her brains out and drained her dry the day after she earned her one-month chip. He made sure I heard the first part and watched the last."

Aaron placed a hand on Tony's face. He said nothing. So many people had told him so many things when he had been mauled and none of those well-meant but hollow words had lessened the pain. He ran his thumb across Tony's cheek, hoping the gesture would convey what words never could.

"I went after him, you know," Tony said as he pulled Aaron's hand from his cheek and held it in his own. "After I graduated from Kapre's boot camp, I went after him."

"Did you find him?"

"He was my first Term." Aaron smiled. "Now ask me if it made me any less fucked up."

"I don't think you're all that fucked up."

Tony grinned. "Again, says the Acqxterm agent slash shapeshifter I hope will be hanging out in my bed."

"Let me get that shower, first, then we'll see." Aaron gave Tony another quick kiss and headed for the bathroom. He turned back at the door. "You know, we need to get some rest for tomorrow."

"We'll get plenty of sleep after we die." The words came out with a wink and a smile, but Tony met his eyes and the mirth faded.

Aaron felt a wild desperation to reassure his partner that all would be well once the full moon was over. But all he could do was stand there, hands at his sides, and shrug.

* * * *

"You can't wear that to work." Tony sidled into the bathroom, brushing against Aaron's bare ass as he did.

"You wouldn't like it?" Aaron teased.

"Of course I would, but you would distract everyone else. And as we're running late already, a distraction would take away from our very, very short work day." Tony ran a hand through his hair. When he saw Aaron was watching him primp he licked his index and pinkie fingers and smoothed his eyebrows in a comical gesture. "Hellhounds and werewolves wait for no man."

"I think I'll follow you in a bit." Aaron put down his toothbrush and turned to face Tony. "I want to try doing multiple shifts first. In case I need to tonight."

"Won't it make you weak?"

"That's what I want to know. When we were in the woods with the Six Rivers clan, I started sensing changes, changes precipitated by Cerberus's presence, I think. Whatever magic he was doing to make the pack stronger also affected me, but I think more so, as I'm his direct descendant. At least that's the theory I have percolating in my head."

"And you think you can shift more than once without consequence because of that connection?"

"I've been getting stronger in leaps and bounds. And last night, when Cerberus confronted me, I felt his power, power derived from the moon. I felt it inside me. I felt... Good."

"Do you want me to stick around in case you run into trouble?"

"No, that's okay. The worst that can happen is I need to take a short nap." Aaron waved him off with a hand. "Just wait until I get there before you talk to Braven."

"Wouldn't do it without you." Tony leaned in and kissed him. His clean-shaven face was as soft as his lips. A surge of desire washed through Aaron. "Go, before neither of us make it to work on time."

Tony grinned. "I'll see you there."

Aaron waited until Tony had clattered down the metal steps and shut the ground floor door. He went into the bedroom loft and found a clear space on the floor. Last night when he had been with Tony, his eyes and jaw had shifted with little pain or exertion. If he could transform his whole body as seamlessly he would have a distinct advantage over the other shifters.

He closed his lids and focused on the power of the moon. Even though it had not risen he could feel its pull. He let his consciousness drift to the horizon, slide down the surface of the earth until the moon glowed bright in his mind's eye. His body gave a massive spasm. A sharp pain recoiled through him, throwing him onto all fours. He watched the hair erupt all over his body. Like the snapping of a rubber band his body contorted, and he was wolf.

Wolf?

Demon?

Furry.

Aaron stretched and padded into the bathroom. He reached up on his back legs and plopped his forefeet onto the vanity so he could see himself in the mirror. His coarse coat was so black he would have believed himself a shadow if not for the deep yellow eyes punctuating the darkness like twin miniature suns. He leaned in closer. While the excessive hair covered the myriad of scars on his body, the fine pale line on his muzzle remained. Although they faded greatly with the shift, the souvenirs of his last great physical trauma never completely disappeared. He shook his head, flopping his long, pointed ears, then bared his teeth at himself. Everything about his form spoke of wolf. If not for the unlikely color of his coat and the dark soul lurking just beneath his skin, he would have never believed he was Cerberus' offspring. The dark thing looked back out at him, pleased he finally recognized his true heritage.

There was a popular myth that if the progenitor of a line of weres was slaughtered then all others would return to human form. It was a lie. The dark thing was a part of him. He couldn't deny it any longer. Aaron studied the telltale scar on his snout a moment longer, then dropped to the floor. He may never get back his normalcy, but Cerberus—and all of his Six Rivers toadies—would die just the same. The beast rolled a protest through him, but he ignored the clamor.

Aaron headed back into the bedroom, concentrating on the shift. This would be the true test of his recent evolution. Instead of pulling his consciousness away from the moon he simply reversed his intent. It was a natural action, one he had given a good deal of thought to in the shower the night before. If he, as Cerberus' own, took the power to shift from the moon, than the direction of that shift, human to wolf or wolf to human, should not make any difference. The moon didn't care if he was furry on not, only he and his demon did. He relaxed his muscles. Another rubber band snap heralded by a sudden pang of short-lived agony, and he was on his human hands and human knees, itching like mad from the sudden retraction of all that hair but otherwise fine.

He stood carefully. The usual side effects might simply be delayed. A minute passed, then another. No wave of fatigue swept over him. He was transformed and fully functional. A smile spread across his lips. This was the advantage they needed. A shifter who could operate in any terrain, any situation. He could run as a wolf, shift to climb, then shift back to continue pursuit.

It was shifter Christmas.

Aaron transformed two more times, just to see if his endurance would wear down. Each time he changed, though, he felt stronger, more confident.

Gifts are never appreciated. That was what Cerberus had said.

Aaron gave the hellhound he was about to murder a silent thank you, and gathered his clothes.

Chapter Nineteen

Baited

Something wasn't right.

Aaron could smell it the moment he walked past the security desk and entered the elevator. A sour, tense fear hung in the lobby air. The dark thing urged him to go back. His own instincts agreed. Images of his last day at Kapre California flashed through his mind. Paralytic panic flowed through his body. His finger wouldn't lift to touch the button. His breath came in short bursts. His knees nearly knocked with terror.

Were they up there? Six Rivers? Would he step off the elevator and find another bloodbath? Heads nearly decapitated, faces mauled to the point of being unrecognizable, entrails snaked across the floor like fallen party streamers? He would have run if his body would obey. The creature inside snarled at his cowardice. A part of him agreed, but it was buried far enough below the fear it held no sway over his actions. The only catalyst that could make his hand incline twelve inches and touch the floor button was the one that popped into his mind.

Tony.

The thought of his partner up there loosened his limbs and sent jolts of motivating adrenaline flying through his bloodstream. He punched the number. The doors slid closed and the lift jolted up. Aaron freed the tab holding his sidearm in his holster. He fingered the snap nervously. The elevator slid to a stop. He closed his fist around the grip. The doors slid open.

A young office assistant was placing bagels on the table in the glass-fronted conference room. The bullpen was bustling with everyday normalcy — agents shuffling papers, chatting near each other's desks, talking on their cells. Director Braven's door was open. Everything was fine.

So why did it feel wrong?

"Hey, Ar," Ellison said as he strode toward him. The foul chemical smell that seemed to seep from his pores came with him, clogging Aaron's nose. He said something else.

"Uh, I…" Aaron trailed off. Ellison's words hadn't made it through the jumble of thoughts in his head. Something was not right. With Ellison barking up his ass, he had no ability to pinpoint it. "What?"

"I said," Ellison repeated, making no effort to hide his irritation, "got a minute? I'd like to chat with you in the break room."

"What?" Aaron gave him a blank look as the words registered. "Oh, now's not…"

"It's about those *werewolves*," Ellison dropped his voice to a whisper with the last word. He stepped closer. "I have some information."

Beneath the toxic scent overlaying Ellison's body was another aroma. Spicy, sweet and undeniably familiar. An alarm went off in Aaron's head. It was the same scent from the brimstone he and Tony had investigated, the same scent that lingered in Cerberus' sparse coat. He struggled to keep his expression even, to keep the knowledge from his eyes.

"Can we do it later?" he hedged. "Braven wanted to see me in her office."

"No, she didn't." A tremulous smile tugged the corners of Ellison's mouth.

"Tony was expecti..." He took a step back. Ellison filled the space.

"Tony is on *our* side."

The room had gone silent. Several agents in the bullpen had their hands on their firearms. The rest watched him with open hostility. Aaron gauged the distance to the door. It was too far to go without being shot in the spine. He opted for retreating to his desk, hoping feigned normalcy would take the agents' edge off, hoping Tony had come clean with Braven and the pair had put their heads together and filled in the blanks about Ellison and were readying an Acqxterm team to take down the duplicitous agent and he only needed a few more seconds to stall. Because that was all he had.

Or maybe they already had confronted Tony, pinned responsibility on him and given him a Term sentence. He shook off the thought as dread threatened to overcome him. Tony was fine. He was just out rallying the troops. He had to be fine.

Aaron made it to his desk with Ellison dogging his steps the whole way. A few of the agents drew their guns, but kept the muzzles down, fingers resting on the side of the barrel, not on the triggers. A hopeful sign. Still, they watched him warily.

"So they gave you super powers in exchange for the blood of Kapre agents?" Ellison's bravado did not cover the reeking fear pouring off him in waves. "Men and women with kids. Good agents. Good *people*. You slaughtered them. And for what?"

"That's the same question I had for you," Aaron said.

The punch came fast. Faster than Aaron would have expected. He dodged the brunt of the blow, but Ellison's fist grazed his cheek. His scar. For some reason that infuriated him. He let out a growl.

Instantly, a dozen weapons rasped from their holsters. Hammers cocked in a chorus of metallic clicks. Sweaty fingers slid onto triggers. Aaron froze. He locked gazes with Ellison.

"And they know you're a werewolf, so don't think these guns aren't all targeted on the base of your skull."

They didn't know he was Cerberus' progeny. Which meant they didn't know he had the ability to turn at any point. Could he shift fast enough to avoid the bullets? Could he run the gantlet of well-trained marksmen with his neck so precariously exposed? Not even Cerberus' gift could give him the speed and skill to try for the door. He sagged against his desk. A drink coaster dug into his hip. He shoved it out of the way, sat on the corner and glared at Ellison.

"Did you think you wouldn't get caught?" Ellison ranted on. "Did you think you could murder our colleagues in California and then come here and slaughter us? We were *friends*, man."

Ellison was laying it on thick. The dark thing snarled for his throat, but Aaron ignored them both. Fighting would add merit to Ellison's lie, arguing would be discounted by the agents who had just heard him growl like a monster.

The elevator dinged. Half of the agents whirled to train their sights on the doors. The other half remained fixed on him. The doors slid open and a handful of fully armored Acqxterm agents swarmed out. He spotted Braven at the back. A familiar form at her right turned the contents of his stomach to lead.

Tony.

Tony, who had held him last night, driven away the dreams that no longer seemed so terrifying. Tony, who had joked with him this morning, who had resigned himself to die with him at the full moon's rise. Tony, who had a high-powered weapon trained on his throat. The old shock threatened to ball him on the floor like a kicked pup. He forced the panic deep inside himself — let the dark thing chew it away. He wouldn't retreat inside himself this time. He extended his hands to his sides, palms out, and stood.

"We had faith in you," Director Braven said from her secure position at the back. "And you were the cuckoo in our nest all along. How many eggs did you plan to kick out, Agent Marvell?"

"All of them," Ellison spit. "We heard about you meeting with shifters, planning your attack."

"An attack will come tonight, with or without my head on your platter, Director." Aaron studied Tony. His partner's face was cold, stoic. He looked back at Braven. "It's not me. You won't believe me, not even when I die defending this office. But that's what I'll do, just the same."

"The only place you're going to die is here, at the hands of this Acqxterm team," Ellison said as he leaned in to give him a hard expression. Aaron caught the traces of relief in Ellison's eyes, smelled the terror on his breath recede. Aaron's imminent death would insure his safety from discovery until Cerberus and Six Rivers arrived to protect him from Kapre.

"Tony —" Aaron began.

"Don't." His partner cut him off. Tony straightened his aim. "I don't want to hear any more of your bullshit."

"Okay." He shuttered off the riot of thoughts and emotions that Tony's cold tone sent swirling through him. Calm. He had to stay calm and keep the dark thing at bay.

"Director, since it was my friends he helped slaughter, I was wondering if I might be the one?" Ellison asked.

This was it. No trial. No jury. Demons and monsters got none of those things. This was Acqxterm. He had been acquired. The only thing left was the termination.

A keening howl carried through the ventilation system above. Agents whirled to train their guns on the registers. Another lupine sound joined the first. Then another, and another. Soon, the floor was filled with wolfish cries. The agents spun this way and that, searching for the location the wolves would spring through and attack.

"But, it's not dark yet," Ellison said softly, clearly confused.

"Your party come early?" Aaron asked. He studied the distance between himself and Ellison's gun, worked out the means to wrestle it from him.

The howling grew louder.

"It's not dark," Ellison repeated.

Aaron knew where the duplicitous agent's thoughts were headed. Before Ellison could say more, he reached out, grabbed the barrel of Ellison's weapon, wrenched it out of his hand and struck him across the temple with the hilt. Ellison crumpled onto the floor.

"Gun!" someone called.

"Wolf!" Tony yelled in response and fired a shot at a vent overhanging Braven's office.

Gunshots exploded around the room as panicked agents fired blindly into the ceiling and ductwork. Braven shouted for ceasefire, but even her authoritative bark was drowned in the chaos. A red light flicked across Aaron's vision. Tony was waving his sight at him. Tony moved the sight from him to the strange coaster on his desk. Aaron looked at it then back at Tony. A grin flashed across his partner's face. He slashed his gun parallel to the floor, indicating Aaron should slide the disk like a puck.

"You coming?" Aaron mouthed the words carefully so no one else saw.

Tony gave a minute shake of his head.

Aaron nodded. No time to beg or argue the dangers of being an accomplice to an escaped werewolf murderer while surrounded by heavily armed people who in the next five minutes would definitely be looking for someone to blame. He had to trust Tony could take care of himself until he could get back to him.

"Be careful." He barely moved his lips.

Tony saw and gave him a small smile. Then he turned and began yelling along with Braven for a ceasefire.

Aaron swept up the disk. It was light, some sort of strange polymer. He flung it across the floor. It skidded into a desk leg. The impact sent a whirlwind of blue light through the room. Light bulbs exploded, throwing the room into darkness. Computer screens went blank and door locks buzzed open. The force flung agents into the air, the crackling electric surge tore the guns from their fingers. Ellison's gun rocketed out of Aaron's fist as the impact pushed him against his desk, but he did not need it anymore. Aaron called up the dark thing and channeled the power of the moon. A hand wrapped around his ankle. One of Ellison's eyelids creaked open. Aaron smiled down at him. The transformation pulled him to his knees as his clothes ripped and fell away. He shifted mere inches from Ellison's terrified face. His demonic half fully emerged and Aaron leaned in to Ellison. He brushed his muzzle against Ellison's nose. The sour stench of urine filled the air. Aaron chuffed in amusement, then turned for the stairwell.

"Shifter!"

The cry took up as Aaron bolted from the shelter of his desk and into the walkway. Twenty feet. The speed granted by Cerberus gave him an edge as the agents found their guns and raised them. A hailstorm of bullets spattered after him, but the electric energy altered their course, sent them flying in dangerous trajectories.

"Cease fire. For Christ's bloody sake, cease fire before we all get shot." This time Braven's voice carried above the din. The room went silent for a moment, then the cry arose from Ellison's mouth — of course.

"Get him."

Tony made a showy dive for Aaron, intentionally tripping over a gun that had fallen near his feet. Tony crashed to the ground, hands barely missing his leg. Tony was on his feet in a flash, the rest of the acqxterm agents at his back. But he had given Aaron the time he needed. Kapre wasn't an exceptionally tall building. Aaron bolted down the first three flights. As the door above burst open he plunged into the stairwell, falling the final three stories. He landed hard, the shock of the impact rattled through his body. One of his paws wrenched painfully. He gathered his legs under him and burst out of the emergency door. Sirens wailed. The backup generators had kicked in.

A ruddy wolf with a bloodied muzzle waited for him on the other side. Carlos gestured with his head and they ran together around the side of the building. A commotion behind them told Aaron the agents had made their way outside. He nipped at Carlos' flank as a warning, and the alpha sped up. Although he could run faster Aaron kept his pace with Carlos' sprint. They bolted past the security gate where the hobbled guard clutched his gnawed Achilles tendon. Aaron flashed Carlos a reproachful look, and the alpha returned his expression in kind.

A delivery van squealed up to the entrance. The side door opened. Two lower level shifters Aaron recognized from Trinity reached out their arms to help the wolves as they leaped inside.

"Got them?" Matthew called from the driver's seat.

"Secured. Go," an older female shifter named Betty cried as she slammed the door shut.

Acqxterm agents swarmed the courtyard as the van peeled off down the street.

Chapter Twenty

The Lupine Army

For Aaron, watching a shifter transform was nearly as uncomfortable as going through it. Carlos' body contorted. His face crumpled and flattened, his arms and legs stretched out of the diminishing fur, forming toes and fingers from the sharply nailed pads. His canine whines turned into human groans as his form settled back into the familiar. Betty immediately handed their leader a set of clothes. Their anticipation leveled on Aaron. They were waiting for him to shift and discuss with them this turn of events. He hesitated. It was one thing to acknowledge his origins to himself, even to Tony and the two leaders of the Trinity clan, but these wolves were not family, not friends.

"It's okay, Aaron," Matthew said from the front seat. The beta had an uncanny way of knowing what was going on in people's heads. Aaron supposed it was what had made him so invaluable to Carlos as a second.

Aaron glanced at the weres circling him like a wagon train one last time, then shifted. What had taken Carlos a full minute was done in less than ten seconds. The weres who had helped him into the van, a pair of men with similar enough features to peg them as brothers, gaped at him. Betty inhaled sharply. Carlos said nothing, but handed him another set of clothes—a pair of loose pants and a T-shirt. He dressed hurriedly and faced his former alpha.

"Tony contacted you?"

"This morning when he arrived at work he was confronted by your Director Braven and Agent Ellison."

"Ellison's the one who summoned Cerberus," Aaron said. "He smelled like the brimstone."

"So we gathered," Carlos affirmed. "He apparently flew into an accusatory rage, citing Tony's complicity in the entire plot. Of course, your director saw the errors in this vein of thought and exonerated Tony on the spot. She was apparently less convinced of your innocence."

"So she ordered a strike team."

"Ellison stuck to Tony like glue while the preparations were being done. It was only by luck Braven called him aside to talk about his participation in the takedown when no other agents were around him. Tony was then able to get out a text message to me. We moved as quickly as we could with what little plan we could throw together."

"Which included howling into the air conditioning vents?" Aaron asked with a smile.

"Well, I howled into the vents. Phil and Bill here" — he indicated the lookalikes—"tossed MP3 players set to Halloween sounds into the ducts."

"We're too young to do much until sunset," Phil said with an apologetic shrug. "Guess we'll never do what you can."

"You did great. I'll bet they'll be hearing those howls all day."

He knew it was best he came clean about why he was so capable in the shifting department. But there would be more weres wherever they were going and they would need to know, too. Aaron didn't know how many times he could repeat the story of Cerberus. It wasn't his favorite topic of discussion, no matter how far he had come in accepting his supernatural side in the past couple of days.

Matthew took the van on a circuitous route through the city, hoping to lose any tails they may have picked up from Kapre. No doubt the agents had alerted the local police about the van. They would have to ditch it quickly.

No sooner had Aaron thought this than the vehicle pulled up to a battered garage.

"Everyone out, quickly," Carlos said.

They tumbled out into downtrodden gloom.

"Over here," Matthew called. They followed the beta to another vehicle, this one a dated minivan. "Betty, you drive."

Matthew tossed the keys to the older woman, who settled behind the wheel looking for all the world like a soccer grandma running to pick up the kids instead of a lethal shapeshifter.

"Everyone else onto the floorboards until we get to the safe house," Carlos ordered.

Fortunately, the cramped ride lasted less than fifteen minutes. Instead of heading farther out of town Betty circled back into the city center. She pulled up to a battered building not far from the Laundromat Tony and he had visited two days prior.

Two days.

Was that all it had been since he had started his first day at Kapre Maryland? Two days since his world had turned upside down once again? Two days since he had met and fallen… His thoughts crumbled. Did he actually…? It couldn't be. They barely knew each other. Tony had abused his trust—

And is now facing a firing squad to save me.

"You coming, *mi hombre*?"

Aaron hadn't realized the van had stopped at a narrow alleyway. He sheepishly met Carlos' inquisitive expression and climbed out of the van. The rest of the shifters were filing down the alley into a door propped open with a broken palette. A burly were, one he recognized as one of his many babysitters, squeezed up the alley against the stream of passengers, taking the van key from Betty as he did so.

"Nice to see you again, Aaron. Look good," he said as he passed. He nodded to his alpha. "Carlos."

"Be careful, Rick," Carlos said.

"Will do." Rick nodded and climbed into the van.

"Rick will take the van on a little tour of the city just to be sure we've lost any trail," Carlos explained as the van pulled away. "He'll leave it near the woods." At Aaron's expression he added, "Far away from Six Rivers' camp. There's another forest on the southern edge of town. Smaller, but just as hospitable to wolves, and a believable hideout. Kapre can waste some time digging around in there."

"Can we afford to let Kapre agents wander too far away when we know what's coming tonight?" he asked as he followed Carlos into the back door of what seemed to be an old office building.

"We have time," Carlos said.

"What if Cerberus changes them into something like me?" he asked, forgetting where he was. "They'll be able to shift right now. The attack could be happening as we speak."

The entirety of Trinity — save for Rick — was inside the building, hunched over battered desks, reading blueprints. Every single one of them looked up as he spoke. There was no need to yell when everyone had super-hearing. There was no reason to try to avoid this any longer.

"One of my co-workers, Spenser Ellison, was behind the Kapre attacks. He summoned Cerberus, either at the request of Six Rivers or on his own whim. You probably know by now that when Six Rivers invaded Kapre California, Cerberus was with them." A few people nodded in assent. "As you also know I suffered many bites. I have since found out one of them was from Cerberus himself. That bite seemingly overrode any chance of becoming a regular werewolf. I am, in essence, his progeny."

"What does that mean?" one of the younger weres asked her pack leader.

"You should ask Aaron, as he is the alpha of this territory."

There was some mumbling at Carlos' statement.

Aaron couldn't fault them for being disturbed. "I know it sounds bad. Most of you were with me when I was at my worst. I was dangerous, suicidal and half crazy. But you can believe me that I am focused now. Ellison, Six Rivers and Cerberus killed my friends and turned me into a demon. Not a were, but a demon. They destroyed my mind and my life as it was. And now they threaten someone I very much care for."

Carlos raised an eyebrow.

"Cerberus' curse is also a gift. I am faster, sharper and I can shift back and forth as quickly as I want without any weakness at all, and I can do it without the aid of the full moon."

"The problem is," Matthew interjected as he abandoned a group of weres and came to stand beside him, "Cerberus might have done the same to all of Six Rivers. We may very well be going into this fight severely outmatched. Aaron is the only one we can hope will bring down Cerberus."

Some faces reflected distrust, others sympathy. Few showed solidarity.

It was going to be a long night.

Chapter Twenty-One

War

The moon had risen slowly, inching above the horizon, ticking away at the sky like the hand of a clock, only reaching its zenith after a torturous wait. The Trinity clan stripped silently, each focused on the upcoming battle. In another five minutes they would spread out around the building and their perimeter ring would alert the Kapre agents. Aaron knew that, as much as Carlos wanted to avoid this additional complication, the wolves couldn't hide in the shadows and still defend Kapre from Cerberus and Six Rivers. They would have to make their stand against Six Rivers in the open and in Kapre's sights, essentially trapping them between two powerful armies. The wolves' and Aaron's only hope rested in the slim chance that Tony might be able to convince the director that Trinity was the least of their problems.

Aaron had little faith in this proposal, but no choice remained. He might be alpha of Grange, Maryland, but he had no pack. Carlos held in his control all of the soldiers, as well as the only battle plan they could come up with. After arguing for hours about whether or not to infiltrate the building, he and the weres decided their energy was better spent setting up a defense on the outside and keeping the battle as close to their natural element as possible.

The minutes ticked by. Aaron stripped off his borrowed clothes and folded them neatly on the hood of the van.

"Are you ready *mi hombre*?" Carlos asked as he approached.

Aaron couldn't help but stare at the form he had not many weeks before been accustomed to seeing walking around naked. With that copper skin, gorgeous black mane, lean fighter's muscles and a generous cock, Carlos was indeed a sight to linger over. Yet, when Aaron looked all he saw was one of many naked men milling around him. Nothing special.

"And what it is you are thinking?" Carlos questioned with a grin.

"Is this how I look to you?" he asked.

"I don't know. How do I look?"

"Like anybody else."

Carlos' grin widened, but a hint of sadness touched the edges. "Ah, so you have gotten over me, then?"

"I guess so."

"It is good, *mi hombre*." Carlos put an arm around his shoulder. "I loved you, but it wasn't the love I feel for Matthew. You understand a little better now, I think."

"Yeah." He turned and enveloped Carlos in a hug. It was the goodbye they deserved, the one they'd never had because of Aaron's crushed heart and pride. "Yeah, I do."

"Should we give the order to shift?" Matthew asked from the shadows.

Carlos pulled away, gave Aaron's face a light touch. "Be careful, *mi hombre*."

"You, too."

"I will give the order." Carlos strode off, his brief moment of sentimentality shuttered and replaced with a shell of unquestionable authority.

Matthew watched his lover walk away, but lingered near Aaron. "Best of luck to you tonight. I wish you and Tony well."

Aaron studied the platinum Nordic god. Matthew was as breathtaking as Carlos. And just as smart. But beyond the traits that made him the perfect beta for Trinity's alpha rested the heart of a truly caring man. Aaron was glad for Matthew's presence, that Carlos had him. He stepped forward and embraced Matthew. The stunned shifter hesitated only a moment before returning the hug with near rib-crushing enthusiasm.

"Take care of him, please," he said into the tall man's shoulder. "And yourself."

"I will." Matthew pulled back. His eyes were damp. "May we all come through this war without harm."

Aaron nodded. The sinking sensation in his stomach told him it was unlikely, that at some point in the night he would lose one of them.

Please don't let it be Tony.

Fortunately he didn't have time to consider the ramifications, both actual and moral, which might arise from his trying to secure such a deal with the universe. Carlos shouted out the command to shift and fifty bodies toppled to the ground, contorting in agony, their muted vocalizations a mix of human and wolf. It was an eerie sound. Aaron let the transformation come. Under the light of the moon it happened even faster, with less pain. It was like taking a breath, natural and easy — from human to wolf in a heartbeat.

The night was looking up.

A few minutes later, wolves, from gray to tan in color, loped forward and spread out around the perimeter of the building. Alarms wailed inside as the security teams caught their movement. There was little time left.

Where are they? Although the words were spoken only in Aaron's head, he could feel them in the tense set of every wolf in the vicinity. They scanned the outlying area — a parking lot with only the front spaces filled, a span of scraggly trees, a snaking drive and a wide veranda.

A wolf yelped in pain. All heads turned in that direction. Several wolves moved to investigate. Aaron shifted back to human form just as they started off.

"Stand your ground!" Aaron yelled.

The wolves stopped, torn between the shouted command and helping their comrade who now bayed frantically with pain. Two broke off to help their pack mate. The others started back to their posts.

Fire flashed just inside the wolves' periphery. Blackness swallowed the air inside the flames. A stream of wolves galloped out of the interior darkness, fangs bared, eyes flashing. In the center of their midst ran the black demon, his lupine pretense all but dropped. Three slavering heads whipped this way and that, snapping and gnashing. Lava flowed beneath his cracked skin. His mouths opened and horrifying, grating wails arose from them.

Cerberus had arrived.

Chapter Twenty-Two

Fang, Fur and Firepower

Thurisaz sigils erupted all over the grounds, throwing jaundiced light across the seemingly endless stream of wolves. Clearly Cerberus and Six Rivers had collected more than one pack on their journey east. Aaron tried to track their numbers but there were too many. Trinity adjusted their position to face the invaders. The Six Rivers wolves leaped forward, teeth bared, jaws snapping. Deep growls poured from their throats. There were at least a dozen enemies to each Trinity werewolf. Death rested in each of those wolves' eyes, and yet none wavered. Carlos lifted his head and howled. Matthew, as pale and massive as his human form, joined. One by one the Trinity clan announced their unwillingness to back down.

Aaron's focus tunneled in. He was dimly aware of shaggy bodies galloping forward, of snarls, yips and growls, but all of that was secondary, the buzz of a television left on in a room and nothing more. His full attention was riveted on the creature now smugly standing in the middle of the chaos watching him. The dark thing responded with curiosity, but the wave of hatred passing through Aaron washed it away. As his legs pushed him forward, he let the shift come yet again. Adapting from bipedal to quadrupedal gait was as easy as the shift itself. Aaron didn't break stride as the transformation bent his back and pulled his arms to the ground, but ran on, his intent focused only on Cerberus. His lips peeled back from his fangs. His hackles rose. Cerberus greeted his aggression with a look of pure amusement. The demon's words echoed in Aaron's mind once more.

Why not?

Aaron sprang. His muscles, filled with the power of the moon, the very power of his target, propelled him with more force than they had ever known. Whatever it was that Cerberus had done to the rest of Six Rivers before this evening had also occurred in his own body. It seemed fitting, the devil dog who indiscriminately tossed around his power taken out by one of its results. This satisfied thought sailed through his mind as he barreled toward Cerberus, mouth open.

Something large and heavy hit him in the back, just below his haunches. He let out a pained yelp as the heavy force ground into his spine and drove him to the ground. Whatever it was landed on top of him. Cerberus made that odd chuckling sound and loped away, his three heads swiveling in search of prey.

"You can be one of us," a voice grated in his ear. Large hands flipped him and straddled his midsection so his paws jutted out like the legs of an overturned turtle. His growl died in his throat as he looked up into the half lupine, blackened face of what was once a young man.

Shock coursed through him as he recognized the former man beneath the monstrous facade.

"Cerberus blessed me. He can bless you, too. We can be brothers, Aaron." The mixed being leaned in and grinned. His face cracked with the expression. Magma oozed from beneath the surface.

A drop sizzled onto Aaron's snout, burning through the hair into his tender flesh. He struggled against the weight, but couldn't gain any headway in wolf form. Forgoing his wolf form he shifted back to human, leaving only his fangs and heightened vision unchanged. The being holding him didn't look surprised at the rapidity of his transformation, but only smiled wider. Like drifting continents, the patchwork of skin comprising his face slid farther apart, revealing more churning lava.

"Brandon Wilkes," Aaron said as the feral amber eyes swept him haughtily

"The new and improved," Brandon agreed. "Like you."

Around them the sounds of battle filled the air. Snarling and growling, agonized howls, meaty thuds. Bodies hit the ground all around them. Aaron did not need to look to know it was Trinity failing. Triumph reflected out of Brandon's inhuman eyes.

"Did Cerberus do this to everyone in Six Rivers?" Aaron asked. He was buying time, he didn't know what for, but a feeling of anticipation in his chest told him to hang on a minute or two more, that help was coming—somehow, in some form. "Did he reward you for bringing him into this plane with this...upgrade?"

"Upgrade. I like that." Brandon stretched back on his heels, but didn't let up on the heavy pressure he exerted against Aaron's shoulders. "I'm the first. I trusted him to raise us up, and so he gave me this as a reward. The others get their 'upgrade' when they prove themselves tonight."

Aaron swept Brandon's body. He was naked, the same as the wolves in the forest, but the claws extending from his fingers were real, and as sharp as honed obsidian. His body, rippling with enhanced muscles, cracked and shifted, showing veins of liquid fire beneath the crusty pitch skin. His jaws were thrust unnaturally forward, his widened, elongated nose a hybridization of human and wolf. No. Wolf and hellhound.

Is this how I will eventually look? The thought shriveled his insides.

"Come on, bro," Brandon said as he leered down. "Your friends are dying out there. They'll be in the dirt soon and you'll be all alone, again. You come with us, you'll have family forever."

"Why does Cerberus want me?" Aaron began to inch his arms toward his body, bringing them as close as possible to the knees straddling him. "He seemed to think my being turned was simply a random occurrence."

Brandon's forehead wrinkled, causing a fiery orange droplet to slide down his nose. Carlos was right. This was not the smartest shifter to ever walk the earth. He watched Brandon process the thought, could almost hear rusted gears turning. He waited, frustrated, but mindful of the patience Carlos had instilled in him. The reply that eventually came out was surprisingly insightful.

"He wants you for what you are now."

"I see." Around him more bodies thudded to the ground. The sound of whimpering became a constant susurration, like the wind through the leaves. "And Ellison? What does Cerberus want with him?"

"Tool," Brandon snorted. "That dude was a drunk and a gambler. He lost money in our casinos and then tried to fake us out with a card counting scheme. He should have been meat."

"But he was a mage."

"Yeah, he had that going for him. Only thing saved his stupid ass." Brandon let up some of his weight, either trusting Aaron more, or forgetting himself in his story. "Cerberus had been banished from earth a while back. Couldn't come without an invitation."

"So you had Ellison invite him. Smart."

"Yeah, it was." Brandon looked pleased. "Problem was a bunch of older wolves, including a couple of my dad's sons didn't see things my way. Cerberus is the new Internet, dude. He's gonna change the game forever."

"You're a good alpha to your pack," Aaron said. The fact Brandon refused to claim his blood brothers as relations showed the depth of his commitment to Cerberus, which seemed somewhere between batshit fanatic and Kool-Aid chugging.

"You can be one of us, too, bro. Hell, you already are. Look at you. You're cut."

"I am." Aaron bucked. The surprise attack caught Brandon off guard. He slipped, just barely, but it was enough. Aaron twisted his hips, tossing Brandon all the way off him. He surged to his feet and planted a vicious kick in Brandon's face, knocking the enhanced were back onto the ground as he tried to rise.

Aaron took a moment to assess his situation. Cerberus had disappeared. Wolves lay dead and dying all around the perimeter. Closer to the doors of Kapre, Matthew's white and Carlos' desert hues flashed among a mass of silver, a pair of leaping and snapping killing machines making quick work of the younger, weaker wolves. Several Trinity shifters, all with some sort of bleeding wound, aided them in their defense. They wouldn't last long, however. The Six Rivers wolves were regrouping.

At least they would all die together, as a family. His thoughts flashed to Tony. Was he the source of his previous odd feeling of hope? If so, where was he?

Brandon struggled to his feet. Aaron looked past him, hoping to catch a glimpse of Carlos once more. When Brandon lunged at him, his first reaction was one of irritation. The idiot wasn't worth his time. Not when his friends needed him. Still trying to contain him instead of kill, Brandon swept toward his midsection in a football tackle. Aaron quickly sidestepped. Brandon careened into the ground.

A howl of pain arose from the center of the now doubled mass of Six Rivers wolves. The hairs at the back of his neck rose. He knew that voice, in human and in wolf form.

Carlos.

Aaron started forward. Brandon tackled him from behind. He crashed to the ground with Brandon on top of him once again. He gave the shifter no time to gain the upper hand, but rolled over, tucking his knees into his chest as he did. Brandon reached for his throat, but Aaron batted his hand out of the way and pushed off with his knees. Brandon, growing frustrated, gnashed his teeth. Aaron punched him in his deformed nose, a jab followed by a right hook. Water sprang to Brandon's eyes as blood spurted from his nose. He howled.

This whelp was no fighter. No alpha. But he had put his entire pack in danger, was now threatening the way of life of all shifters in the country. More so, he was in the way of Aaron's getting to Carlos, Matthew and Tony. He kicked out with his foot, connecting with Brandon's jaw. The shifter fell. Aaron followed and drove Brandon onto his back.

"Cerberus," Brandon yelled. "I summon you, my father hound." He waited a moment. No one came. His expectant triumph faded to dismay. "Cerberus!"

"You stupid kid," was all Aaron said before he transformed into his wolf form.

Whatever Aaron's expression, it terrified the young shifter. It was a pitiful sight, a large, werewolf, hellhound hybrid with magma skin crying in terror and babbling the name of a savior that would never come. Aaron clamped his jaws around Brandon's throat and squeezed. Magma flowed into his mouth, burning throughout, but he held on. Brandon gripped at his fur and pounded his ribs. Aaron channeled the strength Cerberus had given him, the same strength that toughened the hide of—*his brother*? He shuttered off the thought—the demonic shifter who writhed beneath him. He bit down around Brandon's windpipe until the shifter ceased struggling and his heartbeat slowed, then disappeared from Aaron's sensitive ears altogether.

Aaron pulled back and looked at the dead boy. Magma poured from the crevices in his charred skin, blackening the ground. All around Aaron lay the rest of the result of Cerberus' actions, of Ellison's idiocy, of Brandon's hubris. Shifters, a few he recognized as former sitters from his time under Carlos' care, lay bloodied and broken in the dirt. The remaining upright wolves struggled in Kapre's courtyard. He let a long howl flow from his throat. Another howl, weaker, answered it.

Carlos was in trouble.

Aaron sprinted for the battle. The front door of Kapre banged open. Agents in full tactical gear streamed out, weapons pointed. In their center stood Tony, his face barely visible beneath his ballistic face shield. He held his arm extended, showing a glowing red disc resting in his palm.

"Trinity, retreat." Tony shouted. "To the doors."

He tossed the circlet. It spun out into the courtyard, nearly touching the striving throng. It hovered in the air and expanded outward. Like a ring on a toss game it looped over the Kapre building and settled onto the ground, a crimson halo of protection surrounding the entire structure and its immediate grounds.

Despite Tony's shout the wolves did not break ranks. Only one wolf could command that. It was odd to thank the initiator of the horrors around him, but that was what Aaron did as he once again shifted rapidly into human form. Cerberus would die at his hands—or fangs—tonight, but at the moment he was grateful the demon had given him the power to fight this war with such fluidity of shape.

"Carlos," Aaron yelled as he pushed his hands off the ground and propelled upright. He ran toward the center of the battle. A wolf leaped for him. He snatched it out of the air and tossed it against a tree without breaking stride. "We have to retreat. Give the signal. Trinity, when Carlos howls, get to the red light." When there was no response he shouted louder, "Now, Carlos, now."

The acqxterm agents trained their guns. Tiny red dots danced indiscriminately across pelted hides. They were holding fire for now, waiting for the fight to cross an invisible line Braven had no doubt drawn in the sand. Not even the most well trained agent could discern the difference between a Trinity and Six

Rivers wolf. So once the allotted retreat time had expired any wolf remaining in the open with the enemy would automatically be considered a foe. Once the time was up, the agents would riddle them with bullets, allies or not. From the midst of the pack a soft, familiar howl began. It picked up volume, however, as the first wolves responded and broke off combat. It was when the first weres turned toward the halo that Aaron saw Carlos on the ground, bleeding from a gaping neck wound. Matthew ran in circles, nipping at the other wolves, snapping at their heels to urge them into the circle. All of Trinity retreated, except Matthew. He hovered over Carlos and fought off the advancing enemy. Aaron was close, but not close enough to stop the tangle of Six Rivers wolves from taking out both of Trinity's leaders.

"Tony, help," he yelled.

"On it," his partner replied. Tony had a capsule shaped gadget in his hand. "This is a good one, inspired by our washing machine friends."

"Matthew, get back," Aaron yelled as he gestured to the device Tony held.

There was nowhere for Matthew to go. Six Rivers wolves were all around him. Aaron leaped. His enhanced leg muscles propelled him into the skirmish. Canine fangs tore at his exposed human skin, but he ignored the pain. He flung aside furred bodies, threw punches and kicks as he worked his way toward the center where Matthew snarled and growled over Carlos' prone form.

Don't shift, Carlos, was all that went through his mind as he slammed into first one wolf then another, knocking them aside like empty trash cans. If Carlos changed back into human form while down, it was because he was dead. *Please, don't shift.*

"Hold them off, Matthew." He grabbed Carlos and hefted the massive werewolf over his shoulder. The blood dampened fur stuck to his back. "Hang on, Carlos," he pleaded quietly.

Matthew watched his back as he made his way to the circle where the rest of the Trinity wolves waited in a nervous bunch, caught inside the barrier with all of Kapre's fully armed agents. Several Six Rivers wolves tried to infiltrate the circle, but were thrown back by a mystical force. Aaron reached forward to place Carlos on the ground. An electric jolt shot up his arms. He staggered back. Matthew jumped up and placed steadying paws between his shoulders.

"This magic will only let allies inside Kapre bounds. I'm currently not on that guest list," he said to Matthew. The wolf flashed him a regretful glance. "It's okay. Just make sure he's safe."

He laid Carlos on the ground as close to the perimeter as possible. Matthew took his alpha's scruff in his mouth and pulled him into the circle. He looked up at Tony, who stared helplessly at him, his rifle trained on a point just beyond him. His expression said it all.

Aaron whirled around. Six Rivers, three rows deep, had him cornered against the glowing red ring.

Chapter Twenty-Three

Retreat

Aaron let his body shift just a little. Razor sharp claws extended from his fingers. His mouth elongated, his fangs distended. He scanned the opposing group of wolves. He could sense their confusion. Their alpha was dead and the leader of the werewolf uprising was conspicuously absent. It made sense that Cerberus would have wanted just one leader in the clan, just one impressionable, weak shifter to keep under his control. But now that Brandon was gone and with circumstances so dire it would not take more than a few minutes for another wolf — an ambitious wolf ready to prove its worth to the hound of hell — to step up and take charge. Aaron had to make his move before then.

"Little help, Tony?" he asked.

"You're in the way of my toy," Tony yelled. "Any way out?"

"Only through."

He spared a glance at his partner. The usual grin was plastered across his face. If the past two days with him were any precedent, Tony's smile tended to grow wider as events escalated. *Terrific*. His partner already looked like a Cheshire cat.

"Marksmen," Director Braven's voice rang out across the courtyard. "Let's make a path. Do not injure Agent Marvell. He is wanted for questioning."

The aging director, features hidden in the standard riot garb, took first position and aimed. Six Rivers pinpointed on the new threat. Aaron threw himself to the side and flattened out on the ground as the agents' expert aim hit home. Wolves fell to the ground, many dead from a single bullet wound through the neck. The rest turned and retreated to the nearby treeline for cover. Tony passed his gun to Braven, leaped from the steps of Kapre and ran into the courtyard. He tracked the wolves' movement. Aaron watched him advance, transfixed.

The first shifters disappeared into cover. With no time to aim properly Tony heaved the silver object he had brandished earlier. The device sailed through the air and landed at the heels of the last withdrawing pack member. A thick wave of sludge burst from the capsule. It arced into the air and crested over the remaining quarter of Six Rivers who had not yet found shelter among the foliage. Dark ooze splashed over their shoulders and heads, covered the shifters with tar-like fingers. The rest of the glutinous matter splattered onto the ground and spread. Where the viscosity crept the ground lost solidity. The wolves howled in terror as they were drawn down into the pit. One wolf tried to shift, undoubtedly hoping to swim to safety, but only succeeded in being pulled down quicker as he writhed in the agony of transformation. One by one the yelping, panicked wolves sank out of sight. Its work done, the sludge snapped back into the capsule, leaving behind unmarked earth, and no bodies.

Aaron stood shakily. He was no fan of Six Rivers, but that death... He suppressed a shudder. He turned to find Tony watching him, the smile gone from his face. He gathered his emotions and gave his partner a nod.

"Thank you. Nice work."

Tony's expression remained grim. Sometimes, even to an Acqxterm agent who dealt in death, the theory of a weapon was more pleasant than the reality.

The wolves in the treeline howled their rage, reminding Aaron it was not a victory, but merely a reprieve. As if to punctuate this thought, a column of flame erupted just in front of the trees. For a moment Aaron caught sight of a vast nothing in its center, then the dark form of Cerberus filled it. Aaron growled. Cerberus pivoted one head toward his cowering tribe, one toward Aaron and with a snort of utter disdain, turned the last on a spot directly in front of him. The energy field around Kapre began to waver.

"He's pulling down the shield," one agent shouted.

"Op-tech is working against any counter spells this demon might conjure," Braven replied, her voice bounding off the energy surrounding them. "Stand your ground."

But as the disruption grew, a burst of nervous gunfire lit the darkness.

"Hold your fire," Braven barked.

Another agent pulled the gun from the hands of a shaky young man at his right. Probably his first real altercation. The man hung his head and Aaron felt pity for him.

"I'm sorry," the agent said. "I'm..."

"Agent, remove yourself from the field, please," Braven directed.

As the rest of the team watched the shamed agent head with bowed shoulders to the building, Tony approached the perimeter.

"Cerberus isn't moving," Aaron said.

"I guess bullets don't matter enough to a hellhound to make him want to duck."

"It's not just that. He's not moving, but he's doing something."

"What?"

"Look at the sigils from your periphery." Aaron pointed at the Thurisaz marks closest to them. Their brilliance flickered slightly, like an LED string light. "You see that?"

Tony nodded.

"I think he's siphoning off their power."

"Why?"

"I don't know." He turned to Tony. "What happened inside?"

"Braven was not in a mood to listen to anything. You really chapped her ass."

"Me?" he snorted.

"Well, your alleged actions did, at any rate. Same thing at this point."

"And Ellison?"

"Well..." Tony shrugged against his outraged glare. "His story didn't make complete sense to her, but she wasn't open to alternative theories just yet. She ordered him to stay inside."

"Under lock and key?" The pieces began to fall together in his head. A thread of panic began to wind its way around his heart.

"No. Just inside." Tony caught his expression. "Why? What do you think is going on?"

"That." Aaron pointed once again. The light of the Thurisaz sigils funnelled away from their source, streamed toward Cerberus in glowing ribbons. Cerberus traced directions with all three of his heads. The streams wove together, knitting around and around, spiraling in front of the hound and stretching out toward Kapre. A quick flash of light showed the outline of a tunnel, then the air filled with the stench of hellfire. Cerberus inclined one giant head at the wolves hiding behind him. They leaped into the portal, their demon lord close on their heels. A moment later the gate collapsed, leaving only a pile of stinking, smoldering ash.

"Ellison's opened a back door for them. The rest of the agents haven't returned from investigating where we dumped the van, have they?"

Tony shook his head.

"Then there are no field agents inside except for happy trigger-finger over there?" His voice was rising in frustration.

"None."

"So, there's a big building filled with only non-field rated night shift personnel?" Aaron practically screamed the question.

At the sound of his raised voice, his now thoroughly befuddled co-workers trained their rifles on him.

"You tell them," he said to Tony. He raised his hands in the air and tried to look harmless.

"It's Ellison," Tony shouted. "He's made a door that circumvents our barrier. Only someone on the inside could do that."

Braven looked from Tony to Aaron as she gauged her options.

"You have to believe me," Aaron pushed. "Ellison is the one who summoned Cerberus for Six Rivers.

Brandon Wilkes told me they recruited Ellison after he accrued a large debt in their casinos. Brandon slaughtered his competitors for alpha and then had Ellison open the portal to bring Cerberus here so he could transform Brandon and his loyalists into super shifters."

"And Brandon Wilkes can corroborate this?"

"Brandon Wilkes is dead." Aaron swallowed hard, knowing the next words would either save his hide, or skewer it. "I killed him."

Director Braven studied him a moment longer. "Very well. It seems our office personnel are in a grave situation. Those of you Trinity weres who are well enough to fight come with us. The rest of you stay put, try to rest and maintain vigilance."

Matthew looked to Carlos. The leader nodded at his beta, and made a gesture with his muzzle. The healthy wolves jerked their heads in acknowledgment and fell into rank and file behind snow-white Matthew, their new, hopefully temporary, alpha. With a curt wave from the director, the entire mass began the invasion of their home office.

"Agent Harper, come along," Braven called.

"Yes, ma'am." Tony gave him a helpless look. "I'm sorry, Aaron. I have to go. I won't do any good sitting out here with you. People will die while I'm trying to make a point."

Aaron simply stared. There was no time for arguments, but some naïve part of him had been certain Tony would fight for him, fight for his reinstatement as an agent so they could go into battle together. The hurt, the stupid, childish hurt, thrummed through him.

"I'm on your side," Tony said. "I just have to help the people in there. Civilians, unrated agents. They need me. I'm sorry. I really am." He lifted his shoulders in a sorrowful gesture and turned to join the others in formation.

"Director," Aaron called. He spread his hands helplessly, pleading to the last person who could save him from this exile. "Don't do this. Don't cut me off."

"I'm sorry Mr Marvell," the director answered before she entered the door. "I have no idea whom to trust, anymore."

"Trust me," he shouted. When the director didn't respond he yelled again. "Trust $m-$" The imposing steel doors slammed shut, cutting him off.

"Braven!" With a howl of frustration Aaron launched his fists at the crimson field, as if to pound it to the ground. The energy shot into his arms and he was blown back fifteen feet. He crashed onto his back. He lay there, looking up at the stars, fighting back tears of frustration and anger.

"That was utterly useless," Carlos' tired voice carried to him.

Aaron sat up. His alpha had shifted during his temper tantrum. Carlos held a shirt against the slowed bleeding at his throat and stepped through the barrier. Aaron scrambled to his feet and ran to meet him. His former alpha's legs shook with the effort of walking, but he held himself upright.

"If you are finished your grandstanding I have an idea on how to get us inside."

Chapter Twenty-Four

Inheritance

"Us?" Aaron scoffed. "Absolutely not." He paused, considering Carlos' words. A fresh wave of hope filled him. "What's your plan? There's no way you're coming along in your condition, but what is it?"

"We'll see about the rest, later," Carlos said with a tired smile. "First, we need to know if you can get inside."

"You have something specific in mind?" His curiosity was growing by the second.

"Tell me how portals work." Carlos moved to the edge of the clearing and leaned against a tree. Even by the orange glow of the Thurisaz sigils Aaron could see how pale his former lover was, how much blood loss he had suffered. It wasn't a mortal injury, but it would take some time for Carlos to recover.

"Portals appear either when a free being capable of traveling inter-dimensionally opens one, or when a limited being is summoned."

"And can those doors be operated by anyone else?"

"Some demons of higher order and very skilled mages."

"But otherwise the door must be opened and closed by the one who generated it?"

"Yes." Aaron looked away, distracted by a burst of gunfire in the Kapre building. "Is there a point to this, and if so will you get to it? My friends are dying in there."

"As are mine," Carlos reminded him. "Did Ellison make the portal, or simply make it possible for the portal to form?"

"Cerberus can make his own doorways, so I'm guessing the latter."

"That's what I thought. You, then, can open the door into Kapre."

"What?" Aaron scoffed. "There's no way. I've never—"

"You are the direct descendant of Cerberus. You hold his power inside you. His blood is in yours."

"Yeah? So? His blood is in Six Rivers, too." He caught Carlos' upshot eyebrow. "Maybe? Maybe not. He could have enhanced them bloodlessly. Probably did, since they're not like me, or like Brandon was. Not yet. Even so, I can't open a portal just because I have some of Cerberus' blood in my body. Magic can't be tricked."

"Can't it?" Carlos asked. "Blood and tissue, diseases and plagues. All that Matthew said is true. While there is a magical element to our existence, it is also physical. In our bodies. Our bones. Our *blood.*"

"Okay, fine." Aaron scrubbed a hand through his hair. More distant gunfire peppered the night, disturbed the creatures milling under the boughs at his back. "I may have his blood inside me, but that doesn't mean I can open portals. There has been no evidence of that even as a remote possibility. You would think if I had that inclination it would have shown itself at some point during my freak-outs when I was shifting uncontrollably."

"You don't have to open new portal, *mi hombre*. You only have to open the one that is still there."

Aaron looked from Carlos to the pile of ash on the ground a few yards away. He recalled the pulling sensation he had felt inside the warehouse on his first day, the same sensation he had felt when Qi had arrived. He had been drawn to the portals, as if they called to him.

Ridiculous. He snorted, then paced, hands on his hips. How could he open a mystical door? He'd had no training other than having read a few nonspecific descriptions in heavily redacted textbooks ten years before. Only mages were allowed to mess with that stuff, and for good reason. Terrible things had happened when laymen tried to open portals—dismemberment, soul-splicing, flaying, not to mention the unholy litany of beasts waiting on the other side to seize the opportunity to waltz through an unguarded open door.

More gunfire.

Screams muffled by distance and the thick concrete walls of Kapre.

Ghostly suffering howls.

He couldn't do it.

Could he?

"It's the only way." Carlos stayed slumped against the tree, back curved like one of those plant hooks Aaron's grandmother used to skewer her porch columns with.

"How do I do it?" Aaron asked.

"I am afraid this is where my skill set drops me off." Carlos smiled apologetically. "I am nearly one hundred and the alpha of a werewolf pack. I have no experience in magic, and as of the past fifty years, no experience in much of anything other than telling my wolves what they should and should not do."

He was on his own. Aaron searched the courtyard as if the answer to his problem lay somewhere amongst the manicured grass and terrace pavers. He searched his mind for any information that would help him complete his task. Summoning spells, with their complicated symbols, sacrifices and elaborate chants were out. Despite studying them for years he had no idea where to begin. That left natural magic, the kind Carlos so sincerely believed rested inside him. But how to access it?

He focused his thoughts on the pile of ash and thought, *Open*.

The scorched mound of hellfire sat benignly. The Thurisaz sigils carried on emitting their steady glow.

"I want to open a door," he announced to the courtyard.

Nothing.

"Think about it," Carlos said from the side. "*Want* to get in there."

"I do," he replied with irritation.

Carlos humphed but said nothing else.

His sensitive hearing could only pick up the loudest sounds through the thick walls of Kapre, a unified volley of shots, or a particularly loud sound of agony. It was the latter that carried to his ears just then, a prolonged, tortured series of high-pitched screams. Aaron's body went cold. The vocalization was exactly the noise he had made when the werewolves and Cerberus were tearing into him. And the voice—his body grew rigid with terror—was Tony's.

His doubt and frustration evaporated in the presence of his need to get to Tony. The panic of it scrabbled up his chest and filled his throat, emerged as a single, earth-shaking howl of his partner's name. Another were's howl rose up in response. *Matthew*. He was trying to help. But even if he took out the attacking weres, Matthew couldn't beat Cerberus.

"Please," Carlos whispered.

Aaron didn't need to be begged. He screamed again, this time throwing into the sound the desire to tear down the walls brick by brick if necessary to get to Tony. Immediately he was thankful for his nudity. An intense wave of heat consumed him. His skin was fiery, his blood burbled with the inferno raging inside him. He let the power overtake him. His face and hands shifted to partial lupine form. His eyes bulged, as hot as a pair of boiled eggs plucked from the water. His skin turned black.

He howled.

The hellfire ash responded.

Tendrils of glowing dust lifted into the air. It swirled in front of him, tracing the outline of its previous form. It was a slow, infuriating process. But as his urgent irritation grew, the door took on a more defined shape, until finally the embers haloed a deep nothingness. Aaron did not delay, but stepped inside.

A profound emptiness enveloped him. Blind, and with cotton-filled ears, he stumbled forward. His internal compass spun. He staggered in the pitch, if one could actually stagger against a floor that didn't exist. His heart pounded in fear. He was lost in the in-between. He had leaped in unthinking, and would now wander the void forever. With great effort he pushed back a wave of hysteria. Tony. Tony needed him. He had to get to Tony. The darkness did not abate, but rather pressed in, squeezing him as tightly as his panic. He felt a gentle, but certain, nudge and he allowed it to sweep him forward. Just as he moved, he felt a hand blindly clutch at his buttock. He reached back, familiar with that grip. The wounded alpha should not have come, but abandoning him to the vortex was unthinkable. He would have to bring Carlos through.

He secured his grip on Carlos and leaned into the vacuum. His surroundings shifted in a quick, vertiginous flash, then he and Carlos were standing in Kapre's lobby.

"You did it…" Carlos trailed off as they both took in the scene before them.

Bodies lay sprawled across the marble tiles. Agents, guns still in hand, lay oozing the last drops of blood from their bodies. Mauled shifters from both clans sprawled face down or on their sides, lethal bite and claw wounds marring their bare flesh. Carlos made pained sounds as they passed the bodies of his fallen pack members. Aaron recognized a number of them, as well. Burley Bill who had stashed the van that had delivered him from Kapre's clutches lay with his guts spilling across the floor. A younger were with three parallel scars slashed across the left side of her face who had commiserated with him about their violent attacks and subsequent shifts had a mess of tissue and blood where her throat had been. An older lady — close in age to Director Braven — who had ruled as the stand-in alpha female for Carlos when visiting more traditional packs was mauled to almost unrecognizability. They all lay on the cold stone floor, their life, their identity as wolf, torn away. More than the nakedness of their bodies, this lack of fur and fang was the ultimate stripping of their dignity. They were pack no more. Only corpses.

Carlos, his face a mask of pain and disgust, moved toward the elevator. Aaron grabbed his arm.

"The elevator is a perfect trap. We have to take the stairs."

Carlos nodded. His eyes were glazed, unfocused.

"You should stay here."

"Cerberus and Six Rivers have killed my clansmen. I cannot let that lie."

"Matthew is taking care of it."

"Matthew?" Carlos' voice was hollow. "If Matthew is alive."

"He is. You heard his voice."

"Yes, the last time you heard Tony's," Carlos answered. "I have heard nothing since. Have you?"

"They're alive." Aaron propelled Carlos to the back stairwell. "I'm going to get them. But you're half dead."

"I am on the recovering side of that half, however." Carlos gave him a smile that was closer to a grimace. "I will see this to the end, whatever it may be."

"Fine." Aaron glanced up at the security cameras as he pushed Carlos through the heavy fire door. He couldn't linger in the lobby, arguing. Even if Six Rivers didn't have someone monitoring the camera bank, odds were someone would pass by the security station and notice them milling around downstairs. "We'll go together."

He had no intention of holding up to this promise. As Carlos struggled to make the first flight Aaron knew the alpha would not survive full combat. He would have to find a place to stash Carlos. He thought of op-tech. The agents had probably stripped it already. Even if weapons remained, Six Rivers, with Cerberus and his new 'all natural' philosophy, wouldn't deign to touch them. He guided Carlos slowly up the steps, careful not to over-exert the wounded shifter, even though every nerve in his body was screaming for rapid action, for Tony.

The only other occupant of the stairwell was the body of a lone agent, badly mauled, neck broken from her topple down the steps. Aaron looked down at the woman. He didn't recognize her face from the office. She was a night employee. So, where were his daytime co-workers? Still muddling around in the woods where Carlos' man had stashed the van? Why had no one summoned them, or the other off-duty agents? What about the Thurisaz sigils? They should have raised alerts on their mobiles. Had Ellison blocked both electronic and mystical communication? Were the majority of his co-workers sleeping in their beds, unaware their office was under attack? Aaron hoped so. Watching his entire office get slaughtered again would surely land him in the psychiatric ward.

The question was, if Ellison had full homicide on his mind, why would he try to protect his co-workers?

He couldn't think about that, now. Carlos was having an increasingly difficult time navigating the many steps. Aaron turned back. Carlos' lips were blue, his skin pale. Before the alpha could protest, Aaron swept him up in his arms. Carlos gave him and admonishing look, but did not struggle or argue. He was out of strength and he knew it. Aaron carried him up the remaining flight and set him down on the landing. He didn't want to risk making his face a target by popping it into the small rectangular window in the door, so instead he inched as close to the door as possible, relying on his other senses to paint him a picture of the corridor. The heavy stench of gunpowder and terror drowned out all other scents. His sensitive hearing relayed no sign of lingering presence in the hallway leading to the op-tech lab. He creaked open the door and listened for a moment more. No sounds of claws clicking on the tile, no footpads squelching on the floor, no weapons beings hoisted to heavily armored shoulders. The coast was as clear as it was going to get.

Aaron pulled the door the rest of the way open. The hall was littered with more bodies, the ratio of fallen ally to enemy a dismal one. Carlos followed him through, his lucidity slightly improved from his brief rest on the landing. His color, however, remained alarmingly wan.

"This way," Aaron whispered.

He led Carlos down the hall, stopping at the wide double doors of the op-tech lab. The counters were stripped of all weapons, as was the cage of locked weapons at the requisitions desk. The only thing remaining in the room was Robert, the lone op-tech scientist, sitting cross-legged inside a silvery bubble floating four feet from the floor. He had a computer on one knee, a strange glowing tablet on the other and the black squiggle of an earpiece cord dangling from his head. He looked up when they entered. His mouth opened in surprise, then shut.

"Hi, Robert," Aaron said. "You remember me from the other day?"

"The other day?" The distortion of the sphere made Robert's voice burble as if underwater. "I remember you from everyone in the office wanting your head as a desk ornament."

"And what about you?" Aaron asked, eying the tech's fingers as they scurried across the mystical tablet.

"Wrongly placed blame," Robert answered. There was no sympathy or commiseration in his voice, just bald truth. "Doesn't add up. No one wants to hear it from me, though. I'm the geek. I'm supposed to keep my mouth shut and do geek things."

"Like float around in a Sigurddessen Sphere?"

This time Robert did look up. "You know about them?" He was impressed. "I guess you agents think I'm weak for hiding."

"I've read about them, yeah. And it was a good defensive move. The agents took away all of your weapons, which you undoubtedly know very well. Still, you have limited field training and shooting a target is much easier than shooting something sprinting toward you at forty miles an hour. If you were out running around with guns blazing, I'd be worried about you. Since those spheres are damn well impenetrable, I'm not."

Robert flashed him a smile. "You seemed like an okay guy when we met."

"I need a favor, Robert."

"I can't help you find a painless way to jump in the battle, if that's what you're asking. I'm throwing up containments like crazy and as quickly as I do Cerberus just jogs right through them. He has gummed up our mystical security systems and the electrical ones were never engaged. There's not much left in the way of locked doors. This place is your candy jar, man. Stick your hand in. Just be sure where you stick it, or you might lose it. And the rest of the agents have been located and are on their way in, so try not to get a bullet from behind."

"That's all helpful information, but not what I was getting at. I was hoping you would look after my friend." Aaron gestured to Carlos. "He's the alpha of the Trinity clan. He was the one who warned me of Six Rivers coming into the area. We owe him for that."

"I guess we do." Robert gave Carlos a long look. "Unfortunately, I can't let you in here with me. If you do know about Sigurddessen Spheres you know they can only be opened once. After that they dissipate, which would render useless my valiant attempts at not getting eaten."

"I don't need your protection. Only a place to rest." Carlos turned to Aaron, defeated. "I've lost too much blood. I'm holding you back and endangering not only you, but maybe Matthew and Tony. I may not like it, but I know when I'm a total liability."

"Maybe not total," Aaron said. "Look around. You seem to know good ideas when you see them. There might be something in here that can help us."

Carlos scanned the clean-picked room, his expression conveying nothing but doubt, but he nodded. "Yes, maybe."

"Okay. Just lie low until I come back for you."

"Most of the tech has been taken and detonated in this fight. I'm tracking it from here," Robert said. "There's one that hasn't. A special little thing I've been working on since the portals started popping up all over town. It's new and untested."

"That disruptor thing Tony asked you about on my first day?"

"That's the one. He made sure to get it from me when the rest of the Acqxterm knuckleheads were in here scrabbling for bullets and guns."

"He still has it?" A flutter of hope came alive in Aaron's chest.

"He does." Robert tapped the screen. "And it is as yet undetonated. Get it and you have a much better chance of making it out of here alive. We all do."

"I'll do my best." Aaron nodded at Robert. "Thanks."

"No problem. Try not to get your ass chewed off." The tech grinned. "From Cerberus, or Braven."

"It's the latter I'm more worried about, but I'll do my best." Aaron gave him a wave then pulled in Carlos for a quick hug. "Be careful. If they come in, get to a high place. Until then, save your strength, maybe find yourself a lab coat or something. You're distracting, standing here naked."

"You mean disturbing," Robert chimed in, not looking up from his screens.

"As are you, *mi hombre*." Carlos smiled. "But I suspect you will be shifting soon."

"As soon as Cerberus is in my sights, yeah." Aaron flexed his hands, already feeling the claws that would rend flesh. "We're gonna have an old-fashioned dog fight."

Chapter Twenty-Five

The Price of War

The gunshots were growing sparse, distant. The lupine whines and human cries of pain were clearly audible in the pockets of silence. Aaron ran down the hall toward the sound. He couldn't differentiate the noises, couldn't tell if one of them belonged to Tony. But there, in the place where he had started work two short days before, was an abundance of misery and death. Aaron knew it because the dark thing inside him was urging him toward it, driven by the delicious scent of spilt blood and fading life. Aaron snarled menacingly at the part of him he had once loathed. Even now, despite his disgust at the desires of the creature squatting in his chest, he couldn't deny the truth of its usefulness, nor of its inextricable oneness with him. Just as the demon had once controlled him, he would now control it. Any blood it tasted would be by his command alone. Happily, there were several mouthfuls of blood he would gleefully let it relish — especially if Tony was suffering.

The lights flickered as a wash of magic flowed through the hallway. Robert had summoned another spell, maybe to keep Cerberus trapped inside, maybe to help Aaron reach the demon unchallenged. He let the power sweep him forward toward the main offices, toward the smell of death.

The corridor from op-tech and the back stairs led to the heart of Kapre. The door, which usually required a passcode and a fingerprint scan, sat ajar. Aaron eased it open and slid into the narrow hall. Flanked by the broom closet and the staff break room, Aaron cautiously checked first one opening then the other. He closed off the corridor as he cleared the passageway Twenty feet and a pair of reinforced steel doors separated him from Cerberus. He could feel the demon on the other side, hear his chest rising and falling with the fiery gasses that filled his lungs—which meant Cerberus could hear Aaron, too. He was waiting for him. Aaron had no weapons save for the elongated teeth and nails that accompanied his partial transformation. He considered fully shifting before bursting through the entryway and thus providing himself with a greater degree of protection, but if it were locked it would require fingerprints to open, and he would be forced to shift back. It was better to pass through as a biped, then quickly shift once inside, if needed. Aaron turned the handle. It swung freely on its axis. He shoved open the door and faced utter devastation.

Lights flickered. The fluorescents dangled from wires, the frosted Plexiglas lay shattered out of its housing. Overturned desks served as inadequate cover for the mauled agents sprawled behind them. Bullet casings littered the floor. The air wavered with the energy of a dozen spent mystical devices. Naked shifters lay in pools of blood, their spinal cords blown out of the backs of their necks. Here, the number of werewolf bodies outweighed those of acqxterm agents. It seemed the tide had turned in favor of Kapre. The fight had clearly moved on, most likely the rallying agents driving the weres into the main front hallway and down the stairs to the waiting agents outside. In the center of the grisly scene sat Cerberus, all three of his heads fixed on Aaron.

Fear and anger waged war for supremacy as Aaron stepped forward. Cerberus gave another of his gravelly chortles and wagged its massive heads. He pawed at a bloodied mass of black rags beneath his foot. The mass moaned, and Aaron's heart dropped.

"Tony?"

The bundle shifted at the sound. Aaron caught sight of a crimson-slicked shock of hair. Even through the blood he recognized that thick, dark crop as the same he had run his hands through just a few hours before.

"What did you do to him?" Rage boiled inside Aaron. It felt as if it would burn the blood through his veins and flood it to the surface of his still blackened skin. He lunged forward.

Cerberus snarled, shook his heads, and pulled Tony's limp body beneath his with a massive paw. Tony groaned.

"Okay, okay." Aaron pulled up short, hands in the air. "Ease up on him. What do you want from me?"

The room grew hot. The air wavered and a burst of flames appeared at Cerberus' flank. The fire shifted like the parting of curtains, revealing the profound blackness of the void. The demon inclined its head.

Aaron inspected the doorway. Where did Cerberus want him to go, and why? Wasn't he just a mistake? A whim? Why would his creator suddenly want his company? He looked down at Tony, lying limp and in need of medical assistance and decided he did not care.

"Get off of him and I'll go."

Cerberus moved away, kicking Tony aside with contempt.

I'm going to kill you, was all Aaron could think as he stared at the loathsome demon. Aloud he said, "I'm going to trigger a device on his phone to summon medical help." He inched forward, but Cerberus made no move to intervene. He knelt beside Tony. His partner's breathing was shallow. Cerberus' talons had raked clean through the tactical vest. Blood seeped from the wounds beneath.

"You're going to be okay," he whispered as he pulled Tony's phone from his pocket. He made a show of pressing the lock screen key, then hitting the local weather application. He put the phone back into Tony's pocket and palmed the other device resting there. "I've hit your alert app. Braven will know you're in here." He looked around at the bodies. Braven already knew Tony was in here. She had left this room to advance with the rest of the remaining agents and overtake the fleeing Six Rivers weres. He could only hope that the reinforcements Robert claimed had arrived would allow her to shortly send a medic or two back upstairs for the survivors she had been forced to leave behind. Aaron leaned in and gave Tony a kiss on the temple.

"I have to go. But, you'll be okay." He palmed the disruptor, thankful it was not much larger than a USB jump drive. *"We'll* be okay. I promise."

Tony's hand twitched against the floor as if to intercept him, but Aaron pulled back. He turned to face Cerberus.

"We go together. No tricks."

The demon nodded.

Aaron turned to his maker. Standing hip to flank, they stepped into the gate.

Chapter Twenty-Six

The Mind of a Demon

Instead of the riotous dark, Aaron stepped through the portal and into a small clearing surrounded by a moon-washed forest. Crickets and frogs loudly celebrated the sultry night. Cerberus, at his side, chuffed with pleasure and dropped to roll in the grass. With blackened magma legs jutting into the air the beast writhed against the ground, scorching a patch the size of a VW Bug.

"Why are we here?" Aaron asked.

The demon ignored him.

Aaron left Cerberus to his rolling and made his way into the forest. The undergrowth rustled. He caught flashes of silver tails darting between the trees, heard the sound of padded feet against the forest floor. Lupine cries echoed through the trees. The sound coursed such intense pleasure through his body that he forgot everything for a moment. Like water flowing into a glass his body shifted. In an instant his four paws were against the soft earth, his nose low enough to the ground to not only smell the layers of pine needles and browned leaves, but the layers of ancient deadfall underneath. It was a rich, complex, joyous scent. He threw back his head and howled. Several wolfish voices returned his cry.

He bent down and mouthed the disruptor that had fallen from his fingers as he transformed. He poked it gently between his cheek and gum with his tongue, then headed toward a bright patch in the woods.

"I thought you would like it here." The blackened being that was Cerberus in humanoid form caught up with him, matching his lope with a long bipedal stride. The three heads turned this way and that, taking in the scenery with satisfaction.

Aaron didn't trust the words coming out of the three sets of lava-cracked lips, didn't trust the happy-wolf-playground facade Cerberus seemed intent on making him believe. It was all a little too forced, especially with the hellhound standing next to him in a form as close to human as he could attain.

"You must stay here, out of harm's way," the demon said. "My first daughter will now keep you company in the way that man of yours did."

If Aaron could have laughed in wolf form he would have. Not only was Cerberus intent on murdering all of his friends and setting himself up as a god among wolves, he was apparently a raging homophobe, to boot.

Cerberus gestured for Aaron to follow him. Aaron looked back and gauged the distance to the treeline. He could sprint that far, no problem. But Cerberus was bigger, older and more demonic than he. He had to make sure whatever he tried would take Cerberus well out of commission before he tried to escape. He decided to follow the demon for a while. Not only was his curiosity piqued, but the longer he delayed the hellhound in this place, the greater the hope for Kapre, Trinity and Tony.

A beaten swath of vegetation snaked through the trees. A distant rosy glow illuminated the rudimentary path. Cerberus led him toward the light. Aaron's mind turned to Carlos' story of Cerberus' origin. Had it been true? Did Cerberus make the first werewolves? Was this place the past, or simply a pastiche of what he imagined their collective history to be? Cerberus seemed riveted by the illumination, his expression one of expectancy and trepidation. Whatever it was that lay just beyond the last few feet of trees was something the demon feared. And that meant it was something Aaron could use against him.

The trees broke at a small clearing. A large bonfire dominated the abandoned space.

"I left her here." The note of sadness was not lost in the roughness of Cerberus' multiple voices. "She was to take care of you."

Aaron glanced at the hellhound, then back at the fire. While the flames stretched high into the air, there was something odd about them. Like a short movie clip set on repeat, the light flickered at the exact same rate, the tongues of flame stretched only so high before sinking down to reach up again. He touched his nose to the grass and sniffed. No human scent. No werewolf scent. Only the cleanest, most pure forest odors he had ever known. There was no woman.

As if sensing his thoughts Cerberus whirled on him. "She was here. She was to take care of you. Where did she go?"

Aaron tilted his head, questioning.

"Where?" Cerberus' three heads shouted. The nearest boughs shook with the force of the roar.

Cerberus wanted Aaron to shift, to enter into a pointless argument with him. Aaron, however, had no desire to do such a thing. He remained in wolf form and regarded Cerberus with polite interest. This infuriated the demon who began crashing around the empty campsite, uprooting bushes and kicking large rocks, screaming a name Aaron couldn't understand.

Whether from an eternity of roaming the mind-dulling void, or from his very nature, Cerberus was not a sane demon. In an instant the pieces fell into place. Cerberus wanted an army of werewolves not only to follow him, but to love and share time with. There had never been a woman who offered to share her fire, only Cerberus' desperate need for companionship that made him maul his first progeny and turn her into the first werewolf. But instead of climbing into the vortex with him she went off and made her own race, her own family. Weres grew in number while Cerberus roamed the nothing, craving the companionship he had been denied. He must have spent ages dreaming of the time he would bring the werewolves back to him. When Six Rivers became weakened by the untimely death of its alpha, and poor, deluded Brandon called him back from the void, Cerberus struck. He infiltrated the pack, made grand promises, gave Brandon the tools to bring his clan to his feet. When they began exterminating the only people who could stop them, Cerberus had stumbled across Aaron—the one person since his first progeny able to accept his bite, to shift into something close to what he was—and took his shot. And now, it seemed, Cerberus wanted to seal Aaron up in his saccharine version of Werewolf Past so they could be buddies.

Screw that. If the bastard liked his little fire so much, he could go back to it.

Cerberus, still raging, wheeled around toward Aaron. Aaron sidestepped as if readying to bolt. Cerberus headed him off, putting himself exactly where Aaron wanted him. Aaron sprang. He used the massive force of his back legs to push into the demon. He caught Cerberus off guard. Cerberus flew back. His body crashed into the fire. The demon howled with laughter as the patches of magma on his skin absorbed the heat, changed from orange to blue, to white. The black patches crackled and peeled from Cerberus' skin. He snarled at Aaron and sank into the flames. Three lupine heads emerged a moment later, snapping and growling, dripping white-hot lava from their jowls. Suddenly, his idea didn't seem such a smart one.

Aaron raised his hackles and planted his feet, ready for the fiery impact. Cerberus dropped his hips and lunged. Behind him, the flames stretched out, forming a pair of long, delicate arms that wrapped around Cerberus and pulled him back. The demon snarled and turned to snap at the thing holding him. The tongues of fire formed the shape of a woman, who gazed down at the demon with reproach and sadness. All of the fight drained from Cerberus as he looked into those eyes.

Aaron did not bother to question who or what she was — ancient fact or twisted figment — but turned and sprinted for the woods. He let his canine legs carry him toward the portal. All around him the illusion of Cerberus' history was dissolving. Shadows deepened and elongated, swallowing both tree and sky. The void was creeping into Cerberus' sanctuary. The lupine cries around him turned to snarls as the invisible wolves succumbed to the encroaching dark. Aaron pushed himself faster. The void was eating away the ground at his feet. He stumbled ahead, concentrating on the portal. It flashed ahead of him. Twenty feet. The ground slipped away beneath his right heel. Ten feet. The treeline to the right of him disappeared into the shadows. Five. He pushed his front paws away from the ground and let the shift take him. The earth fell away and he leaped forward, hands outstretched as if the door had an actual jamb to cling to. He skidded across the slick grass and into the void.

Not bothering to try to stand, Aaron rode out the slide. He focused his mind on Kapre, on Tony. Like a beacon Tony's presence shined out to him, called him back home. The disruptor — much larger in his human mouth than in his lupine muzzle — threatened to choke him. He dug it out with two muddy fingers and clutched it like a toy. The portal opened on the other end. He saw Tony there, propped against the wall, a familiar figure hunched over him.

Rage boiled through Aaron as he careened out of the portal and toppled across the blood-slicked tiles. He rolled to the side and flung the disruptor into the open gateway. For a moment he thought he saw a flash of fur and fang, but then a wash of brilliant light obscured his vision. He stood and staggered back. An iron like darkness slid across the deeper black, shuttering off the depths of the void like a slammed door. The portal's flames snuffed completely. Instead of ash, a pool of liquid metal dripped to the floor, sizzling as it hit the cool tiles. Aaron felt his features shift to their half wolf form. He let his fangs extend, his claws sharpen, his skin blacken. He turned and faced the man who now cowered in front of his partner with a look of extreme terror etched across his despicable face. A low growl accompanied the name that scraped between his clenched jaws.

"Ellison."

Chapter Twenty-Seven

Cleaning House

"I di...du...didn't..." Ellison stammered. Alcohol fumes rolled off him in a caustic wave. "Ar, man, you gotta believe me."

"Believe you?" The words came out grinding and low, a motor churning through a plant-choked swamp. "You screwed me over, killed our co-workers and helped turn me into *this*. You followed me here and brought Cerberus and Six Rivers with you, and started all over again, all while framing me." His sharpened vision took in Ellison's trembling limbs, then Tony's still form. "Get the fuck away from him."

Ellison scrabbled away, babbling incoherently.

Aaron knelt beside Tony. He placed his hands on Tony's skin. It was feverishly hot, even beneath Aaron's hellhound touch. Tony's eyelids fluttered, but remained closed. His wounds gently oozed blood. He was clotting, but not fast enough to mark a transformation. Aaron's jaw clenched. He turned back to Ellison and let the dark thing's constant fury resurge, drowning his more complex emotions.

"Did you ever think of going to Director Stellart and telling him you were being blackmailed by Six Rivers, you pathetic halfwit?" he asked Ellison. "That would have stopped all of this. Why didn't you?"

"I thought about it." Tears formed in Ellison's eyes. "I did. Did you think I wanted him, all of them, to die? I didn't. I did the spell and then realized what it probably meant for us, having all of the werewolf clans united under a power-hungry demon."

Aaron reached behind Tony's still form for the fallen rifle. Ellison saw him grab it and began talking faster, the tears flowing freely.

"Please, Ar, please. I didn't mean any of it." Ellison wrung his hands like a fretful old lady. "I thought about telling Stellart, but it would have ended my career and I know it was wrong, I know, but I was selfish and stupid and I'm sorry. I'm sorry."

The dark thing snorted in disgust. Aaron let the sound escape from his own lips. "You are selfish and stupid. And you are finished."

Aaron raised the rifle. The dark thing howled in protest. It wanted blood in its mouth. Aaron couldn't think of anything more disagreeable than having the taste of Ellison in his throat. A bullet to the head would be much more satisfying. He raised the weapon. Ellison, despite his years of agent training, did nothing to save himself. He sat on the floor, crying and stinking of alcohol, and pissed himself.

The room shuddered as if from an enormous impact. Aaron staggered as the floor swayed. He caught himself on a desk. He looked at the doors, expecting to see the smoke of a detonated charge, a swarm of agents. The doors remained intact. His stomach dropped, and he turned to the next likely source.

The flames of the portal had begun to rekindle. The air above it wavered like heat from a desert road. Another tremor shook the floor. This time, the space above the flames shuddered.

"He's coming. He's coming. He's coming, he's coming, he's coming," Ellison babbled as he scuttled under a desk.

Aaron caught Ellison's ankle and pulled him back out. "Why isn't the disruptor holding him?"

"It's a temporary fix," Ellison cried as he worked to free his ankle and return to his hiding spot. "This is a big league demon, you can't just stop him from getting through his own portals with weak spells. They won't work. Big demons need big magic."

"Like what?"

"No." Ellison clawed at the floor frantically. "No, I'm done. No more magic."

Aaron released Ellison's foot and let him slither under the desk. He blocked the opening to the snake's hole with his feet and pushed the muzzle of his gun into the space until it rested against Ellison's forehead.

"Rethink that decision."

Ellison began crying in earnest. Sobs racked his chest. "I can't. Don't you see? I screwed up. I wasn't letting Cerberus in here earlier. Why would I? They all want me dead. Here I was safe. All these agents and weapons around me. I wasn't going to leave here, not until you guys got rid of Six Rivers and I got rid of him."

"What did you do?"

When Ellison didn't respond, Aaron banged the muzzle above Ellison's nose.

"Ow, stop," Ellison cried. "He was banished, which meant the only door he could come through was one he was called through. So, I did a spell to get rid of the portals I'd opened here and in California. Or, I thought. I'd had a drink or two..." Ellison shrugged at Aaron's disbelieving snort. "Or ten. Yeah. I had too much, man. I'm sorry."

"You did the wrong spell? Instead of shutting two doors you conveniently mistakenly opened another portal right here on Kapre grounds at the very time Six Rivers was mobilizing to take us out?"

"Yes. I was trying to stop it all. I thought if I could get rid of Cerberus, Six Rivers would lose their motivation and go away." A dribble of snot leaked out of his nose and he scrubbed it away with his sleeve. "You think I wanted him that close to me? I screwed the pooch. I'm sorry."

"I don't believe you."

The room shook, this time with enough force to knock lamps off the few upright desks remaining.

"Does it matter?" Ellison asked. He turned his bloodshot eyes up at Aaron. "Whatever I did, we're here and Cerberus is coming and we're both dead."

"We're not." Aaron lowered his gun and reached under the desk. This time Ellison did not resist when he grabbed his arm and pulled him out. He hauled Ellison to his feet. "You're going to tell me what spell we need and then we're going to do it."

"You won't like it." Ellison jerked his head in Tony's direction.

Aaron's stomach dropped.

"We can do the spell to seal the gateways I made, but that won't stop him from coming back if say Six Rivers decides to find another idiot to invite him into our dimension." Ellison sniffed. His self-deprecation only flamed Aaron's anger. Aaron shook him hard.

"So we kill Cerberus, then? Tell me how."

"The only way to do that is to weaken him enough so you can take him. You're pretty much the only one who can, seeing as you're his direct descendant."

"How do we weaken him?"

"Sever the line of blood. Freshest is best. More power in ones he just made than the ones he did a hundred years ago, if there are any. And it's more convenient." Ellison gestured to the bodies strewn around the room.

"How many are alive?" Aaron asked. He avoided looking at Tony, the deep slash marks on his torso.

"I don't know. I didn't check." Ellison looked at the floor. "Didn't want to know."

"You're a piece of shit."

Aaron roughly released Ellison and canvassed the room. A quick vitals check showed four agents aside from Tony still had pulses. They were the ones whose bodies were fighting the invading shifter disease, the ones who would either turn, or die. It was an unusually high number of potential weres. They all remained like Tony, deeply unconscious. All had bite marks and rent flesh. There was no way of telling if the wounds were werewolf or from Cerberus.

Aaron rocked back on his haunches and studied the young agent before him. With werewolves the transfer of the disease was salivary. Was that the case with Cerberus, as well? Or could he change people with any of his lethal body parts? This kid was twenty-three at best. A new agent. Flushed skin, full lips, thick brown hair. His face was one of those sneakily good looking ones, not the kind to stop people in their tracks, but the kind whose virtues grew more apparent with each glance. And now Aaron was supposed to put a bullet in it.

Aaron passed a shaking hand over his mouth. He couldn't do it. He couldn't play executioner to the four people lying helpless around him. Terrified grief threatened to curl him into a useless ball beside Ellison at the thought of Tony possibly being the fifth. The few intact ceiling lights began to flicker.

"Uh," a voice came over the intercom. "Hey, Agent Marvell, it's Robert. I've got control of the electrical system again. Six Rivers is down. Your Trinity guys and our agents have secured their surrender. The cavalry is coming to you. Just hang tight."

Aaron stood and looked at the speaker over his head.

"I can see you, so nod or something if you acknowledge."

Aaron looked at the corpses scattered through the room, then down at Tony. Soon, the agents would flood the bullpen and Braven would initiate a lockdown. Cerberus would break through the portal, tear through them all, then continue out into the world to find the company he so craved. Aaron shook his head.

"What's that mean?" Robert asked. "You clearly hear me, so you don't acknowledge?"

Aaron looked around for the security camera. He found it in the far corner. He looked directly into the lens and shook his head slowly, deliberately.

"I don't understand. Is there a situation that requires containment?"

Aaron nodded then turned to Ellison, "Help me. Get one of the others. Don't touch Tony. And if you try to run so help me I will shift and be on you in two seconds." He made sure his canines showed when he added, "And I will not let go of you until your little chicken neck snaps under my jaws."

Ellison bobbed his head in compliance and scuttled out of the way as Aaron picked up the young agent and carried him to the doors. He pushed them open with his hip and placed the man gently on the floor. He held open the door for Ellison, who reeked of terror and sped his awkward lurching gait to faster pass him. Once more they each carried a survivor outside to safety. When only Tony remained, Aaron commanded Ellison to sit down. Like a kicked dog, Ellison rushed to obey. Aaron knelt in front of Tony.

"Hey," he whispered. Tony's eyelids flickered at the sound of his voice. "Listen to me. I know it's only been a couple of days, but I just wanted to say I've had a really good time. There's been some messed up stuff, but it's okay. I know you're on my side. And if I had a choice, I'd do it all over again." He touched near Tony's wound. "Except this. I wish I could have spared you this." He bent over and pressed his lips to Tony's. "This'll make that cocky grin of yours return. I think I love you."

In the movies it would have been the part where Tony's fluttering lids creaked open and Tony would look at him and profess his love in return. It wasn't the movies. Aaron scooped up Tony's limp form and carried him through the door. He placed him gently on the floor beside the others. Down the hall, the elevator dinged. With no time left for farewells, Aaron hurried back into the room and shoved the doors shut behind him. He waved frantically at the camera.

"What's up?" Robert's voice filled the room.

Aaron pointed at the doors at both ends of the room and clenched his fists together.

"You want me to lock you in?"

Aaron nodded. He pointed at the portal, which was vibrating with frantic insistency. Cerberus was done ringing the doorbell. He was just going to break in. Aaron pointed again at the portal for emphasis and made a blowing up motion with his hands.

"What about Agent Ellison?" Robert clearly caught his drift. "You gonna let him out?"

Aaron looked back at Ellison, who was looking at him like a puppy hoping for a treat. He shook his head.

"Okay, then." A moment later a reinforcing screen slid through the glass windows, and the bolts inside the door clunked into place. Lockdown. "I can only keep these sealed until Braven gives me an order to unlock them, which is in about three minutes."

Aaron pointed at his wrist.

"Time. Everyone needs time." Robert sighed. "Uh, okay. I can initiate a level ten lockdown. It'll make me lose my job, but I think that's better than getting mauled by Mr Hot and Drippy. Once it's sealed, though, it's sealed. You'll need explosives to get out."

Aaron looked up at the camera and lifted his shoulders.

"Oh." Robert's voice softened. "Oh, man. Well, good luck to you."

Aaron made his way back to the portal. Ellison watched him fearfully.

"I don't deserve to beg for my life." Ellison's voice echoed through the speaker system. Robert had turned it on so everyone could hear. Maybe the tech wanted concrete proof to exonerate Aaron so that when he died he would be given a full agent burial instead of being stuck in a pauper's grave at the county's expense. Robert was a good guy.

"No, you don't," he answered Ellison.

"You think there's anything left to drink around here?" Ellison laughed nervously. He began to open and shuffle through random drawers in upended desks. "I guess this won't be too bad. You're just going to seal the doorway, right? You know, since you put all of those shifters outside?"

"I'm going to face him."

Ellison froze, hands in mid-rifle. He paled. "You don't have the blood to weaken him. You have to have his familial line."

"I do."

"Yeah, but you just shoved them all out the door and locked it behind you."

Aaron ignored Ellison and went to his own desk. It had been knocked several feet sideways and a trail of blood spatter decorated the side. Sitting in the bottom drawer was one of the two personal items he had brought with him into his new workplace, a ceremonial knife with a wickedly curved black blade and horn handle. The horn was from no animal on the earth. It had been a promotion gift from one of his now dead co-worker friends in California.

"What are you doing?" Ellison squeaked in anxiety.

Aaron focused on the gateway. It thrummed from an incredible internal force. If Cerberus wanted to come in, he would let him. He held the blade tightly in his hand.

More pounding, this time from behind.

"Agent Marvell," Braven called through the door. "Let us in. We are here to provide support."

"Sorry, Director, can't," he shouted back.

"What do you mean?" The director grew shrill with irritation. "Open this door at once."

"He only wants me. And I him. Tony and the rest, they're not Cerberus' bloodline. They might not even survive the night. Even if they do, they haven't shifted yet. It's me. I'm Cerberus' bloodline. I'm the end of this."

"He means to use his connection with Cerberus to destroy him," a placid voice carried to his ears through the thick doors.

"Matthew?" There was no need for Aaron to shout, not one wolf to another. "Did you find Carlos? Are you okay?"

"We are both fine, Aaron." Matthew's face appeared in the second door's window. His grieved expression told Aaron he would not try to stop him from what he was about to do.

"Good. Can you do me a favor?"

"Of course."

"Take care of Tony for me. If he changes…take care of him the way you took care of me."

"You have my word."

Carlos appeared between Matthew and the glass. "You need to get out of there, *mi hombre*…"

Carlos was cut off by Matthew, who simply requested, "Don't."

Aaron spared Carlos a long look, then turned his scrutiny to the Director. A range of emotions played across her face, but at least now condemnation was not one of them. He could die an innocent man. He turned away from Braven and mouthed to the camera, "Thank you."

"What about me?" Ellison asked.

"What about you?" Aaron spit as he again faced the portal. "You don't deserve to beg for forgiveness."

Cerberus moved just behind the curtain of distorted air. Aaron felt his presence, the heat flowing off his puzzle piece hide. Aaron watched the flames, imagined they grew larger. In his mind they filled the space in front of him, then began to part like curtains drawn by an invisible hand. As he willed the image in his mind to become the truth he positioned the blade at the hollow point in his wrist. The portal's fire leaped into the air, obeying his internal command. From somewhere that seemed a far distance behind, Ellison whimpered.

In the moment he dragged the blade up his arm and dissected the vein, Aaron's heart desired nothing more than to wander through his life's joys and regrets, to form in his head the perfect picture of Tony's face and hold it tight as his life slipped away from him. But he would not be permitted a quiet death. It would be raw, loud and painful. A flash of intense heat from the portal confirmed this. Instead of fading into the nothing the fire burst out, licking the space around Aaron with blue-white fingers.

Even as the conflagration seared his eyebrows and singed his skin, Aaron stood his ground. When Cerberus stepped through the portal on four massive paws with all heads targeting his direction, Aaron gave the hellhound his best smile, dropped the blade on the floor and let the rest of his body flow into wolf form.

Chapter Twenty-Eight

Desperate Times

He was halfway through shifting when Cerberus slammed into him. Aaron toppled backwards. His front foot, weakened from the cut, slid in the blood pooling beneath and careened out from under him. He slammed onto his side. Cerberus' three heads snapped at him, their jaws spewing frothy magma. Cerberus' massive weight pinned him down, the heat from the demon's body curled his fur into black-tipped tufts. Aaron slashed with his claws, catching the demon across one of its many eyes. The black flesh rent and peeled away. The yellow eye split like a tomato. The wounded head howled. The others joined a moment later. A flood of liquid fire splashed from the source. Aaron quickly wrenched to the side to avoid the spill. The movement brought him too close to Cerberus' other, angered heads. One of them clamped over his bleeding leg. The other dove for his scruff and held fast.

Heat coursed from Cerberus' mouth, slowing the flow of blood. Cerberus began to drag him toward the portal. Aaron thrashed against the mouths' iron grip, but with his foreleg cranked at an awkward angle and his side sliding along the floor, his back feet could only futilely twitch against the slick tiles. As they neared the inter-dimensional doorway, Aaron wrenched his body so his back pressed against the floor. The flesh at his neck tore under the demon's fangs as he pulled it free of the demon's grip. Cerberus growled, but continued dragging him by the leg, the other two heads fixed on the burgeoning portal they faced. With no time left, Aaron pushed his hind legs against the demon's abdomen. His paws sank into the oozing heat. His footpads scorched. Still, they found leverage in the pudding-like mass of liquid flesh. He kicked out against Cerberus with massive force. His foreleg grated along the obsidian canines. With a howl of pain he yanked it free before the heat of the demon's mouth could cauterize the severe damage. He tried to force the pain to the back of his mind as he sprinted away from the portal, but the agony was too much. He made it a dozen steps before his foot gave out. He curled the injured leg up toward his chest and hobbled around to face Cerberus.

He must have been a laughable sight—a shifter no larger than an average werewolf with a profusely bleeding, maimed paw staring down the three-headed creator of all weres. But Cerberus, for once, wasn't laughing. Menacing rage coursed from him with an intensity that matched the fire flowing beneath his skin. It seemed his patience with his wayward child was spent. This time Aaron was the one to let out an amused chuff. Cerberus bristled, reared back and launched. Aaron did the same.

They met in the air, a riot of gnashing teeth and tearing claws. For every one searing mouthful of crusty skin Aaron clamped upon, Cerberus' three separate maws sank in, rending skin and sealing them shut in the same bite. They shook at one another, paws interlocking, mouths searching for the most fragile skin at the base of the throat. The whole time they struggled, the blood flowed from Aaron's wound, drenching his fur and draining his life. Even as he weakened, Cerberus grew no more difficult to oppose. Ellison had been right. Their lives were intertwined, and what was weakening the offspring was having a direct effect on the progenitor. The only question was, how long could he withstand the loss of blood? If he attempted to slay the demon too soon, Cerberus would heal. If he waited too long, he would die before the deed was done. It would be a tricky thing to judge. Aaron tried not to think of that latter part, of how it would end with him lying bloodless on the floor next to Cerberus' corpse. Fortunately, the gargantuan fangs tearing at his flesh were distracting enough for him to deflect the brunt of it.

The inferno raging beneath Cerberus' flesh began to dim. Even though it burned Aaron's lips and gums as he clamped down on it and tore away chunks of gelatinous fire, it did not sear with the same intensity. Aaron, slipping in his own blood, struggling for purchase against the slick tiles, took heart. He drove Cerberus away from the portal, nipping, gnashing and snarling. The tide was turning. Cerberus backed away. The dominant light faded from its remaining eyes. The heads swiveled this way and that, looking for an escape. Aaron smelled the defeat on the flagging demon. Cerberus stumbled. The three necks wavered. The heads toppled like kites bereft of wind. They crashed into one another and melded into one humanoid head. His body stretched on its hind legs, elongating and transforming. The magma faded, the patches of blackened hide sloughed off, imitating Aaron's new half-shifted appearance of black skin and wolfish mouth. Cerberus looked more battered in this form, more pathetic. He stretched out gouged hands.

"See? We're the same," the gesture conveyed. *"Have pity."*

Aaron flattened his ears and snarled. There was nothing in the demon other than selfishness and deception. He leaped.

The object struck him in the back of the head, hard enough to topple him to the ground. Aaron whined and rolled onto his side. Pain coursed through his skull. His stomach twisted with nausea. Through tearing eyes he watched Ellison drop the rifle he had used as a baseball bat against his head and approach Cerberus. The room spun, pinning him to the floor. Between the head wound and the almost total loss of blood, he was pretty well useless. He could only watch as Ellison prostrated himself before the demon and begged forgiveness. Aaron whined again, the closest thing he could come to a warning. Ellison continued to grovel at the feet of the demon he had betrayed. Cerberus placed a hand on Ellison's head.

Aaron struggled to bring his paws under him. He managed to get his shaking legs to steady long enough to push upright. Cerberus watched his struggle, his expression curious. No doubt he wondered why Aaron was trying to save the man who had brought him such misery, because Aaron was wondering it himself. But, asshole or not, murderer or not, Ellison didn't deserve to die the way he was about to. Or maybe other people, like Tony, deserved to have a shot at watching him die. He didn't know. All he knew was Cerberus shouldn't have that particular satisfaction.

He launched into the air. This time no one stopped him. He crashed into Cerberus, who clamped down on Ellison's scalp. The man screamed as he was pulled along between the struggling demon and wolf, caught in a riot of fists, teeth, fangs and claws. Aaron bit down on Cerberus' arm and the demon loosened his grip on Ellison. He kicked out with his powerful hind legs, catching Ellison in the gut and sending him sprawling across the floor. He landed near the portal in a heap, sobbing.

Aaron let his own transformation take him. In an instant the fur and paws receded, replaced by his lupine human form. Cerberus had him by the shoulders in an instant. The large skull crashed into his. Heat broke across his forehead. The pain in his skull was relentless. It seemed as if his brain banged against its bone cage with a persistent metallic beat.

"They're busting through the doors, hoss," Robert's voice came over the intercom. "You gonna do something? Do it now."

Aaron nodded. It felt like shards of glass grinding inside his head.

Cerberus tried to fling him aside, but he clung to the arms holding him. The hellhound had renewed his bid for the portal. Aaron clamped his legs around the demon's waist. It gave Cerberus freedom to stride to the mystical door, but also gave Aaron leverage. He inched his way up the massive boiler of a torso. He clamped into Cerberus' shoulders with his talons, opened his wolf-like mouth and sealed around the demon-man's throat. Cerberus staggered in a languid circle, weakly trying to shake him off. The hellhound beat at his back, plunged razored claws into his shoulder blades. But Aaron, the last vestiges of blood trickling lazily out of his many wounds, clung on. As each drop hit the floor he tightened his grip. As each drop hit, Cerberus' attempts to loosen him grew weaker. Aaron pulled together his strength, knowing it to be his last, then closed his mouth until his teeth met one another. Cerberus screamed. It soon turned to a high-pitched gurgle. With all of the force he could muster, Aaron locked his jaws and flung back his head.

The doors behind them exploded. Aaron's hearing turned to a mosquito whine. Hot shrapnel struck his bare back and buttocks. He leveled his vision with Cerberus, his mouth still full of his progenitor's resected throat. Cerberus stared at him for a moment with a baffled expression, then crashed backwards. Aaron rode him to the ground. He tried to roll away, but only managed to slide partially off the body. The impact had taken away his own breath, or maybe it was simply death finally arrived. Either way, he lay with his feet sprawled on the demon's massive torso, his arms splayed and face pressed against the wet tiles as he gasped for air. The sunset-hued gateway danced in his vision. As the portal faded, a pair of feet scuttled by and disappeared into the void. Even three-quarters dead, Aaron recognized the hideous, over-priced loafers Ellison favored.

Boots crashed around him, encircled the empty space where the portal used to sit.

"We missed him, ma'am. He's gone."

Aaron felt his legs gently lifted and the demon was dragged a few feet away. He watched the body twitch as bullets from five guns riddled the corpse. He understood the agents' need to be thorough, but turning him into Swiss cheese was unnecessary. Cerberus was dead. Aaron felt it inside him, a loss greater than his upcoming demise. A hole. A void just like the one Ellison had just passed into. The dark thing had finally receded.

Does that make me human again? He could have laughed. He looked at his hands, no longer clawed or black. He ran his blood-caked tongue over his teeth. Normal. Was that it how it was going to play out, human again, finally, just in time to lose any supernatural ability to heal? Cerberus was right. Gifts were never appreciated. This time he did chuckle, but it came out of his throat as a groan.

"*Mi hombre.*" The voice beside his ear was soothing in its familiarity. "Hang on. The medical team is here."

He shook his head, or thought he did, at least. Carlos didn't notice.

"They'll patch you up and send you to the care ward to be watched for a few days. That's all."

He heard the strain in Carlos' voice. The alpha was near tears. He smelled Matthew close by, but the beta did not venture close enough for Aaron to see.

He was glad. He didn't enjoy Carlos' platitudes and didn't need Matthew's added to them. He didn't care that his entire blood supply lay pooled across the floor. All he cared about was one thing.

"Tony?" He voice didn't rise above a whisper. When no answer came he struggled to be louder. "Tony?"

"He's going to be fine, *mi hombre,*" Carlos said.

Aaron caught the hesitancy in the shifter's voice, smelled the fear and grief on his body.

Aaron pushed off the ground. Half a dozen hands reached in to press him back down. They could not fight him. Even half dead, even with the dark thing gone, he was still stronger than all of them, at least when it came to Tony. He surged to his feet and lurched toward the door. Another pair of hands caught him, but only to keep him from falling. It was

Matthew. The beta reached around Aaron's bloodied back and held him tight. When Carlos tried to intervene, Matthew shot him a withering look.

"And if it were me?" he snapped.

Carlos backed down.

Aaron ignored their shifting pack dynamic and pressed ahead. His body fought his every movement. He felt light and leaden at the same time. His thoughts were like a cobweb in the wind, trying desperately to fight the breeze that would at any moment permanently unhinge them and send them drifting off into the sky. The only anchor to his soul was Tony. Tony who rested somewhere beyond the rubble that used to be the security doors. He stepped over metal and concrete shards, unheeding. They sliced into his skin, but he had little blood left to offer their honed edges. Matthew guided him around the worst of the devastation. There, in front of him, on a stretcher, pallid and sweating and moaning in his deep unconsciousness, was Tony. He knew without asking the transformation was not happening. The shifter gene was not in his partner. The bite was killing him.

"It was a werewolf bite, we think," Matthew said. "The odds were never..." he trailed off and gave Aaron's side a gentle squeeze.

Aaron shook off Matthew's hands and stepped closer. His chest ached as if he had clawed out his heart with his own hands. An anguished howl worked its way up into his throat and lodged there, choking him. There was no way to get air in, or out.

The room behind him burst into blinding brilliance. He heard Matthew's cry of concern, but his focus remained fixed on the beautiful face locked in a rictus of agony. The heat slammed into his back. He jumped forward and shoved Tony's gurney over. His partner toppled to the ground. The medics let out shocked shouts. The fiery ball struck him square in the shoulders. It burned through his skin, his muscles and his bone. It burrowed straight through until it found the hole left by the dark thing, and filled it.

The medics looked at him and screamed. He screamed back. The sound that came from his throat was deep, gravelly, lupine and otherworldly. He heard Matthew's shouts to be calm, heard the chaos of boot falls and raised guns, and Director Braven's booming command to stand down, but all he saw was Tony. Tony growing larger, closer. His face was all that filled Aaron's vision as he landed directly on top of him.

The new thing inside him was familiar, but bigger. Stronger. Terrifying. But it whispered things that Aaron needed to hear. And while Matthew and the medics seized his arms to lift him off his moaning partner, Aaron dipped down his head, took Tony's arm in his massive fangs, and bit until blood filled his mouth.

Chapter Twenty-Nine

Lost Hours

The lights were too bright. They burnt behind his eyelids, but he could not move to assuage the discomfort. His body cried for a pair of soothing arms and the soft glow of the moon. Somewhere a cub whined. A warm hand brushed his forehead. He fell back into dreams of sorrow.

The next time he came to he was aware of a crazed commotion. Metal crashed to the floor. Wetness splashed against the tiles. People shouted for sedation and extra bindings. A wolf snarled and growled, threatening. Horrible light drenched his vision. A woman screamed.

"For God's sake, just bring his bed in here!" a familiar voice said. Exhaustion suffused the words. "He's not going to hurt him, of all people."

"We have our orders," another person said.

The wolf howled in rage. More crashing.

"Then have your orders changed," snapped the one whose voice he knew. "Or do you wish these to pop up all over your ward?"

The wolf in the room barked and howled. Just as Aaron realized the sound might be coming from his own mouth he felt a new presence beside his bed. A moment later the drugs flooded his system and he drifted off.

* * * *

Tony came to him in his dreams. *He smiled — that same charming, cocky smile — but did not speak. He simply stood there and grinned like everything was fine. But everything inside Aaron was shredded. He was being eaten from the inside out by something he couldn't name. Not the new thing, but something else. It hurt worse than any claw or fang tearing through flesh could. It doubled him over at Tony's feet where he curled in a ball and sobbed until he was empty of tears.*

* * * *

Aaron was in mud. Thick, deep, sticky mud. No. It was more active than mud. Something sought to keep him down, subdued. He knew this, though, had felt it before. In his head he flattened his ears and growled. The thing holding him growled back. He caught a scent in the air, a scent he desperately wanted to believe to be true. He bared his teeth, set his growl to a lower pitch and advanced. He pushed the thing to the recesses of his consciousness, made it relinquish its hold on him. He slid free of its confines and opened his eyes to the harsh fluorescents buzzing overhead.

"Welcome back." Matthew leaned forward in his chair. His surfer boy hair was as rumpled as his dress shirt and slacks. Dark rings edged his brilliant eyes.

"Hi," was all Aaron could muster past the onslaught of distractions that slammed into him. His mouth was parched. His tongue stuck to the roof of his mouth when he closed it. Sand seemed to have collected under his lids. His skin was intensely itchy. Worst of all, he had to pee.

He lifted a hand to assuage at least one issue, the horrific itch, but was brought up short by a thick band wrapped around his wrist that tightened painfully with the movement. A quick survey showed similar bands looped his entire body. Mystic restraints.

"So it was me making all that noise?" he asked.

"Yes. You must be thirsty," Matthew said.

"And I have to pee," he added. This was familiar territory, Matthew watching over him, serving him, while Carlos just made the friendly appearances to check on him. If he had had any sense he would have instead dated Matthew...

"Tony?" He forgot himself and tried to bolt upright. The restraints jerked him back down, tightened. "Tony?"

"He's there, right beside you," Matthew said and pointed to the other side of the room.

Tony's bed had been pushed against the far wall. He lay there, unconscious. His right arm was swathed in a thick bandage. An IV drip hung beside him. A milky substance funneled through the tube running to his arm. A clear wall surrounded his bed. It shimmered gently in the light.

"One of Robert's creations," Matthew explained.

"Like a Sigurddessen Sphere," he rasped. It was becoming difficult to swallow. "To keep me out."

"You wouldn't have harmed him. You only wanted to get to him. They understood that, eventually." Matthew gestured to the door. "I'll get you some ice. You can go ahead and relieve yourself. You have a catheter in."

Matthew pushed a buzzer beside the closed door. Another buzz answered and he loped out of the room. Aaron caught sight of military boots and a lowered rifle in the hall before the door swung shut. Too tired to dwell on the fact he was surrounded by armed guards, Aaron took care of a more basic problem. Unburdened by the worst of his nagging discomforts he turned to his partner. A tinge of pink showed through the white gauze covering the bite he had delivered once the new thing had moved in. It had saved him, no doubt, but for what? When he came to would Tony be as unhinged as he had been after Cerberus' bite? Was his own craziness due to watching his entire office be slaughtered, or was it part of the hellhound's gift? Clearly, Cerberus had been out of his mind for quite some time. Did mental instability come as part of the package? Across the room Tony's perfect chest rose and fell, his face a placid mask of beauty. Aaron decided he didn't care. Just as Carlos and Matthew had helped him regain his sanity, he would help Tony.

Matthew returned with the ice. He only allowed Aaron a few pieces, but they cooled his hot throat and unglued his tongue.

"Where's Carlos?" he asked. He couldn't smell the alpha on Matthew, but pointing out such things was considered rude among the weres.

"He had to return to California." Matthew set the cup on the rolling tray beside the bed and reclined in the chair, ankle propped on his knee. "The rest of the pack was grieving and...antsy. They needed to go home, bury their dead, grieve and resume a normal life."

Aaron regarded the beta. There was a new hardness etched on the kind face, an edge that hinted at something he couldn't quite put his finger on. Matthew patiently bore his inspection.

"Are you two all right?" he finally asked. Directness was something Matthew appreciated.

"I don't know, really." Matthew planted his foot on the floor and leaned forward. "We've drifted apart and together many times. Things may have finally changed."

"I know about change." Aaron smiled.

"You do," Matthew agreed. "I hate to leave you like this, so suddenly after you've awakened, but my own life has been on hold for quite a while, and there are things that need to be done."

"I understand." Although the thought of being left alone in a room with his unconscious lover seemed too much to bear, he smiled. "You've done a lot for me, Matthew. Not just this past... How long have I been out?"

"Two weeks."

"Oh? Oh." He nodded, trying to process this new information. "So, not just these two weeks, but before, when I was freshly shifted. You helped me find myself."

"Carlos cared about you, so I cared about you. And then I came to see you for the man you are, and I cared for you in my own way." Matthew put a hand on his shoulder. "You have changed again. I suspect you know this."

Aaron nodded.

"You are not Him. You never can be. You never will come close. But you have the potential to be something else entirely. Something incredible." He leaned in and pressed his lips to Aaron's forehead, careful not to jostle the restraints. "And you won't be alone in it. Remember that." His eyes briefly flicked to

Tony's bed before returning to Aaron's. "I'll be sure to tell the staff to do something about those restraints on my way out."

"Thank you, Matthew." Aaron looked up into the Nordic were's perfect features and felt a surge of admiration. "If you ever need me for anything, call."

"You can be sure." With a nod, Matthew departed.

Aaron looked past the mystical barrier to his sleeping partner. The movement caused his restraints to tighten. He chuckled, which set the restraints into overdrive. Despite the stabbing needle pain and circulation-terminating pressure, he laughed.

"Alone at last."

The door buzzed.

"Pleased to find you in such high spirits." Director Braven sailed into the room. Her left arm was in a cast, and a patch bandage hovered just above her right eyebrow. Bruises littered the frail skin on her unbroken arm. "You are well?"

"Well enough, ma'am." He shifted to ease the pressure on his back and winced at the restraints.

"I think we've had enough of those," she said to no one in particular. Despite the door being shut the restraints clicked open and retracted a moment later. He was being monitored, of course. Studied. This was Braven's time to tell him he would be transported to a prison cell to await termination. He set his jaw. Maybe his actions against Cerberus would prod her sense of mercy and somehow move her to spare Tony.

"You have presented us with a very large problem, Agent Marvell."

"I understand that, ma'am."

"I know you do." Braven gave him a nod. "You are a very self-aware man. That being said, you did ruin two whole hospital rooms with your antics."

"I'm sor—"

"However," Braven interrupted. "You were not entirely well when you acted as such, and we are somewhat to blame as we ignored you friend Mr Shipley's advice to place your partner in the room with you." Braven looked at him as if she had more to say on the subject of Tony and him, but followed another vein, "Do you know what happened while you were out of yourself?"

Out of myself. That was a new way to put it. Not accurate, but it gave a nice mental image. "I can guess. I became like Him."

"Similar, yes. But, not as repulsive of form, if that concerns you."

"It does, a little. What concerns me more is what I did."

"Did you dream of light?" Braven's mouth quirked.

"I did." He thought back to the dreams, the painful light. The yearning for the moon, and Tony.

"You were opening portals in the medical ward."

Aaron gaped, open-mouthed. He looked down at his freed body, then back at the Director. "I opened potentially dangerous portals where creatures of who knows what power could have crept through and you kept me alive? And you removed my restraints?"

"You would rather I order the guard to put a bullet in your spine?" Braven humphed at his silence. "I thought not. Besides, you did not open doorways to other worlds, only to other places on this floor."

He recalled the dim sound of Matthew's frustrated voice, *'For God's sake, just bring his bed in here.'*

"I opened portals to Tony's room?"

"Indeed. Once he was moved in here you stopped trying to get to him and the gateways ceased to be a problem."

"And now what happens to him?"

"You don't care what I have to say about you?"

"Not as much, ma'am. No."

"That is admirable, agent. But, I am afraid we will have to deal with you, first. The medical staff insists they come in and check on you. They are practically screaming in my ear right now. The director turned her head slightly to reveal a small earpiece. "They say I have one minute more before they start their poking and prodding. They will require you to shift, and you will obey. However, you will not, under any circumstances, open a portal. Are we clear?"

"Is Tony safe?" he asked. He gripped the director's bruised wrist. Immediately an alarm went off. Guards banged into the room. "Is he?"

"You have no need to worry, agent. We take care of our own here in Maryland." Braven gently extracted her arm and waved off the guards. "I understand you will be required to stay an additional night, agent. After that you will report to my new office on the second floor."

"But..." He looked at Tony, who had remained blissfully unconscious throughout the chaos.

"He needs to recover, Agent Marvell. And you need to let him, not hover over him like a chicken with her eggs."

He gritted his teeth against his anger. He forced a neutral expression onto his face and replied, "I will see you tomorrow, ma'am."

Chapter Thirty

Pied Piper

The pen rattled across Aaron's desk like a garbage truck on an uneven street. The clatter of it landing on the tile resounded through the massive space. Aaron watched it roll a few more inches and wobble into stasis. His little wooden desk sat awkwardly at the mouth of the cavernous hallway, a fly on the tongue of a monstrous toad. So much room down here. So much that had been pushed into dark, cobwebbed corners. So much potential behind so many locked doors. Aaron couldn't begin to fathom the power that lay just beyond each. They were all like him, in some way or another—damaged, afraid, strong. And they were just a hair's breadth away from freedom. Only he stood between their confines and a life on the outside. Knowing this should have made him feel a little less alone. A little less scared. But he felt neither.

A week and a half had passed since Braven's visit. Trinity's invasion had nearly demolished the building. While repairs were being made the agents had been displaced to other floors. The shooting range floor now housed the bullpen. The director had taken the range master's tiny office, as the older agent had become one of Trinity's final victims. Robert had been sent along to help Aaron with his task, his desk and equipment crowded into a reinforced storage unit as punishment for his complicity in aiding Aaron and disobeying a direct order to unlock the bullpen doors.

Through all of the chaos and rebuilding, for nearly four long weeks, Tony remained hospitalized. He had awakened six days before, fully aware of his complicated condition, and immediately asked to be sedated. Aaron had arrived too late to see him awake. Since that time Tony's range of consciousness had stayed firmly between un- and tripping balls. Still, Aaron went to visit him every day after work, and had spent the entire weekend sitting in the hard chair by his bedside, his hope growing ever dimmer that Tony would forgive him for what he had done to keep him alive.

It was all he wanted, and to help Tony all he wanted to do, but Braven had made it clear he was to be at work no less than fifty hours a week. It was a condition of Kapre's strict terms for the new Recruitment and Acclimations office — RecAcc for short. Aaron was the lynchpin of this new shift in company dynamics and the hopes of everyone behind the doors his desk now faced rested on him. He sighed and retrieved his pen from the floor. His intercom buzzed.

"You want me to bring out the next one, hoss?" A shuffling of papers followed Robert's question. "This one's behind door number twelve on your right. Stan Grislock. Age forty-two. Psychic vampire." More shuffling. "Not a psychic vampire, like the ones that suck up all your energy, but a vampire who happened to be psychic before he was changed. He'd be handy to have around."

By handy, Robert meant fun to poke with various implements.

"Give me five minutes, Robert, okay?"

"Sure thing." The intercom went dead.

Aaron looked down the row of doors. Thirty prisoners. For whatever reasons the higher-ups had kept to themselves, these particular captives had been spared the extermination part of their sentence. They had been sentenced to life in a tiny, windowless, mystically reinforced cell. None of them full-blooded demons, they each suffered from the condition of being ex-human. And Braven, deciding from Aaron's actions and his impressive physical prowess, had deemed them potentials for rehabilitation. It was Aaron's duty to interview and analyze them, to find out if their abilities would be an asset to the agency, and if they would be moldable to Kapre's standards of conduct. He flipped the small silver plaque on the front of his desk to face him. *'Special Agent Aaron Marvell'*. In larger print below it said, *'Deputy Director, Recruitment and Acclimations'*. The man who would fling open the doors and lure out the monsters with songs of freedom and—relative—normalcy. The Pied Piper of the damned.

"Director Marvell?" The young acqxterm agent who had been mauled during the Kapre attack approached from the elevator bank.

He was Aaron's first RecAcc. A shifter, now, the kid had lost much of his innocent countenance to the wolf inside him, but when he looked at Aaron there was nothing but admiration and gratitude. It turned Aaron's stomach.

"Yes, Agent Finley?"

"You've had a message from the medical ward."

Aaron bolted out of his seat.

"He's awake, sir."

"Thank you." He dismissed the agent. The kid, sensing his distress, beat a path back to the elevators and disappeared. Aaron fumbled for the phone, catching the receiver under his chin and punched the extension. "Robert?"

"You can use the 'com, Aaron..."

"I need you to lockdown for the day," he interrupted.

"But, Braven..."

"Tony's awake," he cut off Robert yet again.

"Gotcha." The sound of fingers pounding the keyboard carried through the earpiece. "Lockdown initiated. Interviews canceled. I'll handle the director if — when — she calls."

"She's going to be mad."

"Understatement. But, she's got a sweet spot for geeks. Back in the day it was a white coat and not a bulletproof vest that did it for our lady of the white hair."

"Too much information, Robert, but thanks." Aaron dropped the phone back on the receiver and ran to the elevators.

* * * *

The guards nodded at Aaron and buzzed him through the secure door. Since his departure, Tony's bed had been moved to the center of the room. Tony was sitting up, nodding at the physician as she asked questions. Aaron hovered by the door until she pronounced Tony, "Good," and promised to drop in on him later in the day. Tony watched her go, seemingly ignoring Aaron's presence until the door closed behind her. Aaron took a tentative step forward, but stopped when Tony's attention riveted onto him.

"I'm sorry." His apology was lame, of course. How could such a simple word cover what he had done to Tony out of pure selfishness?

"I'm not."

Aaron started. He shook his head. The words were too good to be true.

"I mean, I was, for maybe a few days." Tony waved him forward. When he hesitated, Tony flashed him his trademark grin. "What? Afraid of me now? Think I'll bite you and turn you into a hellhound?"

Aaron's limbs refused to function. His mind sped through all of the information facing him, processing none of it. Tony's smile grew.

"You want me to get your kit bag so you can take some swabs or something?"

"I, uh…" Aaron shrugged. "I don't know what to say."

"How about you just come over here and stop staring at me like a zoo animal?"

"I can do that," he said. Although it took a few moments for his brain to convince his legs to move, he found his way over to Tony's bedside. He hovered for a moment then settled in the visitor chair.

"I had these weird dreams," Tony said. "Fire and the moon, people being devoured. When I woke up those were the first things I remembered. I was afraid I was like Him, that the Tony I used to be was gone forever. So I asked them to drug me. But the dreams still came."

Aaron nodded. He knew those nightmares all too well.

"I knew you did it to me. I woke up a little when I fell off of the gurney."

"I knocked you off." He shrugged at Tony's incredulous expression. "There was a fireball coming."

"Oh. Well, thanks, then." Tony looked at his hands resting on the rumpled sheets.

"Turns out it was just coming for me, but I, uh, didn't know that part at the time." Aaron shifted in his seat. The pain of this awkward interaction seemed unending.

"Anyway, I woke up and felt you on top of me. I could smell you. It was strong, almost chokingly so. And then you bit."

"The werewolf virus was in your system. It was giving you all this power, trying to shift you, but your body was rejecting it. Your senses were temporarily heightened while your body..." He passed a hand over his face to cover the unexpected spring of tears. "While your body died. I couldn't take it. I'm sorry."

"Hey." Tony pulled his hand away from his face. "I'm here. With you. That's all I care about."

Tony reached out for him with his other hand. The IV jerked him to a halt. With an annoyed grunt he yanked the needle from his arm. An alarm pitched an ear-piercing wail. Ignoring it, Tony cupped his hand around the base of Aaron's skull and pulled him in. Their mouths met. Relief flooded up through Aaron with such powerful force it swayed his body. Tony, mouth firmly moving against his, steadied him. His grip, strengthened by the demon they both now carried inside them, was like iron. Aaron let Tony guide him on top of him. He hesitated a moment when he neared Tony's abdomen. Tony broke off the kiss long enough to raise his hospital gown and show him the faded pink scars—all that remained of his injuries. The movement also bared the very tip of his cock as it peeked out from under the thin blanket. Aaron took a moment to study the thick ridge hidden by the cotton. His own dick growing hard, he returned to Tony's mouth with renewed vigor.

The doors buzzed and a nurse came in. She paused for a moment, uncertain then said, "Sir, you'll have to stop that."

Tony began chuckling uncontrollably beneath him.

"This is an internal matter," Aaron barked in his best authoritative tone, which sent Tony into paroxysms of laughter. He pulled his ID badge from his pocket. "Deputy Director of RecAcc, here."

"You're the one who helps the agents who are turned?" the nurse asked, doubt edging her voice.

"I'm the one who's going to try."

The nurse looked at him, then at Tony, who was still struggling to regain his composure. She walked over to the IV Drip and punched a series of buttons. The racket ceased.

"Food cart comes in an hour." The nurse turned, snapped shut the privacy curtain and left the room. Through the thick door, Aaron heard her tell the guards to stay outside until dinner.

"Looks like you've found some footing, deputy director," Tony said. "And maybe a fan club."

"I have some openings on my staff," Aaron replied. "Interested?"

"In your staff?" Tony reached down and grasped his cock through his slacks. It jolted under the pressure of his grip. "Absolutely."

Tony stroked the tip with his thumb. The silky fabric of his pants slid across the ridge. He was rock hard in an instant. Aaron pressed his chest to Tony's and pushed him back onto the mattress. Tony curled his arm around his neck and grabbed a handful of hair. Tony opened his mouth to his and slid his tongue inside. Aaron kissed him deeply, feverishly. He ran his hands along Tony's arms, pausing only a moment at the bandage that still wrapped the bite he had delivered. Tony pulled his hand away and placed it on his side, urged his palm to slide lower. He moved away from Aaron's lips, kissed along his neck up to his jawline and ear.

"Thank you," Tony whispered.

A noise, something between a sob and moan, escaped Aaron's throat. Tony covered his mouth with his own once more. Tony worked the buttons of Aaron's shirt with deft hands. When his chest was freed, Aaron reared back and pulled his arms from the sleeves. Tony ran his hands down Aaron's chest to his belt, undid his waistband with the same efficiency and slid down his trousers. Aaron held himself over Tony with one arm as he swiped his tongue across Tony's lips and plunged it into his mouth. He fed hungrily at Tony while he struggled to untie the tiny knot behind his neck. He let loose a growl of frustration. Tony went rigid beneath him. Aaron looked down, afraid of what he had done. But Tony stared back at him with widened, yellow lupine eyes. Another growl came from his throat at the sight and Tony returned it, low, submissive, excited.

Tony yanked the tie free and stripped off his gown so he lay naked beneath Aaron. A bead of moisture rested at the tip of his cock. Aaron growled again. In response, Tony seized Aaron's hips and guided them up to his face. Aaron grasped the bedrails to hold himself above Tony, who flicked out his tongue and ran it across the burgeoning ridge of his cock's head.

Aaron groaned. Tony closed his lips over his shaft and sucked vigorously. Tony tightened his grasp on Aaron's sides and guided Aaron's dick deep into his throat. Aaron arched his back into Tony's ministrations. Tony controlled Aaron's motions with his hands, moving Aaron's hips in a pumping rhythm. Aaron looked down at Tony. Tony's upturned, newly wolfish eyes were fixed on Aaron. Those eyes watched Aaron as Aaron fucked his face. Aaron's body soon took over the rhythm and he thrust down into Tony's willing mouth. His cock spasmed.

"Wait," he breathed. "Wait. I'm gonna come."

Tony moved Aaron back ever so slowly. Aaron's dick scraped gently against Tony's sharp teeth, but a soothing caress of tongue quickly erased the discomfort. Tony mouthed the tip of his dick, lapping up the dewdrops that formed there. When Aaron moaned once more, Tony released him.

Aaron released the handrails and shifted so he was eye-to-eye with Tony again. He kissed Tony and caressed his partner's erection with his thumb.

"What do we have?" he asked as he fondled the tip.

"In the drawer. Usually some lotion or something," Tony gasped the answer.

Aaron reached over Tony, pausing to lap at his erect nipple then opened the nightstand drawer. He fumbled past a shower cap, a spit tray and a bottle of shampoo before he found the tiny bottle of hand lotion.

"Do we need...?" Tony asked.

"We're both beyond human disease, now," he answered. He buried his face in Tony's neck and nibbled at the skin. "One of the benefits of our unfortunate fates."

"What are the rest?" Tony asked as he twisted the lid off the bottle Aaron still held.

"I'll show you." Aaron let Tony squirt the liquid into his palm. Tony was hot against the cool lotion. He began to stroke. "I'll show you everything you need to know. I promise. And what I don't know..." Aaron let go of Tony and pushed him onto his side. He slid his fingers across Tony's buttocks and pushed two of the digits against Tony's hole. "We'll learn it together."

The hot opening yielded to Aaron's touch. Tony moaned and looped his arm back around his neck. Aaron leaned over and let Tony pull him in for a kiss. His cock shuddered against Tony's back. Tony let him go, shook a handful of lotion into his palm, then reached back and slipped his fingers around Aaron's cock. It was Aaron's turn to moan. He worked against Tony's skilled touch, pleasure coursing through the tip all the way to his groin. Tony guided him to his ass and reached back to press his anus against his engorged tip. Aaron collapsed onto his shoulder so they lay parallel, then plunged inside Tony.

Tony cried out in pleasure, repeating soft, almost barking sounds. It made Aaron's already rock-hard dick throb with the need to come. He pumped into Tony and growled. When Tony ducked his head and thrust his ass at him, Aaron bit the back of his neck. He clamped down on the soft skin and growled again.

"Oh god, yes," Tony breathed.

Aaron reached around for Tony's cock. Tony's hand hovered near it and Aaron pushed it away. With slick fingers he grasped the shaft and began working at it with the same urgency he felt building in his groin. Tony pushed against his thrusts as if trying to bury Aaron deep inside him. Aaron responded, slamming into Tony, reveling in the hot, tight passage. Tony's hard-on grew large under his fingers.

"Come for me," Aaron breathed through his clamped teeth.

Tony bucked against him and thrust his pelvis so Aaron's hand worked against his dick. Aaron's cock swelled inside Tony. His groin ached for release. Sweat dripped from his forehead.

"Fucking come," Aaron cried. His voice had dropped to that telltale gravelly sound.

Tony cried out at his command and his body lurched. His skin turned dark gray. Tufts of hair sprouted at his fingertips. Heat swelled up from under his skin. Tony looked back at Aaron with fiery eyes that widened in shock. Aaron glanced down. His skin matched the same demonic hue. His hands were larger, clawed at the end. His cock became massive inside Tony's ass, Tony's cock swelled in his grip.

Tony let out a surprised laugh, showing a mouth full of fangs. Aaron smiled and leaned in to him Tony's enormous erection twitched delightfully in his hand. Ecstasy rolled through Aaron and he slammed through the tight hole with uncontrolled lust. Beneath him Tony clawed the pillow to shreds. He pumped his hips and cock-filled fist to the same inaudible beat.

Tony moaned deeply and threw back his head. A stream of cum shot across the bed. The sight of it brought Aaron's own orgasm crashing around him. He exploded inside Tony. As Tony twitched beneath him, Aaron thrust frantically into his ass. The slickness of his cum covered his cock and he slid through the warm substance a few more times, then pulled out with a howl.

Tony laughed beneath him and pulled his arm around him like a blanket. Aaron pressed his lips into

Tony's neck. Soon, he felt Tony's breath even out. A tiny snore escaped his throat. Aaron pressed his forehead against the teeth marks he had made and closed his eyes.

Chapter Thirty-One

Duty Calls

"Home sweet home," Aaron said as he ushered Tony out of the elevator and into the cavernous RecAcc office.

"This place could use a picture or two," Tony replied.

"At least we don't have to share." Aaron pointed to the small wooden workspace mirroring his own. He looked at the dingy desk facing his and smiled.

"What's that for?"

"Just thinking how last week I was staring down that huge hallway, wondering what in the hell I was going to do. And now I get to look at you."

"And we deal with the guys behind those doors together."

"We do."

"And Robert gets to stay in the janitor's closet." Robert hustled in, his white coat sweeping behind him like a cape. "No, don't worry about me. I like a good storage room. I mean, how often do you get close enough to interviewees to smell every single thing they've eaten in the past month on their breath?"

"Hi, Rob," Tony said. "It's good to see you."

Robert immediately thawed. "You too. Glad you're not too..." He gave an exaggerated overhead sweep with his arms, hands extended into pretend claws. "You know, grrrr."

"Well, I'm a little 'grrrr'," Tony said. He sat down at his chair and picked up the file resting there. "But, not too..." he mimicked Robert's motion with one hand.

"Don't get all that comfortable, there. Director Braven wants you in her office in fifteen."

Aaron exchanged glances with Tony, who tossed the file back onto the desk with a roll of his eyes.

"Do we have to?" Tony asked.

"She did give us two weeks off despite having told me I would be having no personal freedoms for the rest of eternity," Aaron said.

"Fine." Tony kicked to his feet. "Let's get it over with. You know what it's about, Rob?"

"I can guess." The technician came closer. "It has to do with your werewolf friends."

"Carlos and Matthew?"

"Yeah."

"What about them?" A twinge of panic flashed through Aaron. "Are they okay?"

"I don't know. Haven't heard from them. But you remember on the night of the attack when you told Carlos he could stay in op-tech with me and you suggested he look around for something to help out?"

"I do."

"Well, I think he found something else."

"Like what?"

"Some classified things. Things he shouldn't have been able to get a hold of. But, he did. And he took them."

"How do you know?" Tony interjected. "Op-tech was a wreck during the attack. We all ran in, grabbed what we could and ran out."

"I was able to find everything we used that night, either the weapon itself, the shell casings or evidence of detonation. I crosschecked it all against my master inventory list. And those things weren't there. And they weren't even weapons, so no one should have been putting their greasy monkey paws on them."

"If they weren't weapons, what were they?" Aaron asked.

"Can't say. Classified above my pay grade. Braven might tell you. At the very least she's going to hand you your collective ass over it."

"Great," Tony said. "I can't wait."

"Why is she asking for you?" Aaron turned away from Robert to face Tony. "You had nothing to do with it."

"Maybe we get to share blame from now on. Part of a partner-in-all-things package deal."

"I don't understand why Carlos would do this."

"Braven will have some ideas, I imagine." Tony gestured toward the elevators.

"No. I need to know now."

Aaron pulled his cell from his pocket and flipped through his contacts.

"Is this a good idea?" Tony asked as he found Carlos' number. "Braven's not going to like you going off protocol, especially right before we meet with her. You know if we piss her off enough she's going to put *us* behind those containment cell doors."

"I have to hear it from him." Aaron hit the call button. The phone rang eight times, then Carlos' voicemail picked up. He ended the call and found

Matthews's number. The shifter picked up on the second ring.

"Hello?"

"Matthew? It's Aaron."

"I was expecting your call."

"You were?"

"Yes. I figured once the dust settled you would notice something had gone missing from your vaults."

"You knew he was going to take them?"

"I didn't like the idea, but I was beta, not alpha. I could do nothing to stop him."

"Where is he?"

"I don't know."

"Come on, Matthew. Don't treat me like I'm stupid. You two are never far apart. I learnt that pretty quickly."

"Circumstances have changed. Carlos and I no longer see eye to eye."

"You broke up?"

"Yes, and split custody of the kids, so to speak."

"Are you saying you're alpha of part of Trinity?"

"Those who felt we should not meddle in the things Carlos wanted to meddle in stayed with me and made me their alpha, yes."

"And the others?"

"Are with him."

"And you don't know where that is?"

"Somewhere in California, still, if my intelligence is true."

"And what is he going to do with what he took?"

"I don't know. He wouldn't even show me what it was. He'd already stopped trusting me by the time I left your bedside."

"And how can I know to trust you, that what you're saying is true?"

"That's impossible, Aaron. You know that. But, if you come to California I will support you in your search."

"What's he into, Matthew?" Fear twisted his stomach.

"Nothing good."

A horrible realization surfaced in his mind. "Matthew?"

"Yes, Aaron?"

"Did Carlos come to the hospital after I was mauled with the intention of using me to work his way into Kapre?"

A strained silence filled the line. Tony watched him carefully, his expression inscrutable.

"He pushed me not to retire, but to take this job here in the Maryland office."

"He did." Matthew's voice was soft, tired.

"Did he want the attack on this office to happen?"

"A month ago I would have said of course not. I would have defended his intentions to my death."

"And now?"

"And now I am the leader of half of our pack, and he is gone." Matthew sighed. "For what it's worth, I'm sorry."

"You'll be hearing from me." Aaron ended the call without waiting to hear a response.

Carlos had never loved him. He felt dirty, stupid.

"What in the hell is going on? None of this makes sense." Aaron started toward the elevators.

"When does anything that happens with us make sense?" Tony fell into step beside him. "But we'll figure it out. You and me." He clapped a hand on Aaron's shoulder and Aaron squeezed it gratefully.

"Maybe we're going to have to take a trip to California."

"When we're already tasked with turning monsters like us into fully functioning agents?" Tony snorted. "Braven won't go for that."

"Sure she will." Aaron punched the floor button and turned to Tony with a smile. "Any other agent will have to take hours to fly out there. We can be there in a few seconds. And it would be an excellent opportunity to teach you about portals."

"I can't think of any better way to spend my Monday morning." Tony returned the grin and stepped into the elevator with him.

"Sure, I'll stay down here. In the dark," Robert called after them. "Don't worry about me. Plenty of paperwork to do in my broom closet."

The doors slid shut. From the other side came the plaintive cry, "Bring me a doughnut. I know you dropped some off upstairs this morning, butt kissers."

Aaron looked at Tony and he shrugged.

"I do like to kiss your butt," he said.

"As well you should," Tony replied with a wink.

* * * *

Aaron felt the gazes on them before they reached the safety glass of the temporary bullpen. A few agents regarded them with outright hostility, but most expressions hovered somewhere between admiration and fear. It wasn't the most encouraging start to accepting supernaturals into Kapre's ranks, but the agents had a right to be wary. After all, it was shifters who had caused all of this upheaval in the first place. Aaron made a note to bring in more doughnuts.

Braven, enclosed in her Plexiglas cage, waved them over.

"Inside gentlemen," she said. "Close the door, if you will."

Tony pushed shut the door and leaned against the wall while Aaron took the lone seat opposite the director.

"How are you faring? I trust your holiday was lengthy enough?"

"It was very generous of you," Aaron said.

"Do you know why you're here?" Braven fixed them with a glare. Polite pleasantries were finished.

"Trinity has something you want back?"

"Your op-tech ally continues to serve your interests at all costs, I see."

"He worries it'll be an unfair match if he just sends us up here blind," Tony explained with a grin.

"And so it would be. Yes, your little werewolf friends, as grateful to them as we are for helping us with the Cerberus situation, have taken something that does not belong to them. I need to know what they are planning to do with it."

"Maybe if you told me what it was, I could help you a little more," Aaron suggested.

Director Braven's steely composure faltered.

"You don't know what it is."

Braven cleared her throat and adjusted her chair. "The item is a security level above my clearance. I know several items that combined to make a greater whole went missing, but their exact nature and purpose are a mystery to me."

"So, call some higher ups and find out," Tony said.

Braven pursed her lips.

"There's been too much controversy surrounding this office," Aaron said. By Braven's expression he knew he was right. "The Director's job is in jeopardy.

Losing highly classified objects would be the last nail in the coffin."

"Succinctly, if painfully, stated, *Deputy Director*," Braven confirmed. "I can only hope you do not have aims for my seat and you and your partner will aid me in this. I will need you to move discreetly."

"Like without the paper trail of purchased plane tickets or requisitioned vehicles?" Aaron suggested.

"Exactly."

"Consider it done," Tony said. "Although, that means the RecAcc job down there in dingy land will have to wait a little bit."

"Robert can hold down the proverbial fort until you get back."

"You should probably send him some snacks to keep him happy. And maybe give him a desk outside of the closet, or make it a little bigger."

"If you do well in this I will knock a hole in the wall myself."

"We'll leave right away." Aaron stood.

"No one is to know where you are going," Braven said. "Everyone here will believe you are being sent to the Massachusetts branch for supernatural sensitivity training. You will have to move quickly, that training is only two days long."

"Our track record in that time window is pretty solid," Aaron said.

"Indeed. Please replicate that efficiency once more." Braven nodded at them, then passed them bogus orders. "Do leave these handily in the open for curious fingers to find."

They each took their paper and left the offices. The bullpen hushed once more, but Aaron took less notice of it. He and Tony were headed to California. He didn't know what he would find on the other side of the portal he opened, what pain the finding of Carlos would bring, but he had endured far worse. And none of it mattered if Tony was with him.

"You think we'll have a chance to test out just what kind of strength you and I have?" Tony asked as they made their way to the first floor makeshift op-tech department.

Inside the former conference room an intern nodded into a phone piece. "Yes, ma'am. Robert put the security cameras on a looped feed for the next ten minutes. I..." he trailed off as Aaron and Tony approached his desk. "I, uh, they're here. Yes, ma'am." The kid was pale and sweaty and looked like he was about to throw up. He put down the receiver and stared at them.

"Hi," Aaron said.

"You weren't here," the kid blurted. He scurried from the room.

The stores of weapons, depleted from the invasion, still held a few enticing articles. Tony's smile stretched across his face.

"Caaandy shop," he sang in an excited voice.

Aaron laughed and watched his partner move from gadget to gadget, plucking up items and stuffing them into a duffel. When the bag could hold no more and he practically staggered under the weight, Tony moved back to him.

"Should we go to our places and pack some clothes?" Aaron asked.

"What? With your pay bump, *Deputy Director*?" Tony hoisted the burgeoning bag onto his shoulder. "You can buy some nice threads when you get there. Not that you don't look..." He trailed with an appreciative grunt and pulled Aaron in for a kiss.

Aaron savored Tony's lips for a moment, then moved back. "What about you? Should I buy you some new clothes or are you planning to be naked the whole time?"

"Only in our off hours." Tony lightly rubbed Aaron's crotch.

Aaron gently pushed his hand away. He was already hardening. With great difficulty he turned away and led Tony down the hall to an empty space. The battle had touched this room, the contractors had not. The electricity had been turned off. The worst of the rubble was swept into a corner, but bullet holes riddled the walls and faint rusty stains dotted the floor where the cleaning crews had unsuccessfully tried to expunge the violence.

He turned to Tony and took his face in his hands. His partner's blue eyes locked onto his. A shadow lurked behind them, the same that dwelt in his own. He didn't know what he was, or what he had made Tony into. But they were together, and they would handle whatever came the same way. He pressed his lips against Tony's. Tongues of flame leapt into air beside them. The portal hovered, dark and mysterious, within the fire's depths.

Tony gave Aaron a smile and adjusted his bag to avoid the fire. With his usual fearless adventurer spirit, Aaron's lover stepped toward the portal. Aaron's chest swelled with feeling. Tony turned back when he realized Aaron was still standing there, watching him.

"Hey, hellhound. Are you in or are you out?"

Aaron didn't hesitate, but swept forward, caught Tony in his grip, focused his will on California and propelled them both into the portal.

About the Author

Writing stories with fantastical, dark elements is Terra Laurent's passion. Ever since seven-year-old Terra found the Time Life books on the paranormal tucked away in the far reaches of the school library, monsters and demons have pervaded her mind.

She has two published M/M erotic fantasy novellas, Possession, and Trial by Fire. The Beast Within is the first novel in a series of M/M paranormal erotica.

Terra Laurent loves to hear from readers. You can find her contact information, website details and author profile page at http://www.totallybound.com.

Totally Bound Publishing

Home of Erotic Romance